The ARCHITECTURE of LOSS

The ARCHITECTURE of LOSS

Zainab Priya Dala

SPEAKING TIGER

SPEAKING TIGER PUBLISHING PVT. LTD
4381/4 Ansari Road, Daryaganj,
New Delhi–110002, India

First published in the USA by Pegasus Books 2017
First published in the Indian subcontinent by Speaking Tiger 2018

ISBN: 978-93-87693-14-2
eISBN: 978-93-87693-15-9

10 9 8 7 6 5 4 3 2 1

Typeset in Adobe Caslon Pro by Jojy Philip, New Delhi
Printed at Shree Maitrey Printech Pvt. Ltd., Noida

For my daughter

In this work of fiction I have, at times, described the way of speaking of the Cape Malay people. I have tried to maintain the authenticity of this dialect, though it has been modified for clarity to a wide readership. My writing of this dialogue is meant in respect and in no way is a parody of their dialect and mannerisms.

I have also attempted to speak about the imprisonment of a group of women who were activists during the anti-apartheid struggle in South Africa. Any documentation mentioned is not factual in terms of date, name, or place and is written in interpretive narrative form that is fictional, but strongly rooted in fact. I have attempted to treat this narrative with the greatest respect.

–Zainab Priya Dala

PART ONE

BACK TO BRIGHTON

CHAPTER ONE

STALKED BY THE specter of memory, Afroze Bhana drove her rental car into the town on a winter morning. The sun was deceptive. The brightness of its glare belied a bone-chilling sensitivity, its clarity leaving her to wonder at the ghosts at her back. She knew that the car attracted attention. It was too large and too clean. The early-morning bakers and greengrocers stopped sponging down their shop-front windows and watched her glide by.

A man was setting up a table of ascending oranges, bright and glistening with water, outside his vegetable store. The orange at the very top of his pyramid went rolling to the ground. As Afroze drove on she saw in her rearview mirror that a million oranges left their perches and followed her car. Even they were drawn toward her return. Asking the question she felt even the town must be asking, a best-kept secret about to be revealed: why has the Doctor's child returned to the town where she was born, the town from which she was sent away at the age of six?

The town was called Brighton. A Brighton far removed from the other Brighton—the seaside town on the English coast where you licked ice cream cones and froze in a bathing suit, exposing your thighs to unforgiving saline waters.

This Brighton was an antithesis. This Brighton was rugged and arid, a mountain shelf in the middle of rural Zululand, South Africa. The closest town, the even more parched Tugela Ferry, an hour's drive away. Dundee, a veritable metropolis, with an actual ATM and one fast food restaurant, was half a day's drive away.

Nobody remembered the Englishman who came over a mountain in the early 1800s and decided to stick a stake into rock and build this town. There was nothing here, no saleable commodities, unless you considered the hundreds of Zulu tribes that populated the rough mountains as commodities. To the Englishman, Lord Pomeroy, they were just that.

The Englishman was crafty, for he settled here, adopted the fraudulent title of Lord (when he was no gentry at all), and began recruiting, with threats and a gun, the local Zulu men, to send to the labor market in the big cities.

Men would leave their people and travel far away to the City of Gold, now called Johannesburg. The Zulus were a proud people. They did not lose their men easily. But choices belong to the victor—the one with traces of gold and gunpowder. To the City of Gold the men were conveyed, like carts of luggage, where they would descend into the innards of the Earth, disappearing for years. Down in the mines. Forgotten by the world. The wage pittance they sent home the only thing telling their stories, whispering to their women, "We are living. Here is our blood for sale."

A tragic conception will bear a child that carries tragedy inside its genes. The cells of Brighton had begun life in a thick matrix of ugliness. Of loss. These cells would divide a million times over, creating a lineage of loss and heartbreak that would survive the centuries. Brighton, conceived in pain, would only bring pain in different incarnations to all its people. In the years that had witnessed the fall of empires, the rise of apartheid and then the false celebration of freedom for all after years of struggle, Brighton remained quite frozen in time.

A spell, only a powerful spell, would break the curse. Until then, pain became the pastiche composed in self-fulfilling prophecies of Brighton's small populace.

Afroze drove past the old mission hall, hearing the angelic voices of the Norwegian nuns that had once cloistered there, singing prayers to the Lord. ~

For the deliverance of the faithful. The nuns were no longer alive, but their voices resonated through Afroze's gloom. From a tall minaret, another mournful angel sang out the call to another prayer.

For the deliverance of the faithful. She imagined nuns and muezzins praying for Afroze Bhana, calling her by her childhood nickname, Rosie.

Rosie, who hated coming back.

She found her mother's house with ease. It had remained exactly as she remembered it. Thirty-six years had not altered the fairy-tale facade. A fake fairy cottage on the outskirts of Brighton. She remembered once, as a five-year-old girl, trying to bite off a piece of wall, wondering why her mouth tasted of salty blood and not of gingerbread. The witch lived in a gingerbread house. The one who had been trying to fatten up little Gretel. Afroze howled and ranted for days after, when nobody called her Gretel. And she howled from the pain of a broken front baby tooth.

The witch. Her mother. Doctor Sylvie Pillay—that witch who performed miracles of healing for the sick and the dying but could not take away a toothache from her own child.

Afroze was 42 now, on the shelf. No longer the frightened child who used to sit on the stone steps watching lines of bandaged and coughing people snake into the front room of the house. The most beautiful room in the house, the one where the morning sunshine flooded in to comfort, and the afternoon sunshine gave reprieve. Her mother had turned the best room in the house into a surgery, tastefully furnished in nonmedical style. The curves of a cottage-style dormer window reflected the curves of the hothouse orchids that thrived in splendor on the windowsill, gorging on an abundance of sun. On the floors, tiny parquet wooden rectangles in shades that ranged from caramel blond to deep mahogany were arranged in starbursts, the wood varnished to a gloss where people could see their reflections. On the pale walls hung two large Art Deco mirrors facing each other, creating a hall of mirrors that didn't distort into ugliness. And beside both mirrors, Sylvie had sprinkled the walls with framed paintings that were neither landscape nor portraiture, but bright Pollock-styled abstracts of how dreams might paint themselves had they been given canvas. The out-of-place glass cabinets filled with her beloved Swarovski crystal collection stood next to an ugly, peeling examination couch and a trolley of medical supplies. This peculiar medical couch placed among opulence might have disturbed people. But, strangely, all of the doctor's patients found relief in that room, even before she had injected them.

Afroze remembered the smell of cigarette smoke that had wafted under the door of the surgery. Her mother did not care in the least about the stench of the smoke to her beloved patients. She made no excuses. Her ever-present cigarette dangled from bright red lips as she squinted into wounds or shone her torch down throats. The patients never complained to the doctor; they thanked her in adept Zulu for her healing potions and pills. They left presents of fat, live hens at her door, or baskets filled with dewy vegetables glittering like the jewels of queens in their myriad colors. Afroze would linger near the trellis of nasturtiums next to the always opened dormer window listening to her mother's rough, throaty voice speaking perfect Zulu, asking and instructing, diagnosing, and bossing her patients into some form of healing.

Her mother, known to all only as Doctor but whose rightful given name was Sylverani, always wore a sari.

Low-class name, that: Sylvie. Like a shop-girl name, that. Why you throw away your beautiful Tamil name? Call yourself English name, but fall asleep in your drunken daze always in your sari. Why do you always have to be such a conundrum, Doctor? Why?

I gave away my Tamil name, I gave away my Indianness, I gave away my identity because we all were told to be one, a machine. But they watched my defiance in six meters of cloth.

Afroze would watch the morning ritual, folds and folds of pale-colored chiffon floating up among the dust motes, waiting for her favorite moment. In a flourish, her mother would take the folded cloth and flick it upward, unraveling the diaphanous cloud high into the ceiling. Only when it came to settle in a soft pile at her feet would Doctor Sylvie begin the laborious process of pleating and tucking it into a perfectly worn garment. Afroze used to love to stand under the cloth as it fell to the floor. Her mother would ignore the tiny girl with outstretched arms. The girl whose chubby arms perhaps wanted to feel her mother's embrace but who settled for the sandalwood smell of her mother's favorite garment instead. It was many years before Afroze stopped dreaming about the feel of silk chiffon as it fell against her skin, or the way the light caught every ripple in the cascading haze before it fell in soft waves onto the floor.

On the morning the telephone rang, Afroze had been fast asleep. Dreaming strangely of tumbling chiffon on her warm, naked body, feeling the almost-nothing fabric between her thumb and forefinger. The smell of sandalwood, the smell of the old cupboard in which the saris were stored, assaulted her nose, and she woke up sneezing just at the moment the telephone screeched. It was strange, the interconnectedness of people, of genes. She knew before she answered; the message had been carried to her in her sleep, across the plains and mountains of her country.

"Your mother is very ill. You must come."

It is strange, how blood would call to blood when death was flirting.

There was no one outside the fairy house. The walls had now been painted an ugly lavender, and the concrete gnomes and toadstools littered the wonderful garden. Afroze picked her way through the turtles with silly grins, the elves with fishing poles, their fishing lines embedded into a fake pond in which fake fish poked their pouty mouths out of fake water. She stopped only for a second to pay homage to the rosebushes.

Oh, won't you all just die already.

Despite the arid heat of this lost town, those showy roses had never failed to bloom. She hated them. Their garish redness was the last thing she saw before she was sent away. When she used to sit on the steps watching sick humanity come to the doctor for their balms and needles, she always marveled at how every single patient, no matter how unsteady on his feet, would somehow avoid the rosebushes, the fresh lawn, and the long arms of the gladioli. They weaved and careened but always remained on the cobblestone path, the one shaped like two S's saying softly, sweetly, snaky, "Simon-says walk this way to me."

That path was still there. The only addition was a large, gongy wind chime hung from the veranda rafters. It did not move at all. There was, and had never been, much wind in Brighton. Except for the day Afroze had been sent away. That night had been blustery and angry. She felt glad the wind chimes were a new addition. She would not have been able to bear the memory of deep gongs haunting her for years.

The door, still painted forest green, looking ridiculous, swung open with her approach. A tiny waif stood there, holding an armful of sheets. She peeped with large, beautiful eyes at the woman frozen in the collage of the storybook garden.

"Hello, who are you, then?" Afroze said, realizing too late that she had launched into the typical singsong voice adults reserved for children. She remembered this parody voice well. It had followed her for most of her childhood, when she had wondered why adults believed that if you increase the octave and amplitude of your voice, you were somehow less scary.

The little sprite bolted. In a language that Afroze neither understood nor recognized, she heard the girl calling someone.

A tall woman appeared at the doorway; the girl had dropped her dirty sheets and stood behind the woman. Clearly a mother and daughter.

Blood.

"Can I help you?" the woman said, guarding the door with her large, strong frame.

Afroze climbed the stone steps and faltered for a fraction of a moment. She extended her hand; the woman did not take it.

"I am here to see Doctor Sylvie," Afroze said.

"The doctor is ill. She will not see patients," the woman said and Afroze tried unsuccessfully to place the African accent. Was it Nigerian, Malawian? She had no ear for accents.

"No, I mean … I'm sorry, I should have been clearer. I am not here as a patient."

The woman's eyebrows raised and she looked almost ready to shut the door. It seemed as if she had spent a great deal of time sending people away from the fairy house.

"No, wait. It's just that … I received the call. From the Seedat family who live nearby. It's me. I mean … I am her daughter, Afroze."

The woman's face traveled through a range of expressions, at least one of which appeared to be wariness, to see this long-lost piece of the doctor's history. Obviously this woman knew much. About the secrets the doctor kept hidden. With discomfort, Afroze noted that it is very unnerving to meet someone about whom you know nothing, but who by the words on their face tell you that they know everything about who you are.

"Rosie …" The woman breathed.

And although Afroze had not been called that name in over twenty-five years, she answered to it. "Afroze … Yes, Rosie. Who are you?"

"I am Halaima … I live here with Doctor. I look after her. I have been with her for ten years."

Afroze saw the proud jut of the woman's chin. She reveled in her care-giving. She felt that the old doctor was hers. Immediately Afroze knew: she was resented.

"May I see my mother?" she asked, stepping forward. Asking a stranger for the right to open the gates to her own heritage.

Halaima hesitated, looking backward into the dark house, as if she was asking the house for permission. Or perhaps she was asking a ghost in the house for permission.

Finally she moved aside and held her palm upward toward the passageway with a swaying motion. In her movement, she smacked the little girl standing behind her skirts in the face. A loud wail for such a tiny body.

"Oh, now look what you have made me do. Bibi won't stop wailing now, silly child. Oh, Doctor will be so upset. So upset."

And on cue, a hoarse voice followed by a racking cough echoed down the dark halls.

"Halaima! Halaima ... why is my Bibi crying? What is it? Halaima ..."

"Oh pssssh!" Halaima said, flustered. "Look now, what you have done. Just look how you have upset the doctor," she spat out at Afroze, who was trying to work out how she was the one to blame.

Halaima pushed the little Bibi outside and, in her thick language, instructed her to go and complete her wailing at the far fence.

She turned to Afroze, who was rooted to the ground. It had taken her fewer than five minutes in that horrid garden to return to being the five-year-old naughty child, the one made to go and cry in far fences. Some things remain as they were. And they still smell of showy roses.

Halaima had scuttled back into the house, and Afroze heard a muffled exchange. A gruff voice refusing repeatedly. A softer one getting louder. Her mother did not want her there.

Finally, Halaima reappeared with a swish of her beautiful African skirt.

"Go in," she mumbled, and indicated with her almond eyes toward the room on the left down the hall. The darkest room. The one where saris floated romantically to the floor.

Afroze walked with purpose. She was an adult now. A full-grown woman with her seals and medals of heartbreak, mad-crazy-forbidden love, sex, salaries, properties, dinner parties, cars, and nothing much else. There was no need to fear anything. She was a somebody now. But why did she almost trip as she entered the dark room?

The drawn curtains were pink floral. That was the first incongruous thing she noticed. Her whisky-drinking, cigar-voiced mother hated pink floral. But as she looked to the little head poking out from underneath mounds of covers on the bed, she noticed the pink floral pattern everywhere. It was dizzying. She felt the room spin.

"Mother ..." she whispered.

The woman in a pile of pink and satin seemed frail and ethereal, staring with milky eyes at the wall.

"Mother, it is Afroze ..." Again she whispered softly, in a voice reserved for rooms of the very ill and of the already dead.

Her mother did not move. Afroze crept closer and was about to speak again when her mother's voice, in a loud, hoarse boom, spewed lava from her sickly colored bed.

"Rosie! What the hell are you whispering for? I am not dead yet."

"Oh, Mother … I'm sorry. I thought you might prefer quiet … I …" That harsh croak had melted away all the years of steel, and she was a little girl again, watching her mother light a cigar and throw herself onto the lap of a man who had come to visit from the big city. One of many. She saw the clinking ice in the glass and the gleam of admiration in the eyes of a suave gentleman.

"Fuck you, Rosie. You ruined my body, the day you slid out of me. Now, go and see to Bibi because Halaima said you made her cry. Give her some of your money. I hate to see my little girl cry."

CHAPTER TWO

WHAT BEGAN AS an intention to visit for a day began to slowly spiral into the possibility of a night. Despite herself, and the long hours of self-talk she had gifted herself on the drive to her hometown, Afroze felt disgusted but strangely drawn to this house and the women in it. She hated herself for lingering. But she felt that lingering was something she had to do. She reminded herself that one night meant nothing. Only one night, and tomorrow she would leave this horrible town behind—cleansed, purified, transcended, dipped in the pool of deliverance.

Her mother remained on the bed speaking to no one but the bustling Halaima. Afroze had sought out Bibi at the outermost fence, sobbing in the manner that all little children achieve in their early days. Half-hearted sobs. Scratching the dusty ground with her bare foot, she looked up often to the house to see if anyone was watching. When she had convinced herself that maybe an adult was looking at her, Bibi would wail and rack her body with tortured contortions.

She covered her face but kept two fingers slightly open, to watch the effect her drama evoked. She was a cosseted child, and one who calculated her actions by studying the reactions of the two women who surrounded her. But she was a child, after all. And sometimes something more interesting would catch her attention, and her sob performance would suffer.

A red centipede on the ground entranced her. The insect the local Zulu people called *tshongololo* crept with its many legs toward a hole in the ground. Spotting it, Bibi forgot to cry, and forgot to watch if anyone watched her, and she played the game all children play when they see centipedes. She stuck a toe toward it, and watched it curl up into a spiral. The closing in of the creature, its destination postponed, made her happy. She knew that if she crushed it with her heel it would never move again, and it would never reach that dark, cool hole in which it wanted to disappear for good. The strange idea made her happy. Crush the creature. Take away its life. Children can be cruel like that.

Bibi didn't see Afroze approaching. Perhaps then she would have resumed her dry-crying, peppering her sobs with a healthy dose of head-holding and a stuck-out bottom lip. Afroze came to stand very silently next to the child, and watched her try to crush the centipede with a stampy heel.

"Don't kill it, the poor thing," Afroze said, startling the child. Bibi quickly resumed her stance, flat palms raised to her face. Her wailing resumed, their volume exaggerated by Afroze's presence and the discovery of her guilty pleasure of crushing creatures. Within seconds a theater of chest-heaving sobs crumpled the girl's body to the ground. But still, her eyes peeped from underneath lashes, between the tiny slit of two fingers.

"No, please … stop crying. I'm sorry. I'm not angry with you. Please stop."

Afroze wondered whether she was imploring the child out of real feeling for the tearful girl or whether she wanted to quickly pacify her, silence her so that her mother would not hear the loud sobs. Again, she was disgusted with herself. Years had melted away in that pink chintz flower room, and now she was this child—playacting at crying at a fence hoping for comfort, sweets, love, a pat on the head. All the same at the end of it all.

Bibi was savvy. She wailed even louder, sensing Afroze's despair, and perhaps testing a relationship that only a child could sense hung in the balance. The veil of all adult defenses does not extend to a child. A child can feel and see what hangs in the air, needing no words to name it.

Bibi took advantage. She glanced at a rustle at the window, and her crying became a volcano spewing lava that could bury Afroze. A trial by fire. Let us now see who this daughter is, and who has loyalty to her.

Halaima was fast and light, despite some bulk. She flew to the side of the daughter she had shoved away earlier. Again, a play-act. She grabbed her child to her chest, smoothing down braided hair, crooning little clicks and moos. Bibi curled like a cat in sunshine. She knew what drew her mother's love.

"Now what have you done?" Halaima spat, looking up at Afroze with deep hurt in her eyes. The ridiculous situation was enough to make Afroze balk a little. Halaima missed nothing.

"You laugh? You are cruel. Doctor said you would be. What kind of woman laughs at the tears of a frightened baby? A childless one."

"I am not laughing," Afroze said, growing angry at this strange turn of events. Being blamed for making a child cry when it clearly was not her fault was one thing, but hearing hidden secrets spill out of a stranger's mouth was yet another.

"Listen, I said nothing to the girl. I simply told her not to kill the centipede; that is all."

Halaima stared at the empty ground. What centipede?

The one with a thousand-million legs had betrayed its savior and, with those thousand-million legs, had made a clean exit. Afroze sighed loudly, thinking that the centipede's hidey-hole in the ground seemed a nice enough place now.

Afroze opened her mouth to defend herself, to carry on in a high-pitched voice she had not used for years that *it was there, really it was, I saw it, I swear I saw it, don't hate me, I was just trying to help, sorry sorry sorry.*

She stopped herself. To steady her nerves, she looked upward into a relentlessly blue sky. An eagle or hawk sailed high above, scanning the arid aloes for hiding mice. As she looked around, jiggling the keys in her pocket as a reminder of retreat, she saw someone standing at the gate, regarding her car with deep interest.

"Okay, fine. Look I'm sorry. Bibi … listen, I am sorry. Here, I'll give some money to buy sweets."

Both mother and daughter stood straight up. Halaima, with a quick flick of her sharp eyes, conveyed a secret message to her child. All the while, Afroze's attention diverted to the man now walking around her car, kicking the tires and knocking the windshield.

"Here, take it. Bibi. Take this. Go and buy sweets."

Afroze absently shoved a note she had hastily pulled out of her wallet into the child's eager hand and bolted toward her car. She never really knew how much her guilt and fear had cost her. Silencing the child so the adults wouldn't scold was a strange irony.

Bibi looked hard at the note. It was the first time she had touched a hundred rand. But not for long. Her mother whipped it away from her before she even felt the softness of the paper. A revisit to the wailing began to start up in Bibi's chest. Her mother silenced her with a darting eye. This was no time for that. Bibi wandered closer to Afroze, who had started a conversation with the man at her car. She did not have to be told that hugging Afroze would be the best possible thing to do at that moment.

Afroze didn't feel the child steal slowly up and hug her thigh lightly. Her attention was taken by the man. He hobbled around the car, occasionally pushing at it with his fancy cane. He did not look old enough to need a walking aid, but Afroze sensed that he wielded the polished wooden cane with its phallic head for dramatic effect. That he believed it added a distinguished air to his person. A tilted, rakish Panama hat, a deliberately crumpled cream-colored linen suit, and a—yes, unnecessary—cane did make him appear a gentleman.

"Stop. Don't do that to my car," Afroze said again, this time more loudly.

The man looked up myopically and blinked at her, seemingly confused at the order. He was not accustomed to being told what to do. Afroze tried to shake off the hugging Bibi and lunged forward as the man began to push down on the trunk, with more force than he seemed capable of possessing.

"Stop! Who are you? What are you doing? This is my car."

He looked up again. A big smile, the flash of a perfect set of teeth. "Oh, pretty Bibi. Pretty little Bibi fairy. How is my baby girl?" he said.

Only then did Afroze notice Bibi flashing a beguiling smile at her admirer. Bibi relinquished Afroze's trouser leg and sidled over to hug the fawn-colored linen leg of the old man. He patted her head and cupped her upturned chin in his hand. Once again Bibi curled up like a cossetted baby.

"She is rather lovely, isn't she?" he looked at Afroze, regarding her for the first time. Again, it was Bibi's presence that had validated Afroze.

"Yes. Lovely," Afroze said absently.

"Good car you have here. What—a four-by?"

"What? Four-by? Oh … yes, it is a SUV. Four-by-four, you mean."

"Well, that's what I said, didn't I?"

How useless to argue! Splitting hairs with a stranger over a vehicle name. Afroze let it slip.

"What? Toyota? Mercedes? What?" the old man continued. Done with petting Bibi, he circumambulated the car again, not at all bothered by its owner's irritation.

"Hyundai." Afroze replied. She felt the tension, anger, and strangeness of her day settling into her, turning her body to fatigue. This had all been too bizarre. And she had banished all thoughts of the mother she had come to see because the day was too much to bear just as it was. She knew that the moment would come again, that she would reenter that cloying bedroom and do what she had come here to do. Say goodbye. Stay a night, drop a fat wad of fresh notes onto the table, absolving her of any arrangements that would inevitably need to be made. And leave. Swiftly, no emotion, just a clean, crisp farewell. Her mother, the doctor, would prefer it that way.

"Never heard of that model. You sure you didn't steal it?"

"Steal it? That's ridiculous. Look, it's a rental," she told the man, who was now being copied by Bibi in prodding the car.

"Of what relevance is that? Rental … Ren-till. Till what, my dear?" the old man said, pulling on the jutting mirror at the side.

"Please, don't damage it. It's a rental car," Afroze said hastily. Looking closely at him for but a fraction, Afroze knew—with an intuition unlike her usual love for fact overfeeling—that this man's talent for wordplay was just one in a string of talents. The type of talents that came with being a man who lived by the hustle.

The man stood up tall. Suddenly she could see he was not that old after all. Or perhaps he was deft and fastidious in the care of a face and body that he knew were his calling cards. He leaned on his cane, staring at Afroze for a long, uncomfortable time. He deftly removed his hat, revealing a wonderfully styled head of thick, silver hair and an angular, strong jaw, fleshy lips and deep eyes. Afroze almost smiled at him. He seemed to know the effect he was having and enjoyed it.

"You don't look at all like her, you know. Your mother, she was a fiery Diana. My dear, you are rather insipid."

Afroze felt strongly insulted, although she knew she shouldn't be. Yes, a fiery Diana her mother had been, and clearly still was, but Afroze prided herself on being just the opposite. She had worked to maintain a levelheaded ambivalence to her difficult past, and had tremulously guarded this brittle air of nonchalance over the years. It was perhaps this cold detachment to her past and the people of Brighton that made Afroze appear insipid, rather than displaying the actual boiling feelings inside her.

She wanted to be the anti. Yet, in the gaze of this man, she wished for words that did not brandish her blandness. The shameful secret of women is that, though they protest otherwise, when there is mutual attraction, a man's compliments are always welcome, and his rebuff always stings. No matter the woman. No matter the man.

"Who are you?" Afroze ventured, gathering up herself and her composure.

The old man laughed. First a little chuckle, which brought a parody chuckle from Bibi, then a raucous boom that made Bibi double over with child laughter. Afroze felt that she was being mocked.

"Who I am is who I am? And who I am is not a mystery at all."

Afroze was weary. Tired of manipulative little girls who cried with one eye open, of intimidating women in African skirts, of a mother's almost bald head peeping out from pink satin. She had had enough. Why was it that this town harbored people with such eccentricities?

"Please, enough!" She raised her voice. "Enough now. Just be plain. Who are you? Clearly you know who I am. And would you please leave the car alone."

The old man cuddled Bibi for a second before extracting a sweet from his pocket and popping it in the waiting mouth of the child. Bibi ran off toward the chicken coop.

"I am your mother's lover. Sathie," he said casually.

Afroze almost doubled over in shock. Lover! At seventy-one, her mother kept a lover? Afroze had fallen down a hole filled with absent rabbits. She had drunk of a brew that made her small-tiny. She had eaten a poisoned apple. The world was askew.

"You do appear shocked. This and such and such would shock your type. But Sylvie and I have been lovers for years. And as such and such, we shall remain. Did you not hear that Abraham impregnated Sarah at the age of eighty? Are you not schooled, daughter of the flaming Sylvie?"

Sathie spoke beautifully, his voice a velvet amalgam of training, an embodied intonation that arose from deep inside his chest. His words arrived into the world as studied, resonant things of beauty.

Lost, Afroze stared at the man. Not an old man, not a young man. A man who had run the gamut of life, and wore his being like his own crown. He stood with an even more debonair pose now that his status had been spoken out loud.

Looking at the tall, straight-backed man leaning on his cane, Afroze somehow ignored her factual mind, and allowed her heart and body to see. And she saw a man who could have once been one of the great lovers. Looking beyond his body, she glimpsed a handsome man whose attraction lay within and also beyond his form. She shook off the feeling, pulling her rationality away from this whimsy that had taken over her emotions lately.

Sathie knew women better than they knew themselves. He noticed imperceptible things. He noticed a woman suddenly noticing him. And he began to stir inside. Interesting events.

Afroze, despite her attempt at aloofness, found herself blushing and didn't even know why.

When she was five years old, sitting for hours on the steps of the cottage, she saw many of her mother's lovers come and go. The ice in their glasses would keep time with the gramophone, the Indian violin music her mother so adored. They would arrive on Fridays, handing out little presents to Sylvie's little girl, and leave on Mondays at dawn, straightening their ties and jackets, leaving Afroze to silently watch her mother play the melancholic violin records and sit languorously, dreaming on her lounger in the beautiful veranda until her first patients began making their appearances. Sylvie would not speak to the little Afroze. She would only sigh occasionally, smoking her fragrant cigarettes, and perhaps once or twice say words to the morning air. Words a daughter should not hear.

Afroze was happiest when the men came to visit her mother, to stay the night. It was probably because her mother was happy at those rare times, but it was also that the men seemed to feel the need to spoil and indulge Afroze with little gifts of toys and sweets.

She leaned against the car for a minute, the hot sun making her feel nostalgic. She heard the Carnatic violin music drift in from a breeze that did not blow. It was all inside her memories.

"Ahhh, Uncle Logan, throw me up into the air. Come on, throw me up, I want to fly," her child voice rang in the air, and she felt her mother's lover's strong arms hold her tiny waist and swing her off her feet.

"So, you want to fly, do you, Rosie girl," he said and held her by the tummy, sailing her through the air, her arms open wide. She felt like a beautiful and free bird. A swallow. No, a hawk. A hawk.

"Logan, leave the kid. You're just going to make her throw up all those chocolates you gave her." Sylvie appeared, ruining what had been Afroze's only joy.

"Sylvie, you're so hard on this kid," he said and continued to sail her around the rose garden, dodging thorny bushes.

"Leave her, I said leave her," Sylvie's voice, now growing gruff with chain smoking, rang out.

"No, Uncle Logan, don't leave me. I love to play. I love you."

An imperceptible look passed between the two lovers. He stopped flying Afroze through the air; her hair, which had been flying like raven wings, fell flat onto her face.

Sylvie leaned against the wooden post of the porch and lifted a sharp eyebrow. She clinked the ice in her glass of Scotch and walked up to her lover, staring him straight in the face.

"See, I told you. I don't want the child getting attached. What's the point, seeing that you will never get attached to us?"

"Sylvie, stop it. I told you. You know my complications."

He placed Afroze on the ground, and she stood like a mistake between the two adults who were glaring at each other.

"Psssh! Get out of here, Logan. Take your complications and get out!" Sylvie growled.

"Sylv … baby. Come on, I've just arrived. Let's have this weekend. Forget about all this nonsense now. I'm sorry. I'll be more careful, I promise. She's so sweet, looks so lost, your little girl. I just forgot myself for a moment."

Afroze looked up at her mother. She could clearly see the sadness etched into a face that had grown so accustomed to hard lines. She almost believed that she saw eyes glittering with tears.

Sylvie took a long gulp of the straight Scotch. She glared at her lover, handsome and tall with his rakish, long hair and his perfectly shaped beard. Although Afroze could never recognize it, she felt it. She felt things she could not understand emanate like waves from her mother. It felt like a mixture of love and longing, and possible fragments of regret.

"Yes. You and I knew the deal when we got into this. So leave the mollycoddling of my kid alone. Let's go in. I have a new LP with some beautiful ragas delivered to me yesterday. You would love them, Logan. Beautiful sitar and karnatic violin. Come."

Sylvie stared into his eyes, and Afroze saw the things she could not understand pass between them. Logan forgot the tiny girl and placed his hand on the naked flesh between the blouse and skirt of Sylvie's pale blue sari. He licked his lips and smiled. Sylvie smiled too, but maybe Afroze imagined that her mother's eyes were hard. Hard or sad. Both.

They walked away into the house, and Beatrice, the woman who had come to live with them to care for Afroze, came scuttling.

"Baby Rosie, come, I will take you for a walk to the temple grounds. Someone told me they have brought a cow and her calf there. Let us go see it."

Afroze looked up to the window, covered by the flimsiest of lace. She saw her mother with her head on Uncle Logan's shoulder, holding him tightly. He smoothed her long plait and they danced together to the mournful raga. There was sadness in the air. Afroze knew Uncle Logan would be gone tomorrow. Without a goodbye.

Her mother would remain in the darkest of moods for days, doing only her nightly dance with the strange sounds in the *khaya*, and then suddenly, after holing herself up in a dark room, smoking and refusing to see patients, she would emerge in a fresh sari, loudly proclaiming that it was his damn loss.

In time, another man would arrive and be duly warned to not get too attached to the child. Some kept their distance, watching Afroze with apprehension and barely nodding at her. Some were taken by her sweetness, her air of loneliness, that same loneliness that they perceived in their lover, her mother. For some men, this forlorn brokenness was a drug, but once they had had their fill of it, they hastily ran away.

Afroze always blamed her mother for chasing them away, chasing away men that could have been called "Daddy."

Now, the memory of those veranda mornings enveloped Afroze, catapulting her into her five-year-old world, where on one Monday morning crashes and shouts echoed through the air. Her mother's gruff voice was not her own. It pleaded. It cajoled. It promised.

"Please, please stay. She is no trouble at all. Just a child, a silent one. Please stay ..."

And the day had ended with her mother talking to the rosebushes, meaning it for Afroze.

"Maybe you should go to your father in Cape Town. I don't know if I can do this anymore."

But even when her lovers left, taking her dignity in their overnight bags, and even though Sylvie would pour her vexation onto the roses, threatening to send the child away, she never did send Afroze away. Until a horrible night fell like a cloak on her fragile world, and Sylvie finally did banish her child.

It had been a dark midnight. Afroze had never even been warned.

"Please, you have to take her. Take her away. Take her now."

Afroze had cursed the lover who had bewitched her mother's eyes, causing her to exile her only child into a world unknown. But as the years passed, deep into the forest of her banishment, living with a cold, unstable father who explained nothing and a simple but comforting stepmother who knew of nothing to tell, Afroze's curse mutated into cursing the mother who no longer wanted her.

The years droned by in a cautious silence, an eggshell existence. It was as if the day she was dropped into her father's world was the actual day she was born. In her new world, no one believed in past lives. She concentrated hard on the urgency of forgetting. But one image she could only ever remember was her mother's turned back as the car drove off at high speed, not bothering with the crying child and her plastic bags of possessions in the back seat.

Now, this man calling himself her mother's lover grabbed Afroze's thoughts from the past and pulled them with his bare hands into the present. But even here, in the existing now, her mind was racing. Her thoughts gained momentum. Sensing the explosion, the man took her by the elbow. His touch felt cool. Coolness to her rage, coolness to her memories. Heat to her skin.

"Come, let us go in to see my Diana. May she teach her child about fire."

Afroze followed him into the cottage, muttering softly, "Fire razes everything to ashes."

The man, his hearing sharp, turned to look her in the eye.

"Yes. But it is so beautiful."

Halaima, with her laundry on the table that overlooked the front rose garden, watched from beneath the cover of busy hands. Folding and fluttering her fingers in acts that belied her keen attention.

Afroze pulled her eyes away from the unblinking beauty of Sathie. Uncomfortable, she swallowed and attempted to shake herself clean of something she could barely recognize. It took the physical effort of squaring her shoulders and willing her limbs to walk away from him, into the house, to break an infant spell. A tiny, little, newly formed crackle of electricity with a world of potential.

Sathie lingered for a second, watching her march into the house.

"Be careful, my friend," Halaima said, coming to stand quietly next to him, her eyes on the retreating figure.

"I am never careful, my beautiful Halaima. I have never been careful a day in my life."

"Yes, and see where that has gotten you." Halaima shot off, their familiarity easy. Only one who knows you well will warn you if you are heading into your demons' lair.

"Halaima, you know my situation well. I am weakened by my need for a confidante. I didn't expect that you would throw it in my face."

Halaima laughed and pulled Sathie toward her in a light hug. Her affection for this man, despite his showy mannerisms, his sickly sweet speech, and his belief that he was still young and able to turn hearts was strong and unwavering.

"Sathie ... my dear friend. You are silly silly. You think you are playing with these cats, but the cats are going to play with you."

"Cats! Oh, indeed ... you and your little veiled stories. Don't you think it's time you spoke clearly, Halaima of the distant hills?"

Halaima's arched left eyebrow shot up and she smiled in jest. "Oh, really, Sathie of the shadows. Don't you think it's time you spoke clearly too? The doctor laughs at your language; she calls it *proody*."

"*Proody*? What in the bloody world is *proody*? Aah! Parody. Nice to know that you're improving your English. You are most welcome to come to my room at any time for further lessons."

Halaima chuckled and rubbed Sathie's back. "Oh, no no, Sathie sir. I won't be coming to your room for any lessons, unless you let me bring my husband too." She pushed him away lightly.

Sathie laughed, knowing that this woman was immune to his advances. Not that he ever intended to advance upon her. She had become dear to him, a sister and keeper of his worst fears.

Despite his calm appearance, when he saw the doctor's daughter arrive, those large fears came crashing down. And when he looked at Halaima,he knew she was fearful as well.

"I wonder, Halaima, what this rich Cape Town daughter with her fancy clothes and big car is going to do with us. Maybe you and I had better start looking for places where we could go. This daughter has cold eyes; she won't let us linger here like the doctor does."

"Don't worry, my friend. We will be okay. We have nothing, and if we always have nothing, then that is our destiny. And maybe this daughter will be good to us after all."

Halaima, remembering something, patted Sathie comfortingly on his arm, and then quickly started forward and rushed past him to ensure the doctor was dressed.

Sathie watched her hasten away, the ever-faithful maidservant. He was far less confident. He had finally found a home here in Brighton, a place where his creature comforts—fine food, afternoon music—were indulged. He had come to enjoy the sometimes tedious conversation with the doctor, who had finally warmed up to him after months of calling on her, praising her, patronizing her. Now, with the arrival of this daughter from Cape Town, worry and fear began to creep into Sathie's otherwise flawless facade. Would his days of hard-won comfort be taken away from him? He didn't know.

"Destiny means rot. Hope is rubbish. I will make my own hope," he muttered, composing himself in the practiced way that he had learned to cast every thought and fear away before he stepped onto a stage of women in love.

CHAPTER THREE

HAVE YOU MET the great beauty, Sathie?" The doctor's voice echoed through the open door.

Afroze found herself tentatively lingering in the hall as Sathie's ease in her mother's home became apparent. He was a gentleman, his ministrations seemed old world, and more than a bit contrived. He had announced his arrival by calling out in a hearty voice. Afroze had the distinct impression that he used this same call every time. It was trained, the ritual of a method actor.

"Now, where is my great lady love—Artemis, do not hide. I am here and you have never been coy."

A bustle in the bedroom, the sound ladies make when rapidly preening for a man.

Almost a giggle, a waft of the very same perfume she had always worn, the perfume whose scent haunted many days and nights of a child daughter. What was it called? Ah, yes … Cache, Hidden. When she was a little girl and could barely read, the ornate crystal bottle of the French fragrance, shaped like a treasure chest inlayed with gold and boasting a delicately crafted gold lock and key, had captivated her as it reflected morning light, much as the creamy chiffon sari fabric would ripple and dapple with that same morning light.

She could not yet read well but could sound out words and the word *Cache* emblazoned on the bottle in black sounded out in phonetics to *Cac*. Which sounded very much like *kak*, a local word for "shit." And back then, the perfume smelled quite divine. But as she grew older, far away from its smell, its memory earned this misnomer. Crap apt.

The floating perfume scent got stronger and, with a dragging *huff-puff*, Afroze's mother appeared at the door, dressed in a satin nightgown of the deepest red, ruffles tied with ribbons at the sagging drape of her throat, her face made up in a garish heaviness of reds, blues, and pinks. The sight was quite horrific. The scarlet lipstick had been painted on in haste, you could clearly see, but then again, with such a sagging, downturned pair of lips, mistakes would so easily happen. Who had done this? This clown-dressing?

Halaima ...

"Aha, now the blood is beginning to flow in the heart of this mad, desperate lover," Sathie announced, glimpsing Sylvie walking into the passage outside her bedroom. He bowed as low as his stiff back would allow. His every word, his every nuance, was a performance. Afroze, lingering in the passage, looked in puzzled revulsion at the intelligent, abrasive, worldly woman who could stamp out any debate with choice intellectual ripostes, melting under the florid grammar.

What on Earth had happened to this mother, the one who unnerved her dreams with memories of formidable strength? This was not her. This aged doll. This melted wax. Grotesque.

As soon as the doctor bestowed a gummy smile at her lover, she glimpsed Afroze hovering and a scowl came to her face. Afroze quickly slipped in to stand behind her, not wanting that awful childhood feeling to return, where she was a little girl standing between lovers. She ached to just hide away, for a little while.

"Didn't you hear me, Sathie? What do you make of the great beauty?"

Her mouth curled downward. Such a bad taste on the tongue. She was too ladylike to spit, although there had been many times in her life when she had easily lobbed gobs of smoke-scented saliva at anyone who annoyed her. Sathie, her lover's presence, preserved her etiquette. For now.

"Oh, you cheeky old girl," Sathie said. "Silly Sylvie. You are the great beauty. And there is no one else besides."

When he leaned to embrace Sylvie, his eyes lingered on Afroze.

Her mother's painted-on eyebrows shot upward into a terrible, terribly placed auburn wig. Slightly askew on a face that displayed much loss of form and function, the wig, although very unbecoming, somehow rounded off the entire series of brushstrokes of an Impressionist painter. One tiny stroke at a time, creating a complete but messy whole. You would have to be far away to see the big picture. Afroze was too close.

"Well," her mother continued, edging forward with her walking cane, "she is quite bland, isn't she? I often thought that with that milky skin and thick black hair, she would have grown up to be somewhat stunning."

"Oh, my beautiful fiery Artemis. She is not a beauty like her mother."

Sathie winked conspiratorially at Afroze. The wink caught the eye of the hovering Halaima, who clicked her *tsk-tsk* in silent disgust and placed a protective arm around the shambling doctor. Those mynah-bird eyes flashed between two people who had now transgressed all decorum in her world, two disgusting making-fun people.

"You lie poorly, Sathie," Sylvie said. "I can feel the rising of your blood. She is cold and she is flavorless … now. But she is my daughter, after all. She might surprise you when she begins to flame."

"Oh, nonsense and pish-posh, my sweetest Sylvie. How can I be distracted by blandness in brown trousers, when a world of beauty in colors stands here?"

Afroze did not feel insulted, being discussed by critics who clearly did not see things clearly. What cut deeper than the name-calling dissection was the suture on the wound. The passing mention, the offhand comment, her mother had thought of her.

Through the years. Often. When you arrive at a place that has starved you and a hint of the attention that you have hankered after is thrown at you, you take it. Bones and crumbs, despite your pride, tastes very good, after all. This staggering slick of balm on her slapped cheek cooled her, calmed her, warmed her. Her dissolve was palpable and a thick silence encircled this strange gathering at the doorway of a stuffy bedroom. Afroze had crept unnoticed to face her mother in that narrow passage, and into the dissolve, her eyes searched and found Sylvie's. They looked at each other for the very first time since she had arrived, and in this look that passed, Sathie grew anxious and Halaima, who missed nothing, also felt the pangs of uneasiness.

In the silence, Sathie the seducer grinned, not because he felt that grinning was the best thing to do at that time, but because through the stark stare between mother and child, he sensed a door closing in his handsome face. If his Sylvie lost her heart to her restored child, then there would be no room for him. He sensed a gap in the door, and a tiny crack is all an insect needs to get into a sealed house.

His school had been the streets and the bedrooms of virgins, wives, and matriarchs. He knew when he was being displaced. Sensing, like the feral being he was born to be, that a union between these two feminine forces would force him out, he desperately needed to replace the wedge, to center himself in the moment. Sathie, who had run away from every place he had ever been, needed now to secure this one. He was getting too old for running.

In his years as a practicing Lothario, he had learned that all lady-loves, no matter how strong, aloof, or intelligent, could never resist his true asset: that gorgeous, very big smile. He trained his gift on Sylvie. The radiance of that man-smile, the smell of a man in a world filled with women was all that was needed to subvert their attentions from each other.

But it was Halaima who sliced the trance in two, breaking an invisible silver thread that buzzed between a mother and her daughter. The moment dissolved. Perhaps never to reform again.

"Doctor, come. You must sit down. I have laid out breakfast on the veranda at the back."

Her mother shook slightly, a shiver up the spine, and gathered herself up again into brusqueness, taking Sathie's offered arm.

"Yes. Breakfast. Thank you, sweet Halaima. I'm sure you have set the table for three."

"Yes, Doctor. Three."

Afroze shuffled slowly behind the unlikely pair, each supporting the other with the hand free from their canes. Afroze noticed, with a very small smile, that the canes had matching heads.

The veranda at the back of the house was large and had a floor painted a glossy red. Afroze remembered it well. She remembered how it shone when the domestic worker had spent hours on her hands and knees polishing it with lavender-smelling floor wax. The delicious slippery canvas, a temptation for a little child. Afroze had loved to put on pairs of old socks and slide clean across it, crashing into the rows of potted plants at the far end. The one wild game she allowed herself in a house where she spent all her moments creeping and hiding. And the one time her mother had tended to her, the day she had crashed too hard into the wall, missing the plants and fracturing her wrist.

A child with a limp wrist, sobbing in not-fake, wracking heaves, scared and in pain, looked around with a wild desperation for the comfort of a mother's embrace.

You are five years old, you believe in miracles, and in your world, even a broken bone can be healed by kisses. But it was not the mother who came out that day. It was the anxious, angry doctor, who had swept like an irritated animal into the room where Afroze sat, a thick piece of towel wrapped around her wrist, the hasty ice inside it already melted clean away.

"Oh, really, Rosie. Not this now. Not now," her mother had said, hurriedly glancing backward. Ever the doctor, her mother had prodded and poked the massive, swollen wrist, needing no X-ray machine to confirm her diagnosis. Afroze had screamed and wailed. It was so painful. Her mother had cradled her forearm, muttering words like "greenstick" and "radius," and had applied a thickly pasted roll of plaster of Paris to her forearm.

The cool plaster had soothed Afroze, her sobbing was placated by some morphine drops, and she had begun having visions of circling angels. Her mother, the queen of the cherubic seraphs, floated above her, crooning her to sleep. Her mother, a fantastic centaur, the head of a majestic woman, the body of a majestic horse. Archer arms trained to shoot arrows into the sky.

Had she dreamed it all? That night she was tossed about on stormy sheets, the coolness and comfort of her mother's hand on her forehead, stroking her tiny five-year-old chest, calming her down with the feel of skin. Had she dreamed the hugs and kisses?

Maybe she hadn't dreamed that hot mother-tears fell on her baby-bare chest, and a woman crooned many *sorrysorrysorrys* to her in her drowse. Despite it being a painful night, Afroze knew that it had been a beautiful one. The morning had found Afroze looking fuzzily at her mother, fast asleep, crouched at the foot of her bed, gripping tightly to the sheet.

"Ma," Afroze had said in the wake of a morphine stupor. Her mother had sat bolt upright. The always-in-place bun on her head flopping out of its many pins, stray hairs all over her face, tracks of caked mascara making journeys down her cheeks. Tears had ridden those tracks.

Caught in the act, her mother smoothed the sari she had never taken off. She seemed almost ashamed. As if being called *mama* brought untold indignity to her demeanor.

"Rosie. You are awake. Well … You are a very stupid girl, aren't you? Bloody stupid. I'll tell the maid to set you straight."

The swish of sari chiffon seemed louder than a roar. Afroze did her healing in private. She itched and scratched inside the horrid cast silently, never moaning, never fussing.

Some girls from the Norwegian Mission across town came to visit Afroze. Afroze knew the times when her mother went to visit the nuns only by the mood that followed. Sylvie would come back seething with rages of vile bile. Ranting at a world where virginal girls had taken the Order, and had to have babies cut out of them for their troubles.

The small group of virginal nuns, guarded ferociously by a Superior with massive breasts and a very round face, brought Afroze a drooping bunch of blue-purple hydrangeas, a brown paper bag of peppermints from the local grocers, and a Bible. One pretty girl, whose starched, white habit did a very poor job of hiding a halo-shaped Afro, spent a long time telling Afroze how hydrangeas were sometimes blue and sometimes pink, depending on the acidity of the soil in which they grew. When she tried to explain the word *acid* to a five-year-old child, she struggled. Not her native language, English was known to her only in biblical terms. She finally settled on the synonym *bite* to explain what acid did. Acid equals bite.

The best hydrangeas, apparently, were the ones that were neither. They were the ones that were a mix of pink and blue, sometimes with different-colored petals on one large flower. To the rapt Afroze, this long parable of the horticulture of hydrangeas ended in her understanding but one thing: The best things are the ones that have walked on the fine line between having "bite" and having "nothing."

The young nuns sang a hymn for Afroze, a song in accented English that they alone could barely understand, about fishing for Jesus with a Bible and a rod, and took turns marveling at her plaster cast. Only one of them could write. Her Zulu name had been abandoned when she had been given to the Lord. The nuns called her Rachel and she had stopped answering to the name Tombifuti—a name given to her by her mother who had wailed when yet another girl came out of her belly. Tombifuti, in English it meant "Yet Another Girl"! She was asked to sign Afroze's plaster cast. She took the offered black felt-tip pen, scrawling an illegible barrage of curly "Jesus"es before signing off with a flourish, "Love you, T."

Her *T* was shaped like a crucifix and she had embellished it with a few droplet shapes trailing down the cast toward Afroze's itchy fingers. Droplets of blood, perhaps.

Afroze's cast came off just in time for her sixth birthday. Her mother believed this was a present enough, a party in itself.

Sylvie was too distracted to bother about cake. So, it was no cake, just Musa the gardener sawing off the cast in the backyard with his ancient rusty hacksaw, her mother directing the entire process from afar, not even touching the terrified girl. Days later, her wrist still aching, she would be sent away. Many times when Afroze thought about those days that had led up to her banishment, her childhood imagination took her to a place where her Mother stood far away directing Musa to use his hacksaw to hack off Afroze's head. In a warped unreality, Afroze believed that all her mother wanted was to see her dead.

Strangely, Afroze remembered grabbing the Bible from the mission nuns and stuffing it into one of her plastic bags, in lieu of any luggage.

Her mother's mad-rush-scramble to get her out of there, get rid of her as swiftly as possible.

Not bothering much about any type of God, her mother proclaimed to be a communist and an atheist, Afroze had taken the lovely little black book with her to the big big city, Cape Town, where a father who had never seen her awkwardly shook her hand and bundled her into his car, driving like a maniac to the Malay Quarter of town.

Her father's wife, a sweet-tempered Malay woman, hugged the girl to her soft breasts. And later that night when she found the frightened child clutching the black Bible to her chest and shaking like a leaf, she clicked her tongue and prised the book from Afroze's tight fists. Putting it to one side, she padded off in her bare feet, returning with another book.

"This is our book, my child. Not that one."

Afroze looked at the book placed in her hands. She understood nothing of the curving script, the dots above and below, the beautiful calligraphy of the new language.

"Don't worry, I will teach you," the soft woman told her, and held her 'til she fell asleep. Rachel's Bible went directly to the Salvation Army salvage bin the next day.

It astounded Afroze, reeling back to the present, how the simple shine of a red veranda could evoke buried memories. But this entire day had been one of memory. As it should be. She had returned to this place, after all. But nothing had prepared her for all that she had seen in a few short hours since arriving in this arid town. She knew her mother was dying. That was not the difficult part to accept. The incomprehensible things were all the details that made up the bizarre planet she felt she had landed on. It was all deeply incongruous to the woman she recalled. But then, thirty-six years is a very long time.

"May I?"

Sathie had held out a rattan chair with a bright turquoise Hawaiian-print cushion and bowed lightly, offering her the seat.

"That is Bibi's chair, Sathie. Don't you know this?" Sylvie growled.

Afroze was startled out of her trancelike state, induced by fatigue, hunger, and the strange act of her mother waving a piece of meat in the air.

Halaima had indeed set a table for three, but Afroze saw the three did not include her. Two chairs were soft loungers, cushions to soothe aching bones. A hard-back wrought-iron one placed opposite would have been her seat, had little Bibi not taken it, proceeding to precociously rap the plate with a fork and swing her gangly legs.

"Bibi, my sweet child. You are eating with us? I forgot that it is still school holidays." Sathie said, showing surprise, patting her head again. He needed to recover his slight, not wanting to anger the doctor, or the bubbling Halaima, who could spill out vitriol and secrets at any moment. His frantic patting of the child's head continued, rhythmically, too rhythmically. Bibi pulled away from his hands, complaining loudly, "Mister Sathie, you will open my braids. Stop."

He stopped abruptly, and began smiling and cooing his apologies. He had done it many times before. With a quick glance at Sylvie, he noticed with relief that she had ignored the entire mistake and was distracted with her meal. For now.

"Halaima, get a stool for Rosie, will you," her mother grumbled in annoyance.

Even Halaima joined in the remonstration, treating her as if her very presence had caused the greatest inconvenience. Halaima tutted and reluctantly brought the most rickety stool she could find along with a plate and slapped them down. Afroze silently sat down. Sickened by the smell of the meat impaled on a fork, still being waved around by her mother, who was making sure Afroze's nose almost touched the flesh.

"Here, take a bite, Rosie," her mother said, and Afroze looked at the piece of sausage almost shoved down her throat.

She shook her head, her eyes tearing up from the meaty, oily smell of the morsel and more so from the knowledge of what her mother was trying to feed her.

"Best pork sausages in the province," her mother said, "from our neighboring town of Estcourt. I get all my meat there."

Afroze swallowed dry sandpaper; she turned her head away and willed herself not to cry. The cruelty of that food from her mother's own hand, the first meal a mother could offer a long-lost child and it was food that both knew was forbidden.

"Oh, get over it, Rosie. It's only a sausage. It appears your father and his *hausvrau* have claimed your soul for their perfumed gardens," her mother said, the vulgar peacock blue of her painted-on eyeshadow swimming in Afroze's churning brain. The caustic mention of her stepmother brought stinging tears to her eyes. The gentle soul of the Malay woman who had borne a frightened stick-child to her ample bosom needed no insult.

Such a dreadful burlesque show, a scene from the sulfurs of Faust—the 70-year-old painted harlot in scarlet satin, drenched in French perfume that smelled like shit, the grotesque grin of a leering lover with a phallic cane, and the little reed of a child in a yellow sunflower-print dress, humming a nursery rhyme and swinging her legs. The images warped and marbled around her tired brain. She felt faint.

"Mother, I need to lie down." Afroze stood up and her unsteady thighs rattled the crockery. Sathie's full cup of very sweet, very milky tea spilled over. Bibi took the opportunity, as she often did, to stifle a shocked gasp.

"Oh, Halaima. Get her out of here. Look, she has upset Bibi. Let her lie down in the spare bedroom."

Halaima took Afroze's elbow, ushering her as wardens usher prisoners, marching her away from destroying the lovely breakfast.

"I want sausage," Bibi moaned in her loud, high-pitched voice.

"Oh, my little fairy, don't worry. Here, I told your mama to make you the lamb sausages she got from the Muslim butchery."

The last thing Afroze mulled over as she lay on the bed in the darkened room was Bibi's mouth opening wide and pink, taking the piece of unforbidden sausage being offered to her.

CHAPTER FOUR

SLEEP TOOK AFROZE away into the waiting embrace of the woman who had been a mother to her for over thirty years. The woman who had replaced this doctor who had thrown her away.

In her life, whenever Afroze had been in any distress—as a growing young girl, as an awkward teenager, and into the turbulent waters of her adulthood—she would comfort herself with the simple presence of her stepmother. She called her Moomi. Maybe because her name was Moomina, but maybe because she ached to call her Mommy and this was the closest she could come. Her father, Ismail, had taken her from the tiny town in the middle of a dustbowl into the metropolis of Cape Town. No one had bothered to explain to Afroze why she was being sent away.

She had to play guessing games with shadows on the wall and became an expert at eavesdropping on adults' words. Afroze never slept. It was probably because she had trained herself to lay awake at nights, even when she lived in Brighton with her mother. She had always known that this was the time of answers. Stolen answers that she would grasp close to her chest from behind doors that never fully closed. The habit of listening in, of trying to find her place in a torrent of words spoken by adults, became a habit that she would never break.

Even now, in adulthood, sleep was never easy to come by. And even when it did come, it brought with it a barrage of memories and dreams. As she lay spent and ravenously hungry on the single bed in the fairy cottage of her childhood, relegated now to the spare bedroom, the one they used to store things they would never use, Afroze drifted between worlds. Cape Town and its beauty became a magnificent backdrop for a stirring dream, in which she vividly recalled the day she had left to return to Brighton.

Afroze dreamed of how she had crouched low beside the crumbling precast fence. The morning revealed the bright colors of the houses in the Malay Quarter in the steepest of hills in Cape Town. The Malay people, brought as slaves from Malaysia by the Dutch, had suffered badly, but their redemption had been ownership of the best view in all of Cape Town. They could see everything. Everywhere. Their bright, lovely homes, in all the hues and colors of the rainbow, were crumbling, old, and small. But at least they could sit in their rocky yards listening to the muezzin intone the evening call to prayer, and they could enjoy the most beautiful sunsets in Cape Town.

Sometimes, photographers from places like Europe and Australia came up the long hill to the Malay Quarter, sometimes many at a time. And with the sunset dancing for them in all her beauty, they would be so entranced that they forgot their cameras, and just looked and looked. Afroze remembered them, their photographer uniforms of flapper jackets and khaki shorts, their feet shod only in flip-flops, baring their toes even in harsh Cape winters. There was a spot, a rocky shelf carpeted with the local eclectic foliage called fynbos, a viewpoint that gifted anyone who stood there with sunsets that made you believe in God.

The photographers competed with one another for the prime position. The local Malay women, seeing the possibility of business, began setting up tea stalls and informal eateries all around. They sold the most delicious confectionary, a deep-fried plaited donut laced with cinnamon and nutmeg that dotted puffy dough with little speckles of the exotic Spice Islands that the Malay people held close as their heritage. This mouth-watering, sickly sweet donut had started a war in kitchens all across the country. The Dutch women claimed to own it, because they had named it *koeksister.* The Malay women claimed to have embellished what was just a simple deep-fried dough ball into a plait, drenched it in lemony syrup and delicately decorated it with toasted coconut. It retained its Afrikaans name, which translated into "cake sister" from rough Dutch. But Dutch was a language that inverted itself upon itself, and it actually translated formally into "sister's cake."

The Malay men would guffaw and laugh at this moniker, poking each other in the ribs, using that spicy amalgam of English and Afrikaans for which they were famous. "Sister's cake" sounded too rude, too much like a reference to the most private part of anybody's sister, but the women insisted that the delicious confectionary's name meant anything else but that.

The foreign photographers and other tourists who came to the Malay Quarter would return to their homelands, the taste of this delight lingering always on their tongues. They would never be able to replicate its delicate flavor. And they always wondered why Malay women went red in the face when asked what the English translation meant.

The mountain with or without tablecloth, the harbor with its twinkling lights, the city with its hints of decadence. The most beautiful city in the whole wide world. And the Malays who came as slaves now stood over the neighborhood as lords. They possessed what German and French property moguls had coveted but failed to capture. The Germans took Camps Bay, but it had no sweeping view. The English took Sea Point. It was artsy and charming, but it showed no mountain. The French took Hout Bay, which afforded the astounding charms of crystal clear air, happy whales, and perfect breezes. Bantry Bay in lush expanse became the politicians' hideaway. Movie stars tended toward the Cape Winelands district to the east.

But no one had the unlikely gift the happy Malay people had. They had a perch. They were eagles who watched everything that Cape Town could offer. The only drawback was the steeper-than-steep hills over which their homes sat perched. Buses stopped at the bottoms of the hills. And the Malay women had grown good, solid thighs and calves.

Afroze, crouching low, had watched the play of light on the blue, orange, and bright turquoise house fronts. She enjoyed the Matisselike brush strokes on the little patches of God-light. No one had begun their day, cocooned away in autumn sleep; even newborn babies did not yet stir. Afroze breathed the frigid Cape Town wind into lungs that burned, running her cold hands along the thick vine that hid the cracks and the fissures of the wall.

The ice-cold southeaster blew in from the Atlantic Ocean, sparing nothing as it tossed people, rubbish, and rubbishy people in all directions. She blew on her hands and looked up at a sky that refused to turn to full light, despite the ending of dawn. It was always a little bit muddled. But perhaps that was just her vision today.

Her eyes settled on the dark space that was the mountain. For a long while, her eyes didn't stray from its blackness, cast up into the sky. A throbbing energy seemed to radiate from the block of stone, the one satellite that no Capetonian could ever escape, the compass that became due north for beggar and rich man alike. A deep cold emanated from the mountain mass, its dark outline always visible, even in the deepest midnight. You always knew it was there. Like a watcher, a power source, a custodian. The Supreme Witness. In every part of the beautiful city, in every hovel and every ostentatious mansion, no one awoke in the morning without feeling the presence of this mountain. Sometimes residents hated it, for witnessing everything, for keeping so silent and watchful. Sometimes they loved it for the raw energy it seemed to leach into their blood.

Hearing a car engine struggling to turn over, wheezing, Afroze ducked again, despite knowing that there was not really much point in hiding. No one could see anything in these murky waters.

The orange-amber lights of the city twinkled with life, far down below, and slowly as the sky began to turn into purple and then a mild orange, the lights sent messages to one another to turn themselves off. The car in the driveway finally spluttered to a start.

Her father was leaving home, heading for the mosque for early-morning prayer and then to his dubious businesses in the center of town. She knew his routine well. He preferred to stay away from the home he shared with Moomina, grown old now and losing her prettiness.

Afroze knew he would come home only after dusk. And that gave her plenty of time to do what she had been doing for a year now: skulking into his home like a thief, just to spend time with yet another mother she had been wrenched from.

But Moomi was a mother who had not abandoned Afroze.

CHAPTER FIVE

MOOMI CARRIED A basket. It was an ugly old basket. But it was also the most beautiful basket in the world. She could not remember a time when she did not carry a basket. From the soft hand of her mother's mother, it was passed into the reluctant hand of a daughter who did not want to bear grass baskets. Moomi's mother dreamed of days when she would carry better things. But her dreams did not break her grip from the woven handle, and she bore it with obvious distaste. Too soon, when Moomi was a pretty girl who had only turned 13, her mother left the basket at the foot of her bed. Transference of a legacy Moomina would never escape.

Each morning when she awakened, Moomi picked up the handle, her palm fitting neatly into the smooth groove that had been shaped by the palms that had chafed before hers. And perhaps it had been a day when the sun had been shining so sweetly that soft Moomi had come into this world, for she did not mind the bearing of this burden. She was a girl born of acceptance and complete trusting love. She found a love for her basket; she connected with all that was within and all that was without. Moomi understood that it was this basket that had fed mouths, and it was this basket that would bring joy into the world.

For within folds of rough calico cloth, in the depths of this vessel, the women in Moomi's family carried food. Food was such a beautiful thing. Food could heal broken souls. Food sustained their men, and their little babies.

Moomi had learned this from a source closest to instinct. She had inherited a basket that bore sustenance and bursts of spice to the people who needed them most. She had learned the art of cooking even before she realized she was learning it. She knew the art of delicate spices, the orchestra of a world full of fresh, bright vegetables and Cape fruits, and the sensuous movement of rolling, stirring, waiting. A happy hand would bring into this world a dish that tasted only of happiness. Moomi knew how to bring joy. She sold her wares, like the women in her family had always done. Yet she sprinkled within the dishes an added condiment of joy.

She had become a familiar figure on the streets of Cape Town. First, as a young, dimpled girl who carried gleaming bottles of special Malay chutneys and dripping cinnamon-flavored confectionary to the throngs of workers in the office buildings on Long Street. The years had altered her lithe figure, and she had rounded out, spreading outwardly in generosity and girth, while her food spread outwardly in reputation. She was beloved. Her figure arrived at lunchtime to the Koopmans–De Wet House on Strand Street, one of the oldest Cape Dutch–style buildings in Cape Town. Once a home to wealthy Dutch sisters, it was now a museum housing opulent things.

Moomi had learned early enough not to stand too close to the entrance. There are some things that a mother teaches her child that go far beyond the kitchen. Her mother had taught her the best place to stand and ply her offerings. She stood near the sweeping entrance staircase, not too near, but close enough. She clutched her basket of food, which she had spent hours preparing as the sun rose over the city, and she silently waited for people to come and rummage through her wares, thrusting coins into her hand and leaving with the flavors they craved.

When the husband that she loved and feared in one deep inhalation brought home a child and handed this girl to her, leaving her staring and awkward without a bare explanation, Moomi did the only thing she knew how to do: she took the little girl and fed her. She took fresh, yeasty rolls dotted with fennel seeds out of her oven that often misbehaved, and having no butter to spare, spread one with jam made from ripe tomatoes.

"You must eat, child," she told Afroze, who sat stunned and skittish with all that had happened to her. Afroze grabbed the delicious roll and stuffed it into her mouth, and with each bite and each sip of sweet tea laced with condensed milk, warmth began to reenter her little body.

"Who is that man?" Afroze asked Moomi, staring at the closed door through which Ismail had rapidly left. Moomi paused, and her ample chest heaved with a deep sigh.

"Oh, you sweet girl. He didn't tell you anything, did he? Agh, so typical of that man."

"No. He only bought me a cola and a cake. And the car took a long time to come here," Afroze murmured.

"He is your father," Moomi said, unable to meet the child's large eyes.

"I want my ma. I want my Beatrice," Afroze said, and her bottom lip, stained with thick jam, began to quiver.

Moomi did not know reserve. She only knew the art of comfort. An art without artifice. Another woman's child sat in her kitchen. A woman she had never seen but had heard many stories about. Her own childless womb could easily have turned her heart to stone. But Moomi was not designed that way. She grabbed the child into a smothering embrace, feeling the tugs of deep desire. A feminine desire to protect and own.

"Agh now, child. You are with me now. And that is all you must remember."

"But, where is Ma?"

"Your ma. She is gone. That is all, now let me wipe your pretty face. You eat. You eat. Don't think about the bad things. I am with you now." She felt the tiny body struggle against her. The heart beat so fast and strong inside a chest that could not contain its terror and confusion. Moomi held onto the child. She never let her go. And inside the spicy warm smell of her desperate embrace, the stiff, scared body began to relax. Only once she felt a thought come rippling through the child, maybe a memory. Moomi soothed, smoothed soft hair, crooned and kissed wet cheeks. The thought slowly melted away. And it was in this smothered drowning that Afroze began to forget. Nothing mattered any longer. Not the frightening, long car journey from Brighton to Cape Town, one that had taken two days. Not the silent man who stared only at the open road and never at the huddled child. Everything became a distant goodbye inside a hot kitchen that smelled of baking bread. It was a most rapid forgetting.

When the child was full of hot tea, fresh bread, and sweet cakes, Moomi laid her down to sleep in her own quilted bed, ignoring the thought that the man would come home and want his place. She threw a patched-up quilt and a pillow on the threadbare couch in the drafty lounge room. *This is where he will sleep. Always, from now on.*

On her bed and in her arms was where her new child would sleep. It was Moomi's only act of rebellion. The place where each would lay her head and dream of all that had happened, and all that could be. She knew that if she slept next to this child, she would be a custodian of the child's dreams. And like a cleaning woman in a dusty town, she would follow the child into those dreams, wiping and wiping until all that remained was nothing of memory, and everything of possession. Two people who share a bed always seep into each other as they sleep, and soon, after many sleeps together, they begin to belong to each other.

As Afroze slept a sleep that brought nothing but warmth, Moomi sat quietly at the foot of the creaky bed, well into the night. She waited for the familiar sound of a key in the lock. Ismail had come home.

"I don't want to know what happened, Ismail. I don't want to know anything."

She had scuttled from Afroze's curled-up form and set to the task of feeding her husband. He ate noisily. He ate as if he didn't really care where the food had come from. Moomi, who had always found means to bring food to his table and had spent a lifetime asking no questions, decided that she would always prefer to ask no questions.

"Eyy … Moomi, listen to me, here. Don't you start on me. Don't you start your mouth. I am tired." Ismail didn't look up from his plate but pointed a finger stained with thick gravy up at her face.

"Ismail. You didn't hear me, neh? I said I don't want to know. Just tell me one thing—is she mine now?"

"What nonsense you jabbering, woman? She's not yours. She's never going to be yours. Dream baby. Dream." Ismail looked up from his food, chewing with exaggeration, and began to laugh loudly, knowing well enough that food fell from his mouth, half masticated and disgusting. He wanted to be as disgusting as he possibly could. He enjoyed seeing his wife look at the table strewn with his untidy, ravenous disrespect. It was his way of saying to Moomi, "You buy the food that I eat. But I will eat it how I want to."

"Shhh, Ismail. Quiet. The child is finally fast asleep. She was so upset, neh. She said you bought her nothing to eat but a small cake."

"Ja, so? So what?" Ismail challenged her, tearing into a piece of mutton, a cheap cut that Moomi had tenderized and boiled for a long time to make it palatable.

"Ismail, you're an animal. She is just a little girl. You brought her here without even talking to her, telling her why. Agh … I tell you, you is a bloody cruel man. Bloody cruel."

Ismail jolted up from his chair, scraping the metal feet against the cold cement floor with an ominous sound. He swung forward, pushing Moomi hard against the sink. He hovered over her, his face reeking of food, bits of bread and meat falling onto his beard, falling onto Moomi's hair as she was pushed, doubled over, against the metal sink.

"Woman. You shut your big ugly mouth. You know nothing about me. Nothing. I saved you, remember. You were this fat, ugly spinster, selling your chutneys and koeksisters like a slave woman in town. If I didn't marry you, then what? What then? You would've died on those museum steps old and dried up like a bloody hag. So you shut your mouth. And don't tell me what to do with my child. Not yours. Mine."

Moomi pushed hard against him. He chuckled, and stepped away from her.

"Bring me water. I'm going to sleep," he said, and wiped his fingers on her clean white kitchen towel, staining it.

"The child is sleeping with me. In my bed."

Ismail turned again. Sharply. His arm raised, he was about to swing it in a rapid slap.

"Ma … I want Beatrice. I want my Beatrice." The loud crying of Afroze came flying into the moment. The child's cry stemmed the familiar action of a hard, strong blow.

And the child's cry brought fury to the eyes of a once-cowering wife. She squared up to him, staring him directly in his eyes.

"Don't," Moomi growled. "I am going to bed. And she is sleeping next to me."

Ismail swore loudly. He took a few stumbling steps backward, hating the arrival of this child already on the first day. His loathing took an unnerving path. It began its ruthless course with fury against the wife he had left behind in the tiny town where he was born, and where he felt the suffocation of a grave. It exploded toward a child he barely knew as his own. And finally it found its resting place against this woman whom he had always had dominion over. He knew Moomi's nature well, because he had spent years running through streets, studying people's inner hearts.

He knew weaklings, he knew targets. It was how he made his life, prospecting for an easy foil, taking what he could and slipping away unnoticed. He had married this woman, not for her beauty and certainly not for the most alien emotion called love. Ismail had married Moomi because he had studied her long before she knew he was doing it. She was to be his anchor, the one who would keep him comfortable.

And he knew she was docile, with too good a heart to turn on him. Until this day. Now, when a child that he preferred to forget had been thrust into his new world. This child would turn the world of her furious father inside out.

Moomi snuggled deep into the heavy quilt. It was an ugly coverlet, fashioned out of the discarded clothing of the men and women of her family. Thick brown corduroy patches from a man's rough coat were stitched incongruently next to patches of floral cotton from a woman's frock. Pockets became patches. Pleated lilac skirts were ripped open and flattened into harsh squares. There were times when Moomi lay under the quilt, feeling the taut muscles of Ismail nudge into her softness, when she could only look as the rise and fall of the clothing of the generations of people that had borne her thrust acceptance into her flesh, much like the man who covered her thrust into her flesh.

Look, girly. Don't you cry now. This is how we always did it. Be quiet and let him finish.

Tonight, beside her lay a treasure. A softly breathing child, with eyes so large and beautiful and skin so much like milky satin that Moomi could not sleep. She kept opening her tired eyes to stare and stare at this gift. She had never felt love before. She had imagined a moment of love when the tall, wiry Ismail came to court her. But nothing in the world felt like this.

"Oh, you're a pretty, pretty child. My pretty, pretty child," Moomi crooned.

CHAPTER SIX

THERE WAS NO time for getting used to things. Moomi knew that a day without carrying her basket of wares into the streets of Cape Town meant a day without money wrapped in a handkerchief, tucked into her bosom. She woke Afroze from a warm bed and dragged the dazed child into the motions of her world. Soon they would become the accustomed motions of the child's day as well. Packing the food, wrapping the freshly fried koeksisters in brown paper parcels. Two by two. Wrapping the warm rolls into pillows of paper, twisting the ends as if there was a candy inside, they placed them into a thickly laden basket of food that both woman and child could smell but would dare not eat. Eating the wares meant losing money.

Money—warm coins from busy pockets and notes that were so crisp that they crackled like biscuits—that was all that mattered. The basket was heavy. Moomi carried it, so practiced now. But she was older. She transferred the heavy burden from hand to hand. She huffed and puffed, straining her legs to walk down the steep hills from the Bo-Kaap Malay Quarter into the city. She felt strains of pity as Afroze lagged behind, unaccustomed to walking distances. But she refused to pay for a bus. No cent could be spared.

Afroze followed this woman, a stranger but somehow already familiar. She said nothing, asked nothing. Somewhere inside a night of sleep, with the soft breath of Moomi falling on her cheeks, she had fallen into a state of trust. No one had slept next to her before. Afroze's forgetting continued with this simplest of acts: a child sleeping next to a mother. Moomi had willed it so. Be silent. And trust.

Perhaps in awkwardness, or in attempts to comfort, Moomi carried on an incessant monologue. She spoke, wanting no response. The time had not come yet for an exchange, though that time would come. Moomi described each item of food to Afroze, who peered at each treasure with interest. She soaked up the descriptions of the perfect peach chutney, the way in which to break bread into chunks, rather than take an unforgiving knife to it.

She had helped Moomi tie the strings around the little packets of homemade condensed milk cookies, even counting out loud each one that went into a package. And when the basket was full, she followed Moomi's purposely muffled footsteps. A glance at the disarray of long arms and legs emerging from the couch in the lounge room told Afroze that silence was the best thing. The man, this person she now knew as father, lay snoring loudly in a gnarled posture. Spittle dotted his beard, and he had fallen asleep with one shoe on.

Afroze giggled, and quickly put a hand to her mouth. Moomi returned the tiny giggle, her eyes sparkling. They both shared so much more than just a laugh as they looked at the sleeping man who had brought them to each other.

Once outside, the cold Cape Town air sucked the wind out of both their bodies. Afroze had arrived without a winter coat. Brighton was a hot town, winter there had only asked for a light covering of the skin. But Cape Town in winter was a different animal. Moomi knew this. And she had given Afroze an old gray shawl of scratchy polyester masquerading as wool. Afroze itched and sneezed and trudged, dragging her tired body behind Moomi. But each time Moomi turned around to look, she saw Afroze moving. The child was exhausted. But she never stopped walking.

On the steps to the museum on Strand Street, Moomi found her spot. A few feet away from her, another woman stood, similar baskets in hand, similar wares. Flower sellers mingled with fruit ladies, while those who sold crocheted doilies hung behind. An unsaid agreement between the basket ladies from the Malay Quarter wove among them like a strong thread. They only knew the similar things—the foods and cakes that they had learned to make even before they could reach the old coal stoves. So, they sold similar things, same things. Yet each woman would never compete against the other. They would never argue or fight over customers. The businessmen and office workers who could not get through their day without this tasty fare would haggle with these poor women for petty change. Trying to play one woman against the other for a tiny bargain, one that meant nothing to them. But when all the money was counted, it was this haggling that meant the world to each woman. A few cents lost was a sport to the buyer. A funny little game to play. But those few cents lost meant many things to the woman it had been denied. The women protected each other in a silent code and never undercut each other's prices.

Moomi placed the heavy basket on the floor. It would be at least half an hour before the first customers would arrive. The early-morning newspapermen, hot coffee in hand, craving a warm bread roll or a freshly fried donut. Moomi picked the basket back up and tucked layers of the old editions of the same newspapermens' words underneath, hoping that the warm food would be insulated slightly against the ice-cold cement floor. Cold food meant more haggling.

Around Afroze, a group of women formed a little curious battalion.

"Ay, Salaamat, Moomina, what is this neh? Who is this child?" A tall, strong woman said, and poked the reddening frostbite of Afroze's cheek.

"Ja man, Moomi, what's happening?"

Moomi, once quiet, always watchful and ever smiling, came to life surrounded by the sisterhood of women she had known all her life. Finally she could unburden. Finally she could talk to her own. She placed her hands on her hips and, shaking her head, she began a series of clicks and *tsk-tsks* that tightened the radius of her circle of sisters. She didn't have to say a word. Her eyebrows arched up into her creased forehead and her pursed, fleshy lips told them all they needed to know.

"Agh, no. That Ismail se baba, neh Moomi?"

Ismail's child. Ismail's child. The whisper spread as the Cape wind began to blow harder.

"Wait, you just wait here," a small, pretty girl told Moomi, and with a flash of their eyes, the women secretly conveyed the message: don't speak. Not in front of the child.

A few minutes later, the girl appeared with a man at her side.

"Ja Allah, Moomi, it's bloody cold outside for this kinder, this child. Leave her with Oom Dawud. He'll hide her inside the museum neh. What-what Oom, you take die dogter?"

"Yey, Sis Noorien! What, you want me to lose my job what? I kan nie kinders in Wit mens museum bly nie. No. Agh. Nee, nee."

The old man backed away cautiously from the flashing eyes of the gaggle of women. He knew he had lost the battle, but at least he had tried anyway.

The tall woman who had poked at Afroze's frozen cheek stepped forward and spoke directly to the shivering man.

"Dawud. Ek se vir jou … I am telling you. I am your vrou, neh, your wife. If you know what-what is good, tonight in the bed, neh, you take this baby inside the museum."

The women in the group began nudging one another, and a loud giggling emerged from the group. Tall, bossy Reyhana always got her way with her husband, Dawud, who was on duty as the security guard at the building.

"Yo, missus. This is white man museum, neh. Jy weet. You know it's trouble." Dawud tried feebly to change the womens' minds. But they laughed him off. "Ja, but whose kindtjie is this thin one?" He asked and scanned the group.

"Oom. She's my girl. She is Ismail's …" Moomi said softly, looking imploringly into the older man's eyes. He stared at Afroze.

Afroze hid farther and farther behind Moomi's thick jersey. Both her itchy shawl and Moomi's cheap jersey made her erupt into a loud bout of sneezes.

"Ey, you! I'm telling you one time. See this child, so sick, she is in the cold. Now, Dawud, don't make me get angry, neh. You take her inside. You want this small child to catch the nimmonee?" Tall Reyhana bossed her husband. A murmur rippled through the crowd of women. They recalled a terrible bout of pneumonia that had claimed a young boy some months ago.

Dawud looked at Moomi, who looked away. Suddenly, the tears that had been threatening to burst from inside her welled up in her kind eyes. The security guard could do nothing but agree. He tutted and shook his head in a half-hearted attempt to appear angry at his overbearing wife. But he looked at Moomi. They all knew her story well. They knew Ismail; they knew pieces of his dark past. And they saw the stains of his anger on Moomi's skin.

Dawud held out a hand to little Afroze, who clung tighter to Moomi. "Kom now, kindertjie. Don't be frightened of Oom, Uncle Dawud. Come inside. I'll show you the famous rooms before the whites come. It's very nice, neh. Kom now."

Afroze looked up at Moomi, her eyes large and watering from the icy-cold wind. Moomi nodded at her softly and nudged her toward Dawud. Slowly, she took hold of the man's large, rough hand and walked off with him up the stairs into the building. Moomi watched Afroze walk away, the large gray shawl trailing like a train behind her thin frame, and her hot tears could no longer be contained. She began to sob, and there were many shoulders for her to lay her crying head on, and many warm arms to hold her.

CHAPTER SEVEN

THE RUSH OF warmth inside the museum made Afroze shudder like a puppy shaking off a sleep, and she wondered why warmth made her shudder yet the cold outside did not. Her little body relaxed, and she realized how tightly she had been clenching her muscles the moment she stopped. She stood in the large entrance hallway, and the smell of something ancient and wondrous wrapped its way around her. She did not know what it was. Maybe it was the smell of old wood, the scent of books tucked away in library archives. Maybe it was just the clean smell of purity, filled with light and air.

She had suffocated with the smell of the strong spices that hung in the air from Moomi's cooking, hot, cloying smells inside a very small house. The walk to the city from the Malay Quarter was frightening in the semidark of a Cape Town morning—murkiness chased Afroze into every nook, and evil things lurked under every bridge and eave. Acrid smells of stale urine and unwashed beggars who lay passed out, reeking strongly of the cheap wine that they drank. Afroze enjoyed this sudden scent of subtle opulence.

Always a child sensitive to smells, Afroze remembered the strong spicy attar of her mother's perfume and the sharp stink of the medical antiseptics that had haunted her Brighton days. And here, the Cape Town smells of musty kitchens and filthy beggars turned her stomach. This new smell of richness and cleanliness that large ceilings, straight pillars, and arches that spanned into lavender-scented courtyards conveyed etched itself into her mind. Afroze could smell spaces and shapes, as if spaces and shapes could emit fragrance.

The museum was a balm. It was luxury, and beauty. Just a sprite of six, Afroze sensed something grand in the halls and facades. Perhaps it was in the child's nature to seek out space and light, to notice curves and lines in much the same way children notice a new wrinkle at the corner of their mothers' eyes long before anyone else does. When she suddenly arrived at a place that just made sense, who she was and how many years she had breathed didn't matter anymore. A puzzle piece that she had been searching for her whole life now fit neatly into its place. She might be six, but she knew that she was among familiar friends. Afroze drank in the neatness of it. She had a knack for knowing what went where, and why.

"Yessus kindertie, don't you sommer stand and gape, neh, I must put you somewhere sharp-sharp. White man coming now-now, neh." Dawud shuffled nervously around the entrance hall, looking under glossy tables and opening little doors. He silently cursed that wife of his, the strong Reyhana. She always seemed to get her way. And he knew her well. Reyhana took on sad stories and clung to them with her strong arms, willing them with her sheer force to become happy stories.

Dawud was not unaccustomed to coming home from the mosque after saying his evening prayers and stealing a little smoke from a hookah with the men on the street, and then finding strange-looking urchins seated at his dinner table. He would sometimes wake up from a sleep, if he had done the night shift at the museum, to find women he barely recognized scuttling about his home, hair undone, barely covering their battered faces. He had warned Reyhana many times to stop trying to save the entire world and focus on her own nest instead. But she had never changed in all their years of marriage, and nothing would change her now.

Their two sons and daughter had long ago married and left home, but still they lurked around his home daily, unable to leave the glowing satellite that was their mother. Sometimes Dawud's home resembled a soup kitchen, a nursery, a school, and a clinic all bundled up into one chaotic mess, with Reyhana in her bright headscarf barking orders at everyone. Dawud enjoyed the peace of the museum. At least there he could smoke his cigarettes quietly if the curator was not around, and he could softly dream all his strange little dreams.

Now he was saddled with looking after this child, finding a place for the frightened thing to hide, while outside, he was certain, Reyhana would be pounding her palm with a ham fist, plotting how to sort out the problem. He had no doubt at all that Moomi and this child, whom he now knew belonged to that indecent, wild husband of hers, Ismail, would soon become permanent additions to his life. He sighed and shrugged. No one could hear him curse out loud. Reyhana would always have her way because he was weak in her presence, and he admitted sorrowfully that he loved her deeply for all the reasons a man comes to love a woman in older age. He admired her strength. He knew he was a lesser person to her, and her charitable heart would one day take them both through the gates of sweet paradise.

He peered inside a tiny closet, the musty place where the cleaning woman stored her brooms, mops, and smelly liquids. It would have to do. He knew that the cleaning and dusting for the day had been done earlier, and no one would care to look inside the closet for the day.

"Ey, dogtertjie. Ey. Ja ... you. What you dreaming now, white man will mos beat jou blue, neh. Kom hier, kom nou."

Afroze stood frozen to the spot. The ominously dark cupboard looked very much like a place where ogres took children to murder them. Her wide, dark eyes began to well up with hot tears. Dawud glared at the child. He looked quickly at the clock. It was almost time for the curator, the guides, and the official workers to file in the door.

Secretly he hoped that the women outside had thought quickly and delayed them by trying to sell them food. And then he remembered that Reyhana had barked out an order to him as he had led the child away.

"Yey, Dawud, jou skaap, onthou, neh, die dogtertjie verstaan niks van Afrikaans nie. Engels, net Engels, neh. Ek se vir jou."

Reyhana had instructed Dawud that Afroze did not understand a word of the language that he spoke, Afrikaans mixed with a touch of pidgin English—the typical dialect spoken by the Malay people, who had long forgotten their language when they were brought to the Cape as slaves from Indonesia by the Dutch settlers.

Dawud spoke good English. He hated it, but he had learned. The important people that often visited this museum cared nothing for his language or dialect at all and persisted in addressing their orders to him in clipped English or very strong Afrikaans. He began to learn little nuances of all languages well—the museum saw visitors from all corners of the world, and Dawud, in his devotion to keeping this job in the sanctity of the one quiet place he knew, had learned fast. He gestured again to Afroze, who was now sobbing. It had been a while since he had comforted a child, let alone a girl-child. Things like that were left to the women. He had barely hugged his own daughter, even on her wedding day he had shook her little hand in an awkward congratulation.

The fat tears that plopped onto the floor from such a face strangely melted his heart, and he was not accustomed to the tugging inside his chest. He reserved his tears for the days at the mosque when the Imam's lecture would be particularly emotive, describing in a mournful voice the martyrdom of the Prophet's grandsons. The last time Dawud had almost broke into racking sobs was when a visiting Qari from Mecca had read beloved verses from the Holy Book with such intense beauty that Dawud had prayed that such a voice would be the one he hears when he breathes his last. But here, this child sobbing in her thick gray shawl threatened to break all his strength.

He held out his arms; the bayonet he kept at his side for no reason whatsoever, as no one dared come near this place, dropped to the ground as it lost its strap.

"Child, come here. Come here. Don't cry, neh. Don't be scared of Oom … Uncle Dawud."

Afroze looked away from the dark closet he had opened, its musty maw forgotten, aching deeply for a comforting hug. She could hold out no longer. She ran into Dawud's embrace with the innocence of one who has suffered deeply. Her taut muscles relaxed into a fluid union with the strong arms of this man who suddenly remembered how to hold a child.

"Look, my child … what is your name, neh?"

"Rosie …" Afroze murmured, and bit her lip.

Dawud smoothed the glossy hair, tied into an untidy ponytail, tendrils threatening to escape the flimsy ties. He lifted her tiny quivering chin with his finger and smiled in a way that, he hoped, seemed benign. He knew that sometimes an adult's smile could look very much like a grimace.

"Rosie … Ah, what a pretty name for a pretty girl. Like a little pink rose, neh. Stop crying now, I promise you, Uncle Dawud will take very good care of you."

Afroze looked deeply into his eyes. It was the first time an adult had used the word *promise* to her. She recognized the word, and she knew it was a good, trusting word. She liked the word.

"Promise … promise, Uncle?" she whispered and clung to his arm.

"Ahg hierdie kind, sy sal my slegs 'n vroumens maak, sies tog," he muttered under his breath, bemoaning the effect this child was having on him, turning his gruff, manly demeanor into one of a simpering woman. He was helpless in her gaze. This child's eyes could move mountains, and they would.

"I promise. I promise, Rosie, if you go and stay quiet inside this cupboard, very quickly, the time will fly away, and I will take you to your mummy."

"She is not my mummy," Afroze said, her voice suddenly forceful.

Dawud glanced up as a creaking door told him that perhaps the curator had arrived. In all the years that he had worked at the museum, the curator had never been late. And it was exactly eight o' clock. The footsteps pounded on the wooden floor. Quickly, he bundled Afroze into the cupboard.

"I'll come to see you just now-now. You be very quiet, neh, Rosie. Very quiet," Dawud said and rapidly shut the door. He said a silent prayer, hoping that no one had seen him and hoping that those large lamplike eyes that shone out of the dark room would not haunt his dreams.

"Ah, Dawud. There you are. I was wondering where on Earth you had gotten to. The basket women on the street seem to have gotten themselves into an awful state. Do you know what's happened, old fella?"

Dawud stood bolt upright, almost saluting. "No sir, Mr. Arnsworth, sir. I don't know nothing. You know these women, they must have seen a frog or something, very excitable women, sir."

"Yes. Yes, very excitable. Now, Dawud, listen. I'm expecting a visitor at twelve o' clock. His name is Professor Heinrich Opperman, a very famous architect. He's visiting as a professor at the University of Cape Town, you know, and had kindly agreed to come and advise on the restoration of the Music Room. Very exciting, very exciting indeed."

The prim and always immaculately dressed curator puffed out his chest, presumptious in his belief that a security guard who was barely allowed into the opulent inner rooms would know anything of a famous architecture professor.

Dawud knew well enough that it was best to pretend, and he beamed with false knowledge and pride. "Really! Wonderful news, Mr. Arnsworth, sir. Very famous man, very, very good news."

"Oh, indeed, Dawud. Now, make sure you send him straight to my offices, and tell Sweetie to sort out a good tea tray. Only the best for the best, I always say. Righto, off I go."

"Righto. Righto, sir." Dawud bowed slightly as the curator wafted to his upstairs office, plushly furnished and overlooking the flower-lined inner courtyard.

He breathed a sigh of relief and went to peek into the little closet, glad that the little girl did not sob or sneeze while the curator stood there. He found Afroze standing rooted to the same spot, bathed in the shaft of light that entered with the open door. He realized then that she had been in complete darkness, standing there among brooms and smelly ammonia and furniture polish. It must have been a scary place to find herself, but the little thing had not moved a muscle. Dawud had the impression that this child was very accustomed to hiding away in corners and fading away into dark recesses.

He could not imagine what her small life had been like, and he did not have a moment to contemplate it. The rattle of castors on polished wood told him that Sweetie the cook was approaching, bringing the curator's morning tea and breakfast. He wondered if the child was hungry, and decided that she obviously was. He could have included Sweetie into his confidence, but he knew her well. She could barely contain a secret and was known among the staff for her prattling.

Quickly he reached in and pulled the chain that switched on a bare, hanging lightbulb, which flooded the room with harsh light.

He put his fingers to his lips, winked at Afroze, and shut the door quickly, just in time for Sweetie to come around the corner from the kitchen to the entrance hall.

"Morning to you, Sweetie. Dis 'n regte koud dag, neh?" he rambled, then quickly stepped in front of the closet door, trying to hide the slit of light that shone through from underneath.

"Ah, Oom, Dawud. It is so cold today, the coffeepot had to be wrapped in my special blankets, neh," Sweetie joked, gesturing toward the fuzzy crocheted cover that Sweetie had made, an extra-special touch to show her devotion to her job. The loud colors of the crocheted tea cozy clashed with the crisp white tray cloth, sparkling silverware, and pure white crockery.

From underneath a gleaming cloche delicious smells wafted, and Dawud salivated, knowing full well that he had to content himself with homemade jam sandwiches and weak tea. "Oh, Sweetie, you are a clever meisie, neh. Beautiful crochet, beautiful cooking, and so beautiful a face. Must be a lucky man you have for you, neh."

He bantered with the giggling girl, hoping she would be too absorbed in his praises to notice the sliver of light. Sweetie patted her wiry hair hidden underneath a hairnet and a ruffled, white cap.

"Nee, man Oom. You mos nie say this to me, neh. Youz know how I suffer in my Ma se huis, can't find a decent man today and age, Oomie. Just the other day my Tannie Elma bring a very nice man for tea. Agh, he was handsome, neh. He working in the lawyer office on Buitenkant Street, neh. But … Agh, Oomie Dawud, my ma, she chase him with a broom from the house, neh. Down the road, Oomie, so ashamed I feel. I tell you the story why my ma chase so good man away, neh …" Sweetie prattled on.

Dawud silently cursed his line of talk. Everyone knew that Sweetie was a very reluctant spinster, living with her cranky, old mother, and that despite all her best efforts, marriage and suitors had evaded the girl. Talking about her spinsterhood, her mother and all the suitors that she had apparently rejected was a topic that Sweetie relished, and it would be a conversation that could go on.

Quickly, Dawud recovered himself. He pushed the trolley with his foot and leaned into Sweetie, attempting to take her into a confidence. He knew her well enough, she would fall for it.

"Wait now, meisie. Listen, I have big news. Curator sir is having very important visitor today—important professor from university. He is coming to do up the music room, neh. And curator sir says to me that I must tell Sweetie only she can impress the professor with her famous tea and cakes and what-all."

Sweetie's eyes widened and she patted down her apron, smoothed her skirts. "Oh, Oh … Oomie. Thank you. Agh, here I am sommer talk-talk when I have so much to do. Maybe I will make my famous honey cake, neh. Agh, maybe daai watercress sandwiches Curator Sir he loves. Agh, Oomie, nee man, ek kan nie by jou bly vir chat-chat. I must go, now-now."

"Hou op, Sweetie. Go quickly, neh. Curator Sir said he is relying for you to impress important professor. Agh, meisie, and the coffee must be getting cold too—your beautiful dress you knit for the coffee-pot can only do so much."

"Ja, s'true Oomie. Let me run now. Your fault, you keep me here asking me to talk to you. Agh, I have so much to do. Maybe I will get some flowers from the courtyard. Maybe I make scones too. I have the fig jam I buy from Moomi outside. Maybe I … agh, bye bye Oomie. I must … go … I must …"

Sweetie pushed her tea trolley with rattling force, muttering lists of ingredients and dishes in her wake, and Dawud almost doubled over with silent laughter. He wondered if Sweetie would be imagining a handsome young professor who would sweep her away from her droll life and away from the vice of spinsterhood. He was glad she had not seen the light under the door.

The hours slipped by quietly. Dawud did not venture into the cleaning closet; there were too many visitors that kept coming and leaving the museum. He was kept busy handing over the guest book to be signed many times over, and even had to rap his bayonet against the wooden desk when an unruly little boy began to run among the antique blue and white porcelain tulip vases that sat precariously on spindly legged oak tables. He thought guiltily about the large sign outside: no children under 10 allowed into exhibition hall. He thought of six-year-old Rosie inside the cleaning closet, and how he would lose his job if she was discovered.

At one point, he looked outside to the place next to the entrance steps, where the women selling food and flowers stood. He looked with squinted eyes but could not make out his tall wife, who was hard to miss for her height and very bright clothes. He couldn't see her and felt annoyed that perhaps these women had left the child with him and gone off to sit in the rare sunshine in Greenmarket Square. It was unlike Reyhana to be so irresponsible. Something must have happened for them to leave, for Moomi to leave her child there without even a word to him. He would find out later. For now, he did his job with extra care.

At precisely ten o' clock, a gentleman with warm, brown eyes that peered over a pair of silver bifocals stood before him. He had a glorious head of silver hair, worn longer than most men, and he wore a charming tweed coat and brown corduroy trousers. He carried a brown satchel that seemed to have been molded to him along with dark green cardboard tubes filled with plans and designs. Dawud was peeping over his shoulders at the cleaning closet as the man approached and rapped lightly with his knuckles on the desk.

Dawud jumped upward, startled as if he had been caught doing a terrible thing.

"Good morning, my good man," the gentleman said in a pleasantly gruff voice. "I am sorry, have I startled you?"

"No. No. I was ... looking for a ... naughty child here," Dawud recovered himself.

"Oh, there is no such thing as a naughty child. There are only curious children. And all children are such treasures, naughty or not, wouldn't you say?"

Dawud blinked at the man, wondering in his most paranoid way if he had perhaps been set up. He thought it best to be silent. An answer might just damn him.

"Ah, well. I see you are a man of serious business," the man continued. Well, let's get to it. I am Heinrich Opperman, architect. I believe Mr. Arnsworth is expecting me."

"Yes, oh yes, Mr. Professor Architect, sir," Dawud jumped up and saluted the architect as if he were an army general.

"No need for all that Professor Sir business. It's Heinrich. Simple name, but it certainly sticks on the tongue. Blame my old gran; she loved the Germans."

Again, Dawud was lost for words. He was certainly not accustomed to being drawn into pleasant conversation with anybody who visited the museum. Mostly they barked orders at him, ignored him, or, like Mr. Arnsworth, talked down to him and expected supreme adulation.

"Heinrich ..." Dawud tested the sound on his own tongue and found nothing sticking there.

"Yes, that's me. Now ... where shall I find this curator of yours?"

"Agh, he's not mine ..." Dawud blurted out and a loud laugh echoed from the belly of the professor. It was infectious, and soon Dawud was also chuckling.

The loud laugh brought Mr. Arnsworth scuttling into the entrance hall. Clearly he had been lurking in wait for the esteemed professor. He cast a disapproving glance at Dawud, and quickly began ushering the professor upstairs to his office, using his best flowery speech and gesticulating wildly.

As they disappeared into the office, Dawud saw Sweetie peer at him from the entrance to the service quarters corridor.

"So, Sweetie, what you say? Handsome, neh?" Dawud teased.

Sweetie made a face, and wagged a finger at Dawud. "Oomie, jy is sommer naughty, neh. Old man like that! Agh, he'll have a heart attacking him if he see Sweetie dressed up beautiful."

She giggled and disappeared down the passage. Now Dawud had some silence. He toyed with the thought of sitting in his chair and spending his time daydreaming, which he loved to do. But his conscience gnawed at him, and he chose to peep in at Rosie. The little girl was fast asleep amid the tall mop handles, wrapped in her gray shawl.

He felt a stab of guilt. She had probably been starving. He shut the door and went to his desk, taking his large coat from his chairback. He went to the closet again and draped the coat over the sleeping child. She stirred and looked up at him with trusting eyes. He patted her shoulder, and as he did, she closed her tiny fist around his wrist and fell into a sleep again. Slowly, Dawud pried the little fist from his thick wrist and lay her hand softly down on the coat.

CHAPTER EIGHT

DAWUD WAS NOT happy. He was not settled. What began as a day of hiding little Afroze in the cleaning closet was fast becoming a daily ritual. He couldn't even remember how Reyhana had nagged him into agreement. He had put up a good fight, but a futile one. His wife had made up her mind. She riled and regaled him with every parable from the Holy Book she could think of, mentioning names of the Prophet's dearest advisors and how they had sheltered and protected the weak and the vulnerable.

Reyhana was clever like that. She knew that if she appealed to the one thing that was dearest to her man—the love he had for his religion and its principles—then he would have no fight in him. She mentioned how the Beloved Prophet would save the lives of discarded baby girls; she dug deep into folklore and came up with heart-wrenching stories of saints and saviors. She challenged his morality, she harangued at his sense of duty, and finally she had gotten her way. Dawud agreed to keep hiding Afroze in the museum until Moomi was able to sort out a school that she could go to.

Of schools, there were very few. The good-enough schools in the Bo-Kaap were filled to bursting. The schools that had reputations—for being filled with rowdy children of Cape Flats' gangsters, drug addicts and babies possibly born out of the wombs of women of ill-repute—were far away, and not a place to send a girl who had lived a life sheltered in a tiny town. Moomi had the added difficulty of Ismail, who had adamantly refused to acknowledge that the child even existed in his home. He spent most of his time ignoring her, barely looking at her, and gritting his teeth if she walked by him.

Moomi spent her nights waiting for Ismail to come home, because despite his many roamings (she barely wanted to know the details of where he went), Ismail always found his way back to Moomi's kitchen. She never asked him why he had such rage toward the child, yet she ached to ask him more about the woman who had borne her.

In Moomi's imagination, she pictured a woman with the body and stature of a warrior and the face of Afroze, and this was a disturbing vision. She knew very little. She had heard snippets of Ismail's life before he came to Cape Town. She knew he had been involved somehow in the anti-apartheid struggle, although knowing her husband well, she knew that his involvement could not have lasted long.

Ismail was too selfish to give away his freedom and his life to anything that was larger than his own needs. She knew that Afroze's mother was a doctor, and on some nights, Ismail would torture her by speaking of the nameless woman and how tall, slim, and beautiful she was. Moomi could not help but feel twinges of envy for a woman she had never met, a woman who had looks and intelligence but clearly did not have a heart.

Moomi, who had been rendered childless by a cruel God, could never understand how any woman would throw away her own beautiful child. Ismail, in a rare moment of calm, had told her one once that the telephone call he had received that late night, the call that came to the neighbor's home three houses away because Moomi did not have a telephone, had been the child's mother. She had begged him to take the girl away, and she had told him to come quickly, the child was being left at the home of a family friend in their small town. When Ismail told the tale, he curled his lips in anger, telling Moomi that the doctor had cracked, that she couldn't handle the pressure of looking after a child. That she had made a choice and this little girl was not part of the choice she had made. After hearing this, Moomi did not like the doctor at all.

But none of this mattered to Moomi. She swooped down on Afroze and rapidly morphed into an ideal mother. All her frustrated childless yearnings came pouring out onto Afroze. Moomi began to believe that this girl had come from her womb. She treated Afroze like a precious but fragile gift, one that could be snatched away from her at any moment. And Moomi was not selfless, after all. She selfishly chipped away at Afroze's memories, her chisel of smothering love lacerating off pieces and pieces of Afroze's life before. She would only admit to herself in the late hours of certain nights that all she wanted was for this child to forget everything of where she had arrived from.

She would rapidly change the topic when Afroze asked about people back in Brighton. She would coddle Afroze in a blanket of ignorance, driving out memories and questions with a constant stream of immersion into this new life. She tried to make it such that in every moment she shared with Afroze, she ensured that her mind could not drift toward the ghost mother with whom Moomi competed. It was only those times when Afroze was secreted away inside the museum that Moomi regarded with deep anxiety. Those hours, long and painful, were the only times Afroze was away from her bosom. Moomi began to imagine that, alone, inside a small room, glaring at a naked lightbulb, Afroze communed with her past. And Moomi's answer to those alone times, those necessary separations, was to ply Afroze with as many delicious treats from her basket as she could afford. Moomi believed that when Afroze was away from her, it was her food that would keep the thread between them, and it was her food that would act as holy water—the type that exorcises demons.

Afroze forgot very easily. It was not the hardest task in the world. Here, she found things that made her happy and comfortable. She found happy women who cooked and talked and took her into their embraces. They plaited her hair, they dressed her, they fed her, and they listened to her voice. It was something that was entirely alien to her; her life in Brighton had been so different.

There, she had nothing feminine to anchor her. Her daily needs were always seen to, and she had been fed and clothed and sometimes played with by Beatrice. But for the most part, life in Brighton for a six-year-old girl in a home filled with politics and anxiety was not pleasant. She dug at the secrets she knew hid inside crumbling buildings. She spent countless nights staring at her mother skulking in and out of that horrible, forbidden building at the back of the house. And finding no reasonable answer, Afroze—being a child, after all—began to believe that dark, witchy magic went on in that place. She began to believe that her mother was indeed a witch who killed people inside that building; Afroze had heard men scream.

Here, in the tiny rooms of Moomi, Afroze felt that she had been rescued from certain death. Perhaps the witch had planned to kill her next. That was the only logical explanation. So she accepted Moomi's overwhelming, suffocating love, and bathed in the light of the basket-bearing women that were Moomi's sisters, and finally decided that life had begun the day she had been given, Moseslike, to this mother, the one who bore the basket home. Yet she could only call her Moomi, and in terrifying nightmares, she called out the name Ma.

It is surprisingly easy for a child to transfer. A child will embrace the one that embraces her. And Afroze was quick. She loved her Moomi. She sat alone in the cleaning closet of the museum for many days that soon became many months, and her life was happy. It was almost perfect. Dawud grew accustomed to her being hidden there, and he even grew brave once or twice and let her out of the closet during quiet moments, letting her stand and stare at the magnificent rooms, the wide arches and the spiral staircase. He let her wander among the ceramics, and look at the murals and paintings. And in those rarest of times, Afroze felt most at peace.

When Reyhana complained that perhaps the child was too bored in there, Dawud stole a writing pad and pencil from one of the offices and gave it to Afroze. When he went to sneak her out of the room that afternoon, he was shocked to see that she had used up every single inch of the writing pad. Her large, curved drawings arched all over the pages in thick, hard scrawl.

She had been pressing down on the pencil with all her might, forcing snippets of her mind onto the pages. She had drawn the things that she saw. Interpretations of sash windows, arches, doorjambs, and pillars. Sweeping rooms with strangely skewed ceilings, rooms that led into other rooms, hidden passageways, crevices of imagination, and recesses in the walls.

The one thing Afroze had not drawn, and would in fact never draw, was people. The pages and pages were filled until there was no space to even place a series of dots. But not a single person could be found anywhere. Dawud looked strangely at the writing pad. He knew that children always drew little line drawings of stick people.

He had seen his children scrawl Mama, Dada, Brother, Friend stick montages over walls and on tar driveways and cul-de-sac roads. But this child had drawn only things. Things, spaces, and places.

The following day, he gave her another writing pad and another pencil. And she did the same. He supplied Afroze with a constant pile of pages, used-up paper that he found in dustbins, the backs of pamphlets and old calenders. The pile of drawings grew larger and larger.

One day he found her clutching a dirty, old book to her chest while he hushed her down the steps, out to the waiting Moomi.

"Ey, kindtjie, what you have there? No stealing from the museum, you hear?"

"Oom, I'm not stealing. The old man gave it to me."

"What, eh? What old man? Let me see."

She reluctantly handed him her dirty, torn-up treasure. It was an old architecture magazine.

Dawud paged through the faded and crumpled-up pages. He saw nothing there that would interest a child. It looked like trash.

"Oom, the old, nice man. He came into the closet looking for a cloth; he said he spilled his tea. He saw my drawing. Then he went away, and came back with this."

Afroze handed Dawud the magazine.

"What? You spoke to Professor? Oh hoh hooo … we in trouble now, meisie."

"No, Oom, he was nice. He said he won't tell nobody. He said he is a … a archi-test."

Dawud stared at Afroze. He wondered whether his job at the museum was finally over. He decided that it was time to stop taking chances. He would tell Reyhana tonight. The child had to go.

"Agh, what archi-test? What you know about archi-test, archi-test. Go, throw this dirty thing away," he scolded, and crumpled up the magazine.

Afroze screamed and launched herself at him, trying to pull the magazine away from his grip. He was glad they were outdoors, no one had heard her.

"Yoh, wildcat. Relax, neh. Keep your magazine. I'm just saying it must have sommer germs."

Afroze grabbed the magazine from him and clutched it to her chest, staring at him with molten fire in her eyes. "It don't have no germs. And he gave it to me. It is mine. You can't take it away from me."

Afroze's shrill child voice rang out into the emptying square in front of the museum. People stopped to stare. Afroze ignored everyone and stomped off and away from Dawud. He, who had hidden her, cared for her, risked his job for her, mattered nothing at all. All that mattered to Afroze was the beauty she saw inside the magazine. It was surprisingly easy for Afroze to turn her back and forget Oom Dawud. He meant nothing to her in the larger world.

She turned and walked off toward Moomi, who dared not try and take it away. Dawud shook his head and walked off. He felt a slight stab of hurt that little Afroze could so easily cast him off, replace him because of a silly magazine that probably made no sense to her.

"Strange child," he muttered, but then had to remind himself that she did not lead a normal child's life, and perhaps this magazine was all she could call her own.

Their time together had come to its end. Dawud finally was released from the overbearing task of hiding Afroze in the closet. He convinced Reyhana that hiding a child in a cleaning closet was in no way healthy for the child or safe for their livelihood. Moomi, who came under intense pressure from Reyhana, finally let Afroze go to school. Moomi knew that there would be a time for her to let her treasured child out into the world; she just tried selfishly to delay it for as long as she could. But Moomi was not a selfish woman. When Reyhana had found a decent enough school near their home, and had arranged everything, Moomi felt pride on the morning that Afroze donned a new school uniform and walked slowly away. Afroze would begin in the new school year, and would spend her afternoons walking back from the school to her home, where Moomi waited anxiously for her return.

There was dread in Moomi, she knew that she was slowly going to lose Afroze to an educated life, one that she would never be able to match. This was inevitable, because she could not avoid the gleam in the child's eyes when she began to learn that there was a whole world out there. With each new day, when Afroze would come home with books that grew fatter and fatter, Moomi began to fade. Moomi could not read, nor had she ever really looked at a book in her entire life.

It was strange to her that Afroze would spend hours and hours with her face inside these books. Moomi feigned interest, asking Afroze silly questions about the pictures and what the books were about. At first, Afroze tried. She tried to show Moomi what the words were saying; she tried to explain to Moomi all the wonderful things she found within the pages.

"Look, Moomi ... it's a poem about an owl and a pussycat that get married."

"Agh, sies girl. You use bad words. I'll wash your mouth with soap, neh. What-what pus—er, I mean kitty cat—want to marry one owl? Silly things inside your books. Better you don't read so much, you get cow eyes, and the boys they don't like girl with glasses, jy wiet."

But as time went on, Moomi's questions seemed too silly, and Afroze lost patience. She would roll her eyes if Moomi looked at a picture and made a silly comment, or if she started competing with the book with folk stories of her own, the things she had learned sitting in kitchens for her entire life.

Afroze eventually retreated behind locked doors to spend time with those precious books. And Moomi would walk many times past the door, pacing and wringing her rough hands, feeling stupid and inadequate. She began to imagine that with each new book that Afroze soaked up, she was getting closer and closer to her mother, her educated doctor mother, the woman who haunted Moomi's dreams at night. The woman who was thin and beautiful and carried large, important books in her hands.

One day, while cleaning out the little curtained-off haven that Afroze had created for herself in Moomi's bedroom for want of a sliver of privacy in a cramped, tiny house, Moomi found that old architecture magazine. She ran to the bin and almost threw it in. But somehow she just could not.

CHAPTER NINE

AFROZE WAS NO longer a girl. She was a woman. She had excelled at school, bringing home prizes and trophies that found themselves pushed into boxes or collecting dust behind huge, ceramic ornaments on shelftops. Afroze didn't bother at all about the prizes and medals and where they eventually found themselves. There was a burning resolve in the girl as she grew into a teenager, a desire for only one thing—success and its trappings. She had a desire to be seen, to be adored and lauded, and it was a desire that came from a lifetime of invisibility.

As she streamed through school like a silver bullet, brilliant at subjects that brought her the envious ridicule of boys and the hatred of girls, Afroze could not be stopped. Her teachers even feared her. They feared how she would march up to the blackboard in the front of their classrooms, grab the broken piece of chalk from their hands and with nonchalant ease solve a complex geometrical theorem that they had been grappling with for days. It was inevitable that she would be noticed. Her school principal tried to call in Moomi and Ismail for meetings where he could outline all the amazing opportunities such an exceptional girl could have. But Moomi refused to enter the school yard, and no one even bothered to ask Ismail.

When Afroze won a scholarship to study at the University of Cape Town, she didn't mention it to either of them. She marched into the principal's office and informed him that their permission or support was certainly not needed here. She instructed the principal, who stood in awe of this child-woman, to promptly accept. And he did.

When she went home that night, Afroze approached Moomi and Ismail, who were huddled over a very old black-and-white television set that had been a hand-me-down from someone, watching a show about a fancy black car that spoke to its owner and could drive itself. Moomi was fussing over fabrics. As Afroze's school year drew to a close, Moomi had been obsessing over the young woman's year-end dance. She paid particular attention to selecting the head scarf that would cover the mane of hair on Afroze's head. How else would her Afroze get a proposal from a decent Muslim boy if she went around showing off that glossy, brown mass?

"Hey, girl. Move from blocking the TV. We gonna miss Kitt telling Michael who the crook is," Ismail barked.

Afroze rooted to the spot. Michael spoke to his watch, and his car replied in a tinny voice, telling him that the crook was the blonde girl he had been sleeping with all along.

"I'm going to university," Afroze announced.

The silence in the room was punctuated with the beeps and mechanical music of Michael and his Kitt chasing the bad guys through the streets of a deserted city. Michael barked orders to his obedient car.

Ismail stared at Afroze for a long time, his interest in the talking car forgotten. Suddenly he burst out into mocking laughter. "University!" he roared, in between bouts of belly-rolling laughs, "Do you hear that, Moomi? Our girl here wants to do big big things with her life. She's mad. Tell her, Moomi. Mad."

Moomi looked first at the dramatic hysterics of her husband and then up to Afroze, who was standing with balled-up fists.

"S'true girl? You think you going to university?" Ismail asked. His placid tone was ominous.

Afroze nodded, determination written on every taut line of her face.

"Ja, and where you getting money for fancy university studying?" Ismail asked, laughter ceased, mocking still.

"I have a scholarship," Afroze said simply.

"Scholarship, hey? Using so big words now, this stupid girl. Moomi, sort this out. I'm going to the mosque. And, no no no, Madam Big Words, no university."

Ismail stood up. Forgetting that he was in the presence of his wife and daughter, he reached into his pants and adjusted his underwear, doing a funny motion with his leg, high up in the air and then back down as he fiddled with himself. Afroze looked away in disgust. Every reason she could ever think of to get away from that house, to escape this frustrating and ugly destiny, hit her face like bats. She decided. Enough. Enough now.

"Papa, I am going to university. And that is final. It is my decision. I have worked very hard. And I am going. That is all."

Ismail squared up to his daughter, who, like her mother, had grown tall and straight backed. And, like her mother, defiance poured out of her every gesture. Stubborn woman, eyes of steel.

"Hey, you watch your mouth, girl. Don't forget, I took you in when that woman threw you away. I fed you, I clothed you … I will tell you what you can and cannot do."

"Nonsense, Papa," Afroze continued, fearless and strong, "You did nothing. Bloody nothing. Moomi fed me, she paid for everything. Even the very clothes on your ungrateful back. I am going to university. I am going to study, and I am going to become somebody."

Ismail began almost to vibrate with rage. The personal truths—that he was kept by his own wife, that he grew fat and lazy on her broken back—picked at the scabs all over his body. It was enough enduring the jibes of the men at the mosque, the men on the street, who told him how he rode on the sweat of a woman. But to hear his daughter say it, the daughter that he never really wanted in the first place, was enough to make him boil. He lunged at the girl, trying to connect his huge palm with her face.

His age, weight, and days of lazy sitting made him clumsy. Ismail had long ago left behind his street-running days, when he was lithe and slippery like the worst snake, outrunning gangsters, loan sharks, and angry husbands. Afroze simply stepped to one side, and her father landed in a messy lump at her feet. He dared not look up.

Now it was Afroze who laughed. And she laughed. And she laughed. "Stupid, lazy, useless man. I am not a baby anymore. Not the scared little thing that you hid away under the blankets of your car as you drove me here to Cape Town, starving and crying. No, Papa. I have grown up. See, your Afroze is not an insect anymore, hey."

Ismail scrambled to his feet, now trying to dive at the one target that would never evade him. Somehow, he felt that if his fist connected with Moomi's face, everything would be all right with the world. But here, Afroze stepped again in front of him, and she pushed him with force toward the door.

"Get out. Get out of here. No more. You won't touch my Moomi anymore. I am going to university, and one day, Papa, I am going to be rich and famous, and I will take Moomi away from this hole and I will treat her like she deserves. Better than you ever did."

Moomi remained silent, glaring at the fight between the two. A lioness, challenging the old lion that once ruled the pride. Moomi felt strangely afraid. She knew that she should have felt protected and strong, with Afroze baring her new fangs, defending her. But Moomi felt the Earth shifting away from her, and under her feet the movement of the steady plates of the way things had always been shifted. Moomi could not balance in this shift. This new world was not comfortable; it was too new.

Ismail grabbed his old coat and prowled toward the door; he did not look back at Afroze standing with planted feet and tight fists. At the last moment, before he left, he turned to her, and with a sarcastic lip curled like a sour taste, he asked, "So, what you going to study, huh? Medicine? Like her ..."

Afroze looked away. Ismail of the street gangs knew exactly how to push a dagger into a flank. "No. I am going to study architecture."

After Ismail left, Afroze looked at Moomi, imploring her with her eyes to say something, anything. It seemed that Moomi's ominous silence was an even sharper dagger in the flank of this new strong Afroze. She felt secretly that Moomi was ashamed of her.

"What, Moomi? Are you also not happy for me?"

"Agh, my child. I have a soup on the stove, neh. Ismail, he fusses when it tastes burned."

Moomi scuttled away, a crab that could not meet the fire in the eyes of this girl. This girl, who was begging for acknowledgment, got nothing. Even now, after all the years of studying, she was still the Afroze that was unseen. All she needed to hear were a few rare words.

You did good, my child. You did good, my daughter.

Moomi did not return to speak to Afroze. She sat silently in her kitchen, occasionally standing up from the kitchen stool to stir the thick soup, waiting like a faithful hound for her husband to return. The ultimate betrayal. Afroze thought she had been fighting for Moomi's freedom. Now she realized that Moomi did not want to be free. Moomi enjoyed her cage. It was the comforting place that she called home. A sick feeling gripped Afroze and she also grabbed her coat, fleeing out the door, down the steep hill, and toward the bar where she knew some of the students from the university hung out.

Afroze didn't return home that night. In the morning, she tumbled out of the bed of her very first lover, a boy whose name she barely recalled, and took a bus back home. She thought that the walk from the bus stop to the house would sober her, drive away the rank smell of alcohol from her body and hair. But the air had just exaggerated it. In contrast to the freshness of the breeze, the smell of alcohol in a Muslim home in which such smells had never wafted was a damning thing. When Afroze walked into the kitchen door at dawn, on tiptoes—wondering why she even bothered to be on tiptoes as she knew Moomi hadn't slept—the smell walked in before her.

Moomi looked at the girl. A woman knows. She was not this girl's mother, but she had bathed her after her very first period, she had watched tiny buds on her chest bloom into beautiful breasts, she had seen her hips rounding, a woman forming from the clay shape of a girl-child. A woman knows. She knows when her daughter has been with a man and lost her pride to him. The scent of a lover coupled with the ugliest of smells—stale alcohol and cigarettes—and Afroze hid nothing but her eyes as she stood facing Moomi.

Moomi said nothing. She walked to Afroze and slapped her. A hard, loud whack across her face. It was the first; it was the last. It was the only time. It was the worst time.

"Go. Go to your university, whatever. But never enter my house if you drink that poison again. And learn to respect that thing between your legs. Go have a bath."

Moomi had spoken to Afroze in perfect English, not a smidgin o' pidgin. Nothing of the laughable dialect of her mixed-up words. It sounded very disturbing.

Of course, Afroze and Moomi could stay away from each other for no longer than a few aching hours. They patched up their differences in the language of tea and cakes. They never spoke of the slap, and certainly not of the alcohol or the boy. But in this silent understanding, Moomi chose that she would look away. And Afroze decided that she would live her own life. In secret.

Afroze went away to university. She managed to find a room in the girls' hostel. She excelled. She grew proud of herself and swelled in arrogance with each new award and medal that she threw into a cardboard box. She visited Moomi and Ismail on every alternate weekend, bringing them news of life at one of the country's top universities. They listened, nodded. Ismail had mellowed with age and even asked her a few interested questions about architecture—he seemed strangely obsessed with windows. Moomi listened absently, sniffing the newfound arrogance of the girl and praying every night that this overconfidence would not drown the girl one day. She didn't say much, but muttered prayers in her mind and stared at Afroze's face, and, like the mothers of her culture, she blew toward Afroze after she had muttered all the prayers she could think of.

All was well. But things could not stay as they were. Afroze finished her studies and began working immediately as an apprentice in one of the best architecture firms in Cape Town. She began to earn money, and it felt so much like love when she put fat wads of notes in the hands of her father. Moomi refused to accept the money, telling Afroze that it would be more respectful if she handed it to her father. Ismail enjoyed his daughter's largesse. He crowed to everyone he met about how rich she was and boasted every day about new appliances or new furniture she bought. Afroze played the game, telling him, "Papa, I bought a new, special sofa for you. See, it opens out for you to rest your legs."

But really, the soft sofa was for Moomi's tired legs, and the special microwave oven was for Moomi to enjoy, helping her to warm Ismail's food faster when he arrived late at night and pulled her from sleep. Afroze never knew that only Ismail used the brand-new gifts. Moomi still rested her aching legs on an old plastic footstool, and she refused to even learn how to use the microwave oven.

One day, many years later, Afroze arrived home telling Moomi and Ismail that she had fallen in love. He was a cocky, handsome American surveyor who had come to Cape Town to help design the new soccer stadium, for a World Cup that was three years away but already the most highly anticipated event in the country's calendar.

Both Moomi and Ismail disapproved, and they were even more furious when Afroze said that she intended to live with this man but never marry him. They had both heard enough talk in their community; Afroze's reputation as a marriageable young woman was lost a long time ago. Yet they still nursed hopes that she would find a boy, a Malay boy, a Muslim boy. That she would marry according to Islamic law, and not live in the ugliness of sin.

"That man will abandon you," Ismail said.

"Really, Papa, like how you abandoned my mother when I was a baby?" Afroze asked sarcastically.

The blazing row lasted well into the night. Afroze was relentless and brash. She dug up the nastiest of secrets about both the people she had come to call her parents. She ignored their old faces, she ignored their hearts, and she stuck knives into every wound that she willfully opened up. And she left. Ismail stood at the door with tears in his eyes.

"Agh, Moomi. Our girl, she is finished for us now. I don't want her to come here ever again."

Moomi did not argue Afroze's case. She was equally disgusted, even more deeply wounded by the stinging words that lashed her from the girl, once sweet and quiet and now a typhoon of haughtiness and cruelty. Moomi stood next to Ismail, and for the first time in many years she placed her hand on his sagging shoulder. The child had once divided them in their marriage bed. A woman now, the child once—united them.

CHAPTER TEN

THE MORNING AFROZE decided to leave for Brighton after she received the call about her mother's illness, she decided to visit Moomi first. She, as always, parked her brand-new car far away down the hill and trudged up to the house that she grew up in. She saw the familiar car in the driveway, and at the familiar time, the car started with one rebellious choke. Afroze smelled burned gasoline and smoke as her father backed out of the bushy surrounds. Afroze craned her neck to try to catch one last glimpse of the driver, but the fan heater and the large flask of hot coffee had created a veil of condensation. She saw only the glitter of headlights on his thick, old-fashioned spectacles as the battered Toyota turned onto the street. She craved this time to see his face, to tell him of where she was going, why she was going back there after so many years.

But, Afroze had learned a long time ago, her father preferred to leave some things inside a crypt. Never to be opened again. Afroze knew that she was the living flesh of secrets inside this sealed crypt. The reminder of mistakes made. Knew, too, that her father had refused to speak to her for years now because those who are born of mistakes make the worst mistakes eventually. She remained cloistered in the foliage, resisting the temptation to jump out and fall into his embrace.

I'm sorry, Papa. You were so right. I am, after all is said and done, abandoned. Like you always told me I would be.

She wished that, just for today, she could have plucked up the courage to run out of the thorny hideout and knock on the window, hoping to see a smiling face. A father's face. But courage eluded her, and the moment died away with the retreating sound of an old, battered car.

She knew that the gate to the kitchen would be unlocked. It had remained unlocked to her for many years now. She could never stay away from her Moomi and had crept back to her after months of exile. Moomi, being the woman that she was, had welcomed Afroze back into her warm arms. Moomi could forget hurt so quickly. And she could so easily forgive.

Now Afroze was expected, even compelled, to creep into the house, at each and every visit. She had been doing it every morning, and she did it again this day. An intruder. In a home she knew so well. After the dreadful night when her father made her choose and she had not chosen his path, Afroze had kept away for as long as she could. It had not been long. She craved Moomi, and secretly she craved her father as well. He had given her no comforting love, but he was all she had. He had taken in a six-year-old girl and given her a home. And blood remained blood, after all.

Just take her. Take her. Take her away. Now. Please. Now.

Leaving the cover of foliage, Afroze followed her routine. It comforted her. Even the secrecy comforted her. Once safely inside the warm house, she rapidly locked the gate and went straight to the coffeepot, fragrant and simmering on the stove. The recognizable smells of a waking house held her shoulders and soothed the aches from her body. She knew well enough, those aches were not just from crouching in the shadows at the fence. Those aches were signs. Those aches were from a body that was tired and struggling.

Moomi, following her own routine, would hear Afroze at the gate and then hasten upstairs, to appear at the entrance to the kitchen as if she had just awakened. With a feigned nonchalance, Moomi would come downstairs only after Afroze had poured herself a mug of steaming brew that Moomi always made the first thing when she awoke every morning, as a ritual. Afroze seated her long body at the pine kitchen table. It was as if Moomi stood at the top of the stairs, listening for those sounds, before she revealed herself. And whenever she did, Afroze's ice thawed.

She came, softly padding into the kitchen in her slippers full of holes, the thick, fuzzy dressing gown drawn tightly around her girth. Always, when she saw Afroze seated there, she looked surprised, as if this had not been their everyday early-morning routine for almost a year. And always she would pat the stocking on her head, covering uncomfortable curlers, hiding the hair that refused to be tamed. When Afroze saw her slippers, she pursed her lips and rolled her eyes in a game they always played.

"Moomi, why don't you wear the new ones I bought you, huh?"

She waved the comment away and giggled like the schoolgirl she never was. "Agh, Afroze ... what if he saw them?"

"Tell him I bought them ... for you."

Moomi smirked a response and busied her hands at the stove. She could never do that: tell Ismail that she had been seeing Afroze, feeding Afroze. Both of them knew that.

She began to heat up the thick stew at the stove. The aroma of a traditional Malay bredie, a thick, glutinous stew laced with cinnamon and cardamom, slowly wafted toward Afroze as the old tin pot started to heat the rich tomato gravy and chunks of cheap lamb cuts. This smell of bredie, always beloved by her as her favorite dish, now seemed too strong and pungent. As a child, and then as a woman who was sensitive to light, space, and smell, Afroze sometimes felt that her heightened senses were her blessing and curse. Now they seemed only a curse.

It used to irritate her that Anton persisted in spraying his cologne near her when he knew the smell made her retch. But now she thought nostalgically of Hugh, the American surveyor—a man she had loved with mad devotion, at a time when she was happy. Hugh had been the reason she had left her father's house, and then Hugh had been the one who had left her after the stadium was not even built. His job had been to estimate its costs. The finished product did not matter to him. When he left her, she was torn to pieces.

Anton had been the power that Afroze craved, the most successful partner in the architecture firm where she had begun her climb to the top. He had been trying to seduce Afroze for a long time, and after Hugh walked away from her, she turned to Anton in a silly act of rebound, trying desperately to fill up the empty space. Afroze knew she would never love Anton, but pride and fear of being alone kept her close to him, and she began to enjoy the social prestige and security that being with him gave her. She was a better architect than Anton, but she had never been offered the partnership that he had gotten. And this irritated Afroze, even when she tried to truly love him during their nights together. Anton was astute; he sensed that Afroze was not in love with him, and he began to grow cold and distant. His slow emotional disconnect from her began to devastate her, not because she missed him, but because abandonment terrified her deeply.

When they came apart at the seams, with the unraveling of her mind, Anton retreated from her. Afroze, who had always prided herself on keeping a strong and stony composure, secretly had been struggling with a deep depression from her teenage years. She recalled a furtive visit to a psychiatrist some months ago, when she finally broke down enough to admit that alcohol, expensive street drugs, and men did nothing to push away that ennui.

Anton had stopped coming home to the fashionable apartment furnished with the latest international flair that he shared with Afroze in the trendy, hipster suburb of Cape Town called Camps Bay. He avoided Afroze when she was awake. And being awake from the drugged sleeps she drowned in was rare. She had found another partner—sleep. Anton was not very patient. He missed society, parties, and laughter. He hated staying home in their claustrophobic apartment, watching Afroze fall to pieces, not telling him why. And one day, when Afroze had come home to tell him something he did not want to hear, he had simply picked up his already-packed bag and left. He never looked back at what he was leaving behind. He had important places to be, and very uncomplicated people to see. She spent the next few weeks, lying under the covers of her bed, flitting from one unwanted memory to the next.

Now all that mattered was Moomi's simmering lamb stew, and Afroze realized she was starving. But her stomach wouldn't allow her to bear the meaty unctuous stew. Too early in the morning. In her mind she gorged herself, though she knew she would barely manage a few mouthfuls. How much she missed food. Good food. The taste of things would never be the same again. She avoided Anton, he avoided her, and in the coldness of their once-bustling world, she sank into a place where nothing felt good, nothing tasted good, nothing looked good. Afroze was numb. She had lost her joy, and although she had never been described as a bubbly woman, the smile that could light up a room had drained out of her.

When the beauty and magic of Cape Town, which could banish the darkest melancholy, failed to lift a smidgeon of this gloom from Afroze, she realized something had to be done. She could no longer walk around with a mercurial monkey on her back. She decided it was time to consult a psychiatrist.

Dr. Singh's offices were in a part of the city where no one Afroze knew could see her enter and leave on her twice weekly appointments. Despondant though she was, she still tried to maintain the false mask of composure while among her colleagues. Her position as the only woman in the architecture firm was tenuous, because she was the only woman who had come close to being offered senior partner, and she was sure that "women troubles" such as depression would quickly destroy her reputation among the male partners. They had no time for such troubles.

Dr. Singh was good. Astute and kind, he slowly teased out Afroze's blocked memories and treated her with gentle but strong therapy.

"Afroze, you do realize that you are suffering from major depression," he told her on their second consultation.

She knew. Inside, she knew. But she resisted the diagnosis. "Look, Doctor, I am a busy, active, and very balanced person. I doubt it is something as serious as major depression."

Dr. Singh leaned back in his wingback chair, looking every bit the psychiatrist. He was silent for a long while, regarding her. She felt uncomfortable.

"Afroze, forget the label, the diagnosis, for a moment. You have described to me in very brief detail your childhood. Why is it that you cannot talk more about it?

"Well, what's the point, Doctor? Talking about it won't change it. My mother abandoned me when I was six, threw me to a father that didn't want me. The only person I truly have is my Moomi. What's there to say any further?"

"Blocking it out doesn't make it go away, Afroze. It gives it even more importance and space in your head. You need to let it all out. You have so much anger in you."

"I'm not angry. I'm fine. I just want some pills or something to feel better, so I can continue with my hard-earned life and work."

"Well, if all you came here for is pills, then you have come to the wrong doctor. I don't believe that popping a few pills will be a magic bullet that will cure anyone. You need to talk about your past."

"My past … my dreadful, dreadful past." Afroze sighed and leaned back in her chair facing the doctor. He smiled at her and wrote something down in his yellow pad.

"So, what's that you're writing, Doc? That I am a difficult woman? A pain to have around? Tell me …"

"Do you think you're a pain to have around Afroze?"

She looked in silence at the hourglass that the doctor kept on his desk. The tiny white grains of sand slid slowly downward, telling the time. Counting down to the moment when he would send her out of his office into the big, bad world and probably sigh with relief.

"Well, what I think doesn't matter, does it? Everyone else thinks it and then they eventually get rid of me. Like you … with your hourglass …," she said sarcastically.

"I want to help you. I am here to support you. I can see how frightened you are."

"I am not frightened," she spat back, sticking out her chin. But she did feel fear. The fear of a child who was rootless, unwanted, cast away.

"You are very frightened, my dear," he said simply.

She remained silent and drummed her fingers on the armrest.

"Oh look, the hourglass is almost empty. Time to go, Doc," she said, and again the cynicism dripped from her.

"Afroze, why did you come here? What do you hope to achieve by having consultations with me?" Dr. Singh asked with an even voice. He pointedly ignored the hourglass, and folded his arms.

"I don't know." Afroze breathed out, and suddenly her tired shoulders slumped forward. That steely exterior was cracking. Could she allow it to? Was this hard facade not the gate that kept the ugliest demons inside their cages? It was exhausting to spend days and nights batting away ugly memories. She felt afraid to let them out, but she knew that the doctor was right. Keeping them in was eating her alive.

"Listen, I will give you a prescription for an antidepressant. Not because you asked, but because clinically I really think you need it. And I am giving you some pills to calm your anxiety, help you get some rest. Maybe you should spend a few nights in the hospital, get proper rest away from life."

"No. No hospitals. I have no time for it."

"Okay, Afroze. Here's the prescription. But you have to come in twice weekly for therapy sessions. The pills don't work on their own. You are young. You can heal this part of your past and live a fulfilled and complete life."

She grabbed the prescription paper and held onto it like a lifeline. Absently she nodded and agreed to return twice a week for psychotherapy. She left Dr. Singh's office feeling tremulous but relieved that something was being done. She promised herself she would go for the therapy sessions and booked them.

After two weeks, the pills began to work. But their side effects made her numb, and just as the doctor predicted during one of their sessions, they were not a magic potion. The numbness was good: it made her function, it even brought small smiles to her face. But the demons still lingered.

She spoke about them in apprehensive monosyllables to the probing questions of the psychiatrist. Secretly she had hoped for a great, golden moment when she would break through from the shackles, but the moment hadn't come.

"It is a slow process, Afroze," Dr. Singh assured her. "You have to stick to it. Keep up with our sessions. The breakthrough will come."

But Afroze was done. She walked away from Dr. Singh's office one day, feeling ice cold, but her mood had lifted and she could live with that.

"What's the point in revisiting that awful past," she muttered to herself, and never went back to the doctor again.

The pills would do her fine.

But a call to revisit her appalling past had come after all. A literal telephone call in the middle of the night, but also a fearsome inner call within her. It was time to lay ghosts to rest. Swallowing more and more pills than necessary to giver her fortitude, she steeled herself with their chemical amalgam.

Devoid of sensation, a sourness remained. Seated in Moomi's kitchen, she wished there were a spell that brought life to the living dead. An anxious knot, always present in her chest, began to swell as she thought of her impending trip to Brighton to see her dying mother. To comfort herself, she turned to Moomi, and to the stories that comforted her as a girl. She prayed that they would be the magic that would work.

"Moomi, do you remember how you taught me that my name was Afroze?" she teased, wanting to grasp onto a happy memory.

"I remember, girl. And I remember how I begged you to stop calling me Moomi ..."

The word "Mommy" hung in the air. Both pretended not to notice.

"Tell me the story again, Moomi. The story of Afroze."

Moomi chuckled softly and settled herself in a chair across the kitchen table, repeating a story she had told this child many times.

"Oh, dear girl, I remember the day your father went away and didn't return for a week. And when he came back, I was standing at the kitchen door. Ismail walked up the driveway with so many plastic bags in his hands. Like he had gone shopping and had bought you. And there you were. So tiny, thin, and scared. You were creeping like a little spider behind him, your big eyes looking everywhere.

"Ismail handed you to me. I looked at you, peeping at me from behind your thick eyelashes, and I loved you from the very start. Ismail left you with me, and you sat on the sofa, at the very edge, not moving. As if moving might cause you to be in trouble. I made for you a mug of cocoa and you looked shocked. I knew that it was the first time you had tasted hot cocoa. You drank and drank. You asked for more, and I gave you extra sugar, too, this time. I asked you what your name was and you said in this small voice, 'Rosie.' But Ismail told me your name was Afroze. So I told you that Afroze was such a beautiful name, a name for a princess. I told you to forget Rosie, and from now you would be Afroze. My Afroze. Your name means 'light.' And you have become my only bright light. My Afroze."

Moomi trailed off, never tiring of repeating the same poetry again and again. She always told it the same way, never changing a word.

Afroze looked at the dark green flannel of Moomi's back as she buttered hot toast, not wanting to tell her that all her indulgent efforts were in vain. She felt a wave of guilt, knowing that perhaps Moomi was using up the last of her precious butter on the slabs of brown bread. *Save it for yourself, Moomi*, she ached to tell her. But she knew that feeding her gave Moomi comfort as much as eating Moomi's food gave her comfort in turn. When Moomi faced her with the toast, she saw the puffiness of her left cheek.

"Did he hit you again? What is that man's problem, Moomi? What?"

"Agh, no Afroze … forget it now," she covered her cheek with her hand, "Just eat now. Don't worry about me, he gets as much as he gives, neh."

Afroze loved how Moomi always ended her sentences with the typical Cape Malay suffix "neh." A piece of a word that could mean a million things. Acceptance, asking, wondering, sulking, swooning. A neh for all occasions.

Moomi slapped the butter knife into her palm, smiling slightly at the gesture. *He gets as much as he gives.* He gave her nothing but blows.

"No, Moomi. He should not be taking it out on you … what I did …"

"Afroze … it's not about you. He … has so many other … ghosts …"

"I know …" Afroze murmured to herself, but she knew Moomi had heard the words.

CHAPTER ELEVEN

IN THE SILENCE that was broken only by the clink of the spoon on her chipped plate, Afroze looked around at Moomi's attempt at beautification. Her lack of money did not mean a lack of finesse. She had somehow turned that old, ramshackle house into a home, with her dainty crocheted doilies and her cheap, plastic flowers placed everywhere. Somehow Afroze preferred the fakery of acrylic roses to the large, real ones she had left behind in her childhood. She saw that Moomi had spent long hours cutting up old newspapers into pretty shapes, using them patched together as a tablecloth. She recognized the kitchen curtain. It was a pieced-together dress Moomi once wore, in a time when she bothered with wearing pretty floral dresses.

Her heart ached, knowing that all of Moomi's efforts would be laughed at by the trendy friends whose parties Afroze used to attend. Back when she was invited.

Her tumbling mind could not settle. Each thought she landed on became a symbol seducing her into yet another memory. She recalled a New Year's Eve party she had once attended, a year after she had gained her degree from the University of Cape Town. Twenty-three years old, edgy, and cocky, she fell into a group of equally cocky friends. Among her very rich, chic friends were beautiful models who had taken to the trends of drinking alcohol and using cocaine.

It was a "Bergie" party—a party where the high-fashion guests were asked to come dressed as the cheap-wine-drinking beggars and drug addicts who dotted the Cape landscape. The beggars had become known for having no front teeth. Despite being ridiculed by most Capetonians, male Bergies took a rebellious pride in their appearance and believed that those who had no front teeth would give better blow jobs.

Afroze, wanting to show off as one of the "in" crowd, had fished out torn, brown corduroys from the gardener's plastic basket at the expensive town house she shared with friends in Claremont. She had enjoyed all the preparty revelry as her friends sipped good wine and took turns tearing up and dirtying their clothes, comparing costumes and celebrating those that were filthier and uglier.

Afroze was in the heady throes of being a newly qualified A-class architect, graduated at the top of her class, the poor girl done good. She had been pursued and seduced into the most coveted internship at the largest architecture firm in Cape Town and her arrogance had reached its peak.

Her troubled childhood, her fractured lineage, all had combined exhilaratingly with fast money and a place on the socialite list. She had become dangerously egotistical. Placing a filthy cap backward over her tumbling mass of curls, she had applied black permanent marker to her two front teeth, and paraded with her guffawing, fashionable friends using the slang language that only the Bergies used.

"I'll blow you skelm, suckie-suckie, neh neh …" she parodied.

Everyone roared with laughter. At the party, amid the incongruent feast of sushi, cassoulet, and umami canapes, a cocaine-addled girl in torn stockings and a maid's outfit dirtied by grass stains, torn in strategic places that revealed her bosom and her hips, went around loudly singing, "Jou'z want me now, neh? Ize knowz jou'z getting hard for Shamiema, neh. Jou'z come by me and I'll suck jou lekka now skattie."

It sounded disgusting.

Afroze recognized her. She was a model, who had once dated a South African rugby fly-half—a prominent player—and then had rapidly replaced him with a cricket captain—the fly-half was too top heavy and crushed her when he was on top. Despite her best efforts at looking like a vagabond, she still looked as sexy as hell. She had now replaced the cricketer with a German businessman, whom she knew for certain she would marry. She chewed at her mouth in a sloppy, slurpy in-and-out motion, as the Bergie women with no front teeth did. The movement was nothing short of orgasmic. Filthy, with dirt on her face and a stink to high heaven, she was grabbed and groped by men and women alike.

The party had ended badly. Someone suggested, long after the old year had been au revoired, that they go down to where the real Bergies hung out, maybe try to score some fun and games there. They had all taken a minibus taxi, something as alien to them as irregular facial appointments, to a bridge near the Cape Flats. The beggars huddled around paint drums of fire, blissfully unaware and uncaring about old years and new, saw them coming, and soon enough a fight broke out. It seemed that real beggars didn't particularly like being parodied by rich kids. Who knew?

As the revelers poured out of the minibus, one tall, muscled beggar with a scar that ravined across his head, so deep that it looked like his head was two large protuberances instead of one skull, grabbed at the young model.

"Yah pussy, jou want to see what-what a real man can fok, neh, come suck this," he said, pushing her hand to his crotch. The cocaine suddenly wearing off, the young model panicked and looked around wildly for her German soon-to-be fiancé. Seeing his blond flower being picked, the German had gone mad and ran like the fly-half the bombshell had left behind, careening into the thick body of the beggar.

Both fell forward into a pile of dust, and suddenly it became a free-for-all. Even the model tried her hand at a bitch slap. Fake dirt was replaced with real dirt. Clothing that had been ripped for costume effect got ripped even more, and one very hip, young peacock who owned a French restaurant in the waterfront had his two front teeth really knocked out. Bloodied and grappling with his cheap white T-shirt that said "I heart CT" he held the broken teeth in front of him in disbelief, and the Bergie who had kicked them out laughed hysterically.

"Come now, jou ma se poes, come fight this. See what a real man got," the maniacal Bergie howled and began to open the already broken zipper on his smelly trousers.

The now front-toothless restaurant owner, who always prided himself on his perfect appearance for his rich guests, scrabbled about in the dust and made off at full speed, leaving his teeth behind.

Everywhere she looked, Afroze saw ghoulish figures, a scene out of an apocalypse, a Dante's inferno melding movie images from a cheap projector with visions of the mayhem before her, bleeding into one another, and strangely thinking of a painting she had seen on a trip she had taken as a visiting architecture scholar at University College Dublin.

The volcanic black and orange landscape of *The Opening of the Sixth Seal* by Francis Danby rose in front of her, and in the haze of fear and the wearing off of drugs, she couldn't exactly make out what was real and what was a painting of souls in the midst of the apocalypse. The Earth opened its maw and souls were sucked into the abyss and swallowed and swallowed and swallowed.

"Kom, I do you good, my gorgeous, better than anyone do you ever."

When Afroze began to feel as if she was being grabbed by the ankles and pulled toward the angry volcano, where Faustus stood in a rose garden and toasted her rapid rise to success with a goblet made from a skull, she backed away from all her friends, who were being beaten to a pulp. She heard the swearing and other horrid words that rebounded off the urine-soaked bridge and ran away.

She thought of the gangs of teenagers she had watched on television, always punctuating fighting-talk with an insulting reference to someone's mother. She wondered why fights and rage always brought in a mother.

"Jou ma se ..." Your mother's ...

Running as fast as she could toward town, desperately looking for a taxi cab on New Year's after midnight, she realized she could easily be in deep, deep trouble. She had met another gang of merry-rich partygoers who took her for a real Bergie woman and began taunting her.

It took frantic explanations and a name drop or two, and soon she found herself holed up in another after-after party in a Camps Bay mansion. Again, the drugs were aplenty. And she remembered nothing much more of how the night had ended or with whom she had ended it.

When she had woken up and cleaned up well enough and gone to face Moomi the Monday morning after, bitterness rose in her throat as Moomi spoke. Afroze recognized the reality behind that fake put-on accent of the model who had been offering blow jobs at the party. She balked and retched at Moomi's table and Moomi rubbed her back, gently saying, "Agh, pretty Afroze girl. You is such a weakling. You must eat more, neh, you too skinny. Never mind, you leave Moomi's bredie now, and go lie down on the settee, neh."

Afroze looked into Moomi's face and saw the chewing motion she made with her lips as if she were eating up her own mouth and had run into the bathroom to retch loudly. Moomi stood by the door, handed her a towel, and kissed the top of her curls. But Afroze was disgusted by her own self. Reviled. Without even looking at Moomi's face, Afroze had bolted clean out the door.

After she left Moomi's little house, she went home to the apartment she shared with two models and an artist, burned the gardener's clothes, and bought him new ones from a proper boutique in town. The gardener, not at all impressed with Abercrombie and Fitch, had ripped the sweatshirts at the sleeves, and even had cut out the coveted fashionable "A" and was contented with yet another torn outfit. He felt it suited him better.

"Aber-what-what se ma. Ugly shirt!" he muttered and pruned the bushes.

The news of the fight between Bergie beggars and rich kids hit the newspapers. But of course, most of the rich kids' fathers owned those newspapers, and everyone in Cape Town was appalled and shocked at how badly behaved Bergies could be. A rich-kid state of emergency had been called, and every Bergie from Hout Bay to the

Cape Flats was looked at with suspicion. Which really didn't bother them much. Nothing new.

Afroze stopped going by Moomi's house for at least two months, but then one day she had arrived at the unlatched back door as if nothing had happened.

The following New Year, the theme was "Harry Potter." Much better that way. Afroze reluctantly went to that party wrapped in a cloak telling everybody she was invisible. The ennui had begun that year, after the party of beggars.

It was how the depression crept in. Feeling like a fraud, a bastard child, someone who did not deserve all that she had been given. *More trouble than you're worth, you are.* Her mother's words, which had been hiding in the catacombs, came gushing out. *More trouble than you're worth.*

It was then that she met Hugh, another bright young star, a man she loved madly. She initially hid her depression well from him, and even convinced herself it didn't exist. Until the day her father threw her out of the house for sleeping with a white man. For refusing to choose his religion. And even though she tried, even though she loved Hugh, parts of her were empty halls of echoes. Hugh sensed her emptiness and wondered why she hated herself so deeply. Enough to make herself suffer.

Now she went to no parties. And she relished the small patched-up home of her youth. Moomi's little house. But she could never go back there to live. It was too late. Her father would not have her back. She had been his greatest embarrassment among the Islamic scholars and religious men that he spent all his time with. This shameful daughter from his shameful past was not accepted. Another parent now denied the existence of Afroze, his child.

Only Moomi had accepted her for all that she was and all the choices she had made. But always, subtly in their little conversations, Moomi would throw in little dashes of suggestions about how Afroze could return to the straight path and be accepted in the community again. Afroze ignored the suggestions.

She felt no conviction for anything at all. But she felt shame like a spear. Once, she had been ashamed of Moomi, of this place with its pawn-shop furniture and Moomi's silly attempts at painting the walls in odd colors. Now she tried to imprint every single mismatched item on her tired mind.

"Afroze … eat, child. You never eat lately. You don't like my cooking, neh? Maybe it's not the fancy Camps Bay restaurant food you're used to …"

She reached her hands forward and cupped Moomi's face. She stroked the aging skin. "Moomi … I …" she trailed off. She held her hands tightly and looked deeply into her eyes.

"I know," Moomi simply said and blinked back easy tears, "the pills are not good for you, child."

"I have to take them, Moomi. They bloody cost a fortune anyway."

"What depression nonsense, Afroze? What? I say to you, go and get married to a nice man. Not that white man who treats you like trash. Find a good Muslim boy, make *nikaah* and have babies. Babies will sort out all the depression story."

Babies. They are not a magic potion.

A nice, decent life didn't feel like it would be in her future. Afroze had received the telephone call the night before. Maybe if she stood face-to-face with the ghosts, they would be exorcised. And then, maybe she would be free.

Nothing else worked. The bag of pills had become a habit. Expensive, frothy vegetable juices remained untouched on the kitchen counters, some friend's rose quartz crystal hanging around her neck, sniffs of lemon oil that followed her everywhere, reiki, massages, strange cleansing rituals. Nothing worked.

Afroze had to face the past. And a dying mother was probably the best way to do it. It was time to leave. To go home. To Brighton, after thirty-six long years. Back to "Dry Bry."

Dust. To. Dust.

She found tears stinging her eyes and had to look away at the old-dress patchwork kitchen curtain. The minutes ticked by. The thick stew remained uneaten in her bowl.

"When?" is all Moomi asked when she was told, and the word lay heavily between them.

"Today, Moomi. Today."

Moomi sobbed without attempting to hold it in. She had never cried openly in front of anyone, least of all Afroze. But today, something stiff and unbendable inside a strong woman broke, and she didn't care if Afroze saw her cry. Afroze returning to Brighton meant losing her. Maybe forever. And Moomi was in no way prepared to let her go.

Their little morning dance had begun when Ismail had thrown Afroze out of the house, but ironically this had drawn the two women much closer together. They shared their own little world, in which Afroze would creep into her kitchen at dawn. She knew Afroze led a lavish lifestyle, and earned a good wage, enough not to be in need of her cheap food.

Moomi stood next to Afroze and quickly brought her head to her ample bosom, crying and knowing exactly why she was crying.

"Afroze … Afroze …" she crooned.

Don't forget me …

"Moomi, I am …" Afroze whispered.

"Shhhh girl … quiet now. Don't say anything."

"But Moomi …"

"Afroze, go to her. It is the right thing." Sharply, Moomi turned her back.

Later, braving the winds as she climbed up the hill that led to her luxurious apartment, Afroze wished she had given Moomi something, some token of love, or another appliance or gadget that would make her life easier.

But she knew her Moomi would never have accepted it.

PART TWO

DRY BRY AGAIN

CHAPTER ONE

OUR ALLAH HAS created the djinn and He has created the djinn out of smokeless fire and our Allah has created man and he has created man out of a lump of clay. Both man and djinn receive His holy message. Both man and djinn submit to His will. Both man and djinn will face Him on the day of Qiyamah, when all deeds will be brought for judgment, and our Allah decrees that the djinn can see Man and that the djinn can interfere with man, both in very-very bad and so-so good and just plain disinterested so-so involvement in the affairs of man but man of clay will not see djinn and may never interfere in life affairs of djinn and maybe that does not seem very fair, actually. In fact. Because. But.

But it is so. It is so.

And be watchful of the tall trees. Never walk near them at nighttime. The djinn live in the tall trees and sometimes they just can't help themselves.

Halaima told the tale of the djinns, a story that was familiar to her sleeping child, one that she knew always calmed Bibi, whose mind was constantly active. When a woman's voice becomes a lullaby, when she cradles her half-asleep child in her lap, she rocks herself without realizing it, mimicking the rocking of oceans and waters. For maybe they made the man out of clay but they made the woman out of water.

Even when the child has fallen fast asleep, a woman who tells a poem-lullaby to the child takes a very long time to stop rocking herself, because the act has been both fortifying and a corporeal drowsing for both mother and child. A child may not need to be rocked. A child may content herself on a voice and a buttery smell. A woman will still rock. Herself.

As she now sat on the veranda of the cottage in Brighton, taking in the fresh, clear air with only the sounds of the surrounding bush, Afroze was drowsing even though a long sleep had been banished by a coffee the strength and color of tar. The back veranda was to blame for this underwater lull, cozy now in a moonless night, embers from a long-serving fire bringing smoky fumes to the air's cocktail.

It could take Afroze a thousand and one sleeps, the sleeps of Scheherazade's lover, to finally squeeze the last ugly drop of life-tired from her bones and blood.

The blood of hers, the one whose blood had leeched into her body via a strangulating umbilical cord, had long since been put to her bed. Her mother lay like a baby bird. A bald one, a toothless one, opening gummy mouth every now and then to flap out a snore. Someone, probably Halaima, had covered her thickly in blankets of tasteless colors; they clashed with every object in the room. Afroze wondered how many nightmares one could count in that heap. But the sleeping mother seemed content, her bald turtle-bird head poking out, the only evidence that underneath that pile of strelitzias, Snoopys, and sunflowers lay an actual person.

Her cheap wig hung on a chair back. Vanity finally banished for comfort. Afroze shuddered to think of her mother sitting for hours, being petted by Sathie's linguistic lauding yet itching to scratch her scalp. And for decorum and style, not scratching her itch even once. Luckily her mother was alone. Undoubtedly, Sathie was capable and virile, but he did not stay the night. Afroze dreaded the thought that he might have stayed, or slept in her sick mother's bed. Cinderella did not have to fear being discovered. Sathie had sauntered away long before midnight. This mother–Cinderella did not wear glass slippers. Afroze knew. This mother wore slippers of lead. They banged their way on wooden floors. And banged their way toward wooden doors.

I am coming for you. Don't make me come over there.

On the back veranda, next to the fire, Bibi slept the sleep of the innocent on her mother's rocking lap. After Halaima had rounded off her djinn story, she sighed and stretched out her arms high above her head. Her lovely, long neck rolled from side to side and cracked alongside the crackle of burning logs. Afroze roused from her doze. Both the women watched the slumbering child.

The offending breakfast still turned Afroze's stomach, for no other reason than having an overwhelming sense of an unbearable day—with a bizarre septuagenarian love affair being played out in perfumes and lipstick, and a child who wanted to kill a centipede.

It was not the pork sausage. It was not the pork. Afroze was a woman of the world, a bright, young thing. Cape Town parties had taken wildly to the trend of pulled pork. She had kissed mouths that had smelled of meat. But, as it should be, the child returns and the child-adult becomes the child-child, smacked with a stick and told to repeat all the evil things Shaitaan brought into this world—pork being one of them. She had never tasted it in her life. Though perhaps Sylvie had fed pork to her when she was a young child, before she had sent her away to a home that abhorred everything about the animal. In Moomi's house, you could not even utter its name. Pig.

"How do you cook it, when it is forbidden?" Afroze blurted out.

"Doctor likes to eat it. And I cook what Doctor likes."

"You and Bibi, have you been with my mother a long time?"

Halaima clicked her tongue against her teeth, a question-and-answer session not welcome at this quiet time of her night. She showed her irritation with a sigh. But deep down, the woman in her needed to talk to another. Too much of her world was a child, a loquacious man, and a demanding doctor. She had forgotten that sometimes women sit late into nights and share their stories. She had forgotten that this was a beautiful and powerful thing to do. Something inside of her opened up.

"I came to this place with my Uncle Abdur-Rahman. We came from Malawi, my town is Mzuzu. My mother died of a very bad illness, and I was 13 years old. The men told my uncle that I must marry, but my uncle made a promise to my mother that he would send me to school. But the men were very strong, and they were so angry. My uncle took me to school and he waited there for so many weeks, the European people who taught at the school listened to my uncle and they took me into the school. But the men from my father's place came to find me, they said to my uncle that I must marry. I am a woman. There was much fighting. They said to my uncle that I can read books and maybe I am a witch. I am a woman now, I must be a wife. The European lady, she told the men that I would finish my school. But my uncle was very scared; he told me we must run to South Africa. He will work in the mines. But the South African at the mines was not happy to give the job to Malawian man. Praise be to Allah, I turned 17 and we ran to so many places: Johannesburg, Durban. My uncle met a man at the masjid during Jummah, or Friday prayers.

"He told my uncle to come with him to this town, because my uncle knows about fixing buses. This man, Seedat, he owns many buses between Dundee and Durban. I came to this place. And here I am very happy. Now my uncle, he is buried and he is very happy. He sees that I have my daughter now. May Allah grant him beautiful gardens in Jannat, our Paradise."

Halaima spoke like a chant. Her mesmerizing voice took Afroze deep into a world of love between an uncle and his niece. Living on the fringes, hiding in townships, waiting for a day when they could stop their hearts from banging against their chests in fear. But Halaima spoke of it in a matter-of-fact way, far removed from the actual pain of it all. Life was good now. There was no need to recall the past. People suffer, good people and bad. The best ones just keep moving. And the best of the best will walk in the gardens of paradise.

"How did you come to live here with my Mother? What do you want from her?" Afroze asked cuttingly, putting an end to the tiny little bond that Halaima had felt forming.

Sathie was right. This woman was cold as ice. Halaima shot Afroze a dark look. She picked Bibi up in her strong arms, Bibi's gangly limbs dangling out akimbo. Halaima swept past Afroze, her skirt making a dismissive rustle.

"I must put my child in her bed." Halaima said, walking swiftly away. She turned slowly at the doorway to the house, looking at Afroze again, this time her dark eyes finding and holding Afroze's gaze. She looked like a queen, lit by the orange light, and Afroze felt Halaima's strength in that brief moment when their eyes met and lingered.

"Your mother is a good woman," Halaima said, and then she was gone.

CHAPTER TWO

THE MORNING FOUND the women in the fairy house in a fluttering tantrum. It began at dawn with the loud howls of the doctor. Afroze, who had fallen asleep in the lounger on the veranda, lulled by the dying fire, sprang up, knocking over the empty coffee mug she had been clutching as she slept.

She bolted toward her mother's bedroom, expecting the worst, not wanting to see it. But she found her mother sitting upright on the edge of her bed, clutching something in her hands. Ugly, gray tendrils. Fronds of weakness. Strands of hair. Barely there.

Again, her mother screamed. The type of scream that was half disgust, half terror. Carrion cry. It was her hair, after all. What was left of it. All falling out, all clumping together, everywhere. Her hands itched with the horror of some sort of contagion. She wondered in her own private rage at how much she hated parts of herself. Even the parts that had left her, and fallen off.

"Halaima! Come, come. Halaima, there is more. Come." She ignored Afroze, who had run to her side.

"Mother, what is wrong? What is it? Are you in pain?"

Her mother was staring in shock at a long, silvery strand that lay on her lap. She began to moan in fear, pulling at the almost undetectable strand, trying to pick it up. But her fingers shook with tremors.

The situation was getting frightening. Afroze had to do something. Where was Halaima? Halaima would know what to do. Afroze felt inadequate. She did not know any means of comforting her mother.

Her mother began brushing at her body, violently. Scratching at her skin, pulling the overstretched folds until they fell back in red puckers. Every attempt Afroze made at holding down her hands sent deeper howls into the morning. The old woman had gained taut muscles in her anxiety, fighting Afroze with force.

Afroze made a clumsy attempt to hug her, to make her stop. The hug was met with a violent twist that found mother and daughter sliding to the floor. Her mother lying on top of her, Afroze could feel how light her frame had become, how age had bitten holes into once-formidable bones. The smell of her was strong and pungent. Afroze knew the smell of soiled sheets.

Her mother felt no shame. She clawed into Afroze, going first for her mane of untied wild hair, pulling at it with her balled fists. Tufts of dark, beautiful hair ripped out, clutched in clawed, aged hands. Her mother glared at the tufts and her keening intensified.

"The witch. The witch has taken my youth. My hair. My hair. She cursed me. Curses. Curses," her mother moaned, and the words brought fresh, foamy spittle to her toothless mouth. Her scalp afire, Afroze felt that she was suffocating, and pain made her try to push her mother off of her. But the old woman would not let go. She grabbed at Afroze's fresh skin, pinching at it, like she had pinched at her own; the pain was sharp. In disgust, Afroze noticed that her mother's nails were long and painted maroon.

"My hair. My hair. Collect. Keep. My hair." Her mother ranted, clutching tufts of Afroze's long hair, and Afroze could not breathe any longer. When her mother's hands began snuffling her nose and mouth, smelling of musty, old skin and a hated perfume, Afroze pushed with all her strength, and her mother rolled off her and lay panting on her side, her limbs splayed.

It was only then that Afroze looked up to the door, realizing that Halaima had been standing there all along, watching mother and daughter fight like cats in a cage. Afroze saw a faint smile linger only for a second on Halaima's lips. And then it was gone.

"Doctor, I am here. Are you okay? Doctor, it is Halaima. Come let me help you up."

Too late. Too little. Halaima had watched the horror for too long before acting. Afroze saw it as Halaima's cruel calculation.

Halaima saw it as giving a mother and a daughter a chance to hold each other.

Afroze kneeled on the horrible carpet, gasping for air. She reached forward, an attempt to assist.

"Stop!" hissed Halaima. "You have hurt her enough."

Slowly, in the most caring of grasps, Halaima pulled the frail, old woman to her feet, and hugged her close to her chest. She gently placed the old hands around her neck, and she circled the little waist. In a waltz, they moved to the bed, where Halaima laid her softly down.

She reached for one of the many blankets that had fallen in piles on the floor. Afroze tried again; she handed Halaima the blanket closest to her. It was bright blue. Snoopy danced in a cloudless sky, musical notes dangled in the air. Halaima batted away Afroze's hands.

"Go! Go now. I will get this sorted out."

Afroze backed slowly out of the room, only realizing that she still had the Snoopy blanket clutched to her when she sank into a chair in the kitchen.

Bibi appeared at her side. A tiny apparition in overall pajamas. The tufts of her puff-ball hairstyle stuck up like antennae.

"My blanket," Bibi said petulantly, and pulled at the Snoopy. She dragged the large blanket away, and Afroze watched the girl disappear into the darkened passage.

Afroze had barely caught her breath when, again, like a little morning nymph, Bibi came back, holding a beautiful Chinese lacquered box in her hands. She blinked innocently at Afroze and indicated that she should take it. Afroze, steeped in confusion, took the box from the little hands and immediately opened it. She was met with the horrific sight of hair. In revulsion she shut the box and swallowed hoarsely.

"It is Doctor's hair," Bibi said matter-of-factly, the way only a child could speak of something so bizarre.

"What?" Afroze asked.

"Doctor collects all her hair. She says it is for her dead day."

Afroze opened her mouth to question when Halaima stalked into the room. She picked up the dusting cloth that had been left on the table. She made rapid dusting movements, making an exaggerated theater of the work. Afroze waited for her to say something. She said nothing at all. She just dusted.

In its pristine state, the mink-colored, corduroy sofa cushions covered with thick plastic had to be dusted meticulously every day. And most important, so did the large, overbearing imbuia cabinets with the mirrored inner walls that contained the doctor's treasures—the beautiful Swarovski crystal ornaments of mythical creatures, strawberries, trees dripping with tiny golden pears, and perfectly cut vases that glittered. Afroze had a hazy remembrance of breaking a swan once. But she did not recall her punishment. Halaima seemed intent on the punishment of silence. She focused her attention on the room. The museum. Or now, a mausoleum. A crypt filled with the most beautiful things.

"I have brought your bag inside from your car. You must bathe. Sathie will be here soon. You look like a mess." Halaima said after a long silence, concentrating on dusting a beautiful red-crystal unicorn. It glittered with fire as the morning sun rose and streamed into the room.

Afroze stood up to leave.

"Do not use all the water. Restriction starts at seven and I still have to bathe Bibi and Doctor."

Afroze nodded like an obedient child. She placed the lacquered box with its strange contents on the table and walked away.

CHAPTER THREE

SATHIE'S ARRIVAL WAS again met with a girly commotion. He swanned into the house at exactly eight o' clock, dressed again to perfection in dark trousers, crisp, white shirtsleeves, and a tweed waistcoat, very much the dandy brandishing his smile and his cane. Bibi ran up to him, clearly in love, accepting the fawning he advanced on her. He made a show of a magic trick in which he pulled sweets out from behind her ear and Afroze, who was watching from the front door, rolled her eyes at the oldest trick in the book. Bibi skipped into the house, loudly singing his arrival, and again from the bedroom there came the flutter of debutantes getting ready for the ball.

This time Afroze didn't linger to watch. She could not bear to see again how her wigged, limping, old mother melted and flirted in his presence. Afroze had bathed with Halaima's strict cautions ringing in her ears, using barely half a bucket of lukewarm water to splash her body down. She felt dirty still, sure that the sparse allotment of water she had been given was totally unfair. She had heard Bibi splashing about in a full bathtub with squeals and songs.

Dressing hastily, she realized that she had packed only two sets of clothes. She had not intended to remain in that house for longer than a night. Afroze was just thankful that she had packed her large bag of pills, but then, she always had the bag with her and went nowhere without it. Swallowing her doses of calming pills was a balm to her frazzled brain. How beautifully bitter they tasted on her tongue. So familiar. She knew there would probably never be a day in her life when she would not take them.

"Ah, there she is. The fainting Rose," Sathie announced, standing up with a gentlemanly sweep when Afroze finally came to the breakfast table.

She saw her mother seated in her usual place, dressed, powdered, and painted again. This time a different ugly wig. But still the same bright lipstick. All traces of the woman who had been keening and scratching banished; she looked composed. Serene. She turned a glance at Afroze, taking in her plain black jeans and white shirt, her bare face and tight bun. She frowned deeply.

"My dear Rosie, you should have made some effort at least. There is a gentleman at the table, after all," she said.

Afroze looked at the table. A place was set for her at the farthest end of the table.

"Far enough away from the pork, are you?" her mother said pointedly, and stabbed a sausage with her fork.

Afroze did not respond. She slid into her chair and gratefully grabbed a slice of toast. Halaima appeared, placing a mug of strong tea before her. Sathie, who had taken his place at her mother's side, whispered something to little Bibi and they both giggled loudly.

Afroze remembered her mother hating giggles or silliness at the table. But now she smiled benignly at the laughing pair. "Share. Share the joke, you two," Sylvie said.

"Oh, it's nothing, my dear. Just some silly talk from an old man," Sathie said and absently picked up her hand to kiss it.

"Mister Sathie said that Miss Rosie makes her mouth like a chicken's backside," Bibi announced.

Afroze's mouth went into a natural pout, one she now became very self-conscious about, and her mother burst out into loud laughter. Even Halaima stifled a chuckle.

"Oh, my darling Sathie, what would we do without you? Us boring old girls would probably just wither away and talk about flour and sugar. You are our dearest light," Sylvie said, turning a flirty eye on Sathie, who puffed up even further.

"Yes, my sweet Sylvie. But truly your daughter should learn to smile more," he said.

"Agh, Rosie. Always with a pout. Born with a pout. Probably why she is still a virgin," Sylvie said.

Afroze spat out a mouthful of tea. "I am … not. I have … I mean, I am not a … virgin, Mother," she stuttered, drawing more laughter from the two.

"Well, Rosie. You could have fooled us. You walk like a virgin, my dear," her mother said.

"What's a virgin?" Bibi asked, and this reduced the two lovers to fits of laughter so absurd it was a comedy in itself.

Halaima appeared then and shushed Bibi quickly, ushering her from the table with a piece of thickly buttered toast.

"Not for the dogs, you hear. For you, little Bibi angel. So you can grow big and strong and very, very clever and become a doctor like me," said Sylvie.

Bibi batted her lashes and hugged the old woman, skipping away to a tune in her pretty child voice.

Sylvie's eyes followed the little girl until she was out of sight, growing misty and soft as she watched the child. Afroze's eyes never left her mother. She glared at her in hateful disbelief.

See how you love a stranger's child, Mother. See how you do.

Sathie looked from mother to daughter, and theatrically cleared his throat. "Rosie, my dear. As a gentleman and as the one who is closest to your dear mother, may I ask the one thing we all would like to know? Dear girl, why have you come here?"

"It's actually none of your business," Afroze said snippily.

Sathie, clearly insulted, maintained his composure well, that mask of a smile never leaving his face. He felt the fragility of his place in the doctor's home shake the ground beneath his well-shod feet.

"She has come to watch me die. That's why she is here. But here I am, disappointing her by being full of life," her mother said and waved her fingers at Afroze in dismissal.

"I have not come here to watch you die, Mother," Afroze said defensively. "And perhaps if the adults in this house begin behaving like such, instead of giggling teenagers, you would know that I came here to see how you were. When your neighbor, old man Seedat, called me in Cape Town telling me you were ill, I booked a flight immediately."

"Very generous, Rosie. Leaving your fancy Cape Town to come to this dump to see me," her mother replied.

"I wanted to see you, Mother." Afroze said and fell silent. Even Sathie had no retort.

Sylvie sat still for a fraction of a second, her thoughts running into places no one could read. And with a start, she shook herself a little and her masklike face reappeared. "Do you want a medal then?" she muttered and stabbed dramatically at her sausage, which she shoved into her mouth. She chewed noisily, in an arrogant show.

"Well, I am leaving today anyway," Afroze said," I'm driving back to Durban after breakfast, Mother, and my flight back to Cape Town is at two."

"Can't wait to run away, can you?"

Afroze's eyes blazed now. Anger and frustration bubbled over. The last twenty-four hours bared their teeth. "Enough! That is enough. What do you want from me? I come here to see you, hearing news of your grave illness. I am laughed at, scolded, blamed, treated like an intruder into this … this strange world you've created for yourself. Well, there, Mother. I did my duty. Which is more than you have ever done for me. So yes. I do want a medal. I do."

Sylvie put down her fork with a clatter. She stared at her daughter's angry eyes, her flushed skin. For a long, long while, she just looked at her. Afroze refused to drop her eyes, and returned the burning scrutiny. Two women, a million unsaid words like an electric cable connecting them, alive with the energy of every wild thing that has never been let out of its cage. And somewhere in the middle of it all, the salty, old woman began a knowing chuckle.

It simmered first inside her chest, little flutters of a rib cage. It rose quickly into a mighty roar. It engulfed the circle the two women had drawn around each other, the bright orb. Not to raze. To create. For creation begins from a point of light, a crazy, static, rubbing together of two atoms that should not even be in the same room together, energy created from aggrieved matter. Creation. But of what?

Sylvie knew. It was the strangest of emotions. She had never felt it before. But Sylvie knew what this electric storm had done. It had created pride. And pride trumped guilt. It had the power to dig trenches, fill moats, throw wrecking balls at walls.

Afroze felt it as well, though she could not name it. She had never experienced it before. She was young. And she called it "anger." The name stayed. Anger old began to beat at pride newborn with large, ugly sticks. Afroze felt powerful. She felt it tentatively, as if power was a new feeling in the world. She squared her shoulders and brandished herself, enjoying the new emotion, this virgin dominion in a world in which she had never tasted such things. She knew she had won.

"Goodbye, Mother. Thank you for your kind hospitality."

She stood up to leave. Sylvie knew that it was now her serve. She could deliver a stinging volley, aiming strong the blow to her child's head. Or she could place her hands upward and refuse the game. Where is maturity at a moment such as this? The second that defines the course of love or hate that would run inside veins for generations. The cowards turn away. They neither play nor concede. They look away.

Had Afroze lingered for but one second longer, she might have seen the slightest of movements. Her mother's hand, reaching ever-so-slightly toward her. But it did not happen that way. Afroze marched. Sylvie grabbed her fork. All beauty dissolved. Possibilities were ended.

And yet moments such as this always call for a knight in shining armor. *Oh, Charming, where are you, Prince? Ah, there you are. Naughty man. See you looking at the young flesh, the new flesh, the child of your benefactress. Glimmer, glimmer, sigh … Oh, but she is such a beauty after all. You just can't help yourself, can you? That high color finally comes to her cheeks. What on Earth is wrong with me? My Diana's daughter. I see fire in you yet, my dear. Shall I have a sip?*

Finally taking up his long-awaited knighthood, dapper Sathie stood, accepting the scepter borne unto him. Now was the time for a man to stand between these two women. Time to take control of this war. A woman at war is a marvelous thing to behold. He had been waiting for a moment like this for most of his life.

"Rosie, dear Rosie. Stop now. Just hold on there for one minute, you hellcat you."

"Sathie, what do you want?" Afroze was fuming now. For a fraction of a second, Sathie lost some nerve, but composed himself very quickly. Honor was at stake. Manly honor, dash of stirred loins, an old man awakened. Vivid life enters into his world. He laps it up like the dog he is. It's all a bit wild now, animalistic. The lionesses are fighting. Can you smell the heady smell of pheromones?

Sathie knew he was a cowardly man, and had been one for his entire life. He thrived on his handsome face but was always the first man to hide under a table in a bar fight. Haranguing women frightened him. He had been brought up by harpies, made it an educated existence to avoid a crazy-mad woman. And he knew that the day would come when his smiles would fail the situation. And this day seemed to have come.

Sathie realized that the arrival of this daughter into Sylvie's life probably signaled an ending of his world of creature comforts, but as a man, he also felt a longing inside him just by looking at Afroze. He knew he should not, but he did. He had always been a man who sensed attraction in the air and could tell by just one look that conquering a woman would be easy. When he had seen Afroze bossily instructing him not to touch her car, he had suddenly felt awakened from a dormant state. It had been many years since he had felt such stirrings. Something about the unattainable air that emanated from Afroze intrigued him. He knew he was aging, and the headiness of conquering this unreachable beauty made him desire his youth again. His life with Sylvie held no passion; it never could. But seeing her daughter made curiosity flare into something greater. Sathie braved the possibility that Afroze could destroy his pampered peace, and advanced a way to make her remain in Brighton for just a little longer. Purely to indulge an attraction that he needed to feel alive again.

"Rosie, Rosie … come now, girl. Just stay on for only an hour more. I have something very important I want to speak to you about. We … have. Sylvie and I … both."

Sylvie shot Sathie a dark look. A confused look that also smacked of lifeline.

The knight had cast his lance and one piece of wall came crashing down.

Afroze again pursed her lips without realizing she was doing it. "Okay. Fine." She returned to sit at the table. This time, Sylvie looked down at her plate. Her heart was beating a little too fast.

"Madam Architect," Sathie announced and swept low to the ground, bowing in flourish to the perplexed Afroze.

She shot him a rolled eye and lifted an eyebrow. No time for melodrama when she had just enacted her own.

"You are an architect? Yes?"

"Yes," she responded.

"You will help us build."

"Build what?"

"Your mother desires to build something, anything. With her name on its doors. A school is what she is thinking of. But it could be a clinic, a crèche, even a little community center for women to come and sew and do things that busy women do. It's not about the building, Rosie. It is about the name on its door. How wonderful, is it not, my Sylvie?"

Sylvie hesitated. Things had taken a sudden turn. In all her life she had never hesitated, but in her dotage, something was shaking inside her bones.

"Oh, my dear, Sylvie is just overwhelmed with the possibility that her plans will now come to fruition. But I know my beloved Sylvie better than anyone. Her deepest desire is to demolish the khaya, and to turn that place into a school."

Afroze looked out to the old, crumbling building at the edge of the backyard. The khaya.

Khaya, the Zulu word for "home."

CHAPTER FOUR

IN THE DEAD of midnight the child could not sleep. The night owls and the frogs ignored her when she attempted to join them. She lay very still on a coverlet embroidered with butterflies; she had never seen a real one yet in her life. She moved toward the window. In the light that only darkness could give, she bunched up balled fists, her palms holding thickly onto thin lace. The curtains were not shields. They were created for beauty, something feminine for a bedroom of a child. This lace, these butterflies, were a display that a little girl slept here. A hope that if she lay her head upon a pink pillow with a butterfly motif, then her girl-childness would be acknowledged in a world not made for her. Despite the attempts, the hardness of the room reflected the hard world in which the child walked. A few butterflies and a smattering of lace did not do their jobs. She had to live a difficult, little life.

Her shoulders sat near her ears. They always did. Telltale signs of an anxious child. Easily she startled. Easily she welled up. Sensitive to smells—she could never bear them well. She knew emotions and events by the many smells that brought them into her life. In the dead of midnight, in the dead of every midnight, she listened and sniffed. She knew long beforehand when something was happening. Something always smelled like it was happening.

The adults had tried to be careful. They hadn't realized her secret power. They, like all adults, believed that if they whispered, she would not know. But she smelled what was on their breaths even when she heard no voices. Just scratching sounds, the sounds that raspy whispers made when they echoed against walls. Others might have easily thought it was just mice, scratching their mice claws against the hardness of wooden floors. But she knew it was not the mice that skulked. She knew it was the people that skulked.

How silly they were! They had placed her little bed against a window. They did not know how she would awaken from a sleep that was never really there and move the lace aside. The lace that smelled forever of crying. She knew that tears have smells. Everyone's tears smelled the same. Some just lingered longer.

Her mother could not help but rustle. It was her calling card. The child would forever know her mother by the sound of rustling leaves. Always this way and that, in and out of rooms, down passageways, into the yard, away and about and all the way around. No footsteps. Just whispery, crackly, swishy, swooshy. Skirts and fabric. The child once lifted her mother's chiffon sari to answer a plaguing question: Did this mother have feet? The child received a little shove with a foot in response.

"What are you doing under there?"

"Get out from under my skirts."

"Such an odd child."

But her mother sailed onward and forward. She sailed on footless steps during the day. And she hurried in harried steps at night. She came alive then. In the dead part of midnight. Never a sound, but busy and with her greatest purpose. Only in the darkest of nights. The child smelled gasoline and smoke. Always the same broken-down old car. Always the same hushed whispers.

A moaning mound of blankets, told a million times to shut up.

"Quiet! Be quiet, you hear, or I am going to knock you out cold."

"Just shut this one up, will you, or my child will wake up. And this place is so silent, everyone will hear."

"Ay, wena. You … I'm telling you now. You shut up. You hear me?"

"Look, he's going to scream when we move him. I'm knocking him cold. Told you to give him all that brandy. What? You went and drank it all, huh?"

"No, missus. I promise, missus, I didn't touch the brandy. I give him all. It not working."

"Oh, for bloody hell's sake, here. Go inside and fetch me the bottle on the table. I'm going to make him pass out. I have a child here. He's got to shut up."

"Yes, missus. I go fetch it, missus."

"Don't you touch a single drop, you hear, or I swear I will cut you straight like a pig, up your gut."

"Ayyy, missus. Not a pig, missus. No, missus. Yes, missus."

A peeping child. The blanket is gray and it writhed and moaned. Her mother took the bottle that was much fuller than when she herself had drawn from it earlier. The man's gait told on him, that he has drunk of the bottle too. The child had seen this man many times before. But in daylight he didn't talk to the child or the mother. He filled their tank with gasoline and chewed a matchstick, stinking to the heavens of fuel. Then in night's veil, he fluttered around the doctor, clearly drunk but still, was all the doctor had for help. This drunk would have to do.

Both poured the liquid into the blanket mound, maybe there was a mouth there, inside. They waited, they breathed, sometimes he said things like:

"There's three more to come to you, Doctor."

"One was taken away last night, Doctor. We lost one."

"No hope left, Doctor. We are losing too many."

And she said things to him in return.

"Okay, bring."

He brought mounds of moaning blankets, lying down and writhing on the back seat of the car. This one had taken an entire bottle of brandy. Sickly sweet amber brandy that they could barely afford. They both prodded the blanket mound. No moans.

Like a man, the woman doctor with arms of steel and a frame made of solid, straight rods carried the bundle into the khaya. Like a man, the strong woman lifted and lugged a heavy body into the dark rooms. She was no shrinking violet.

They did not know, or had the time to realize, that the little child was awake and watching them through a tiny crack in the lace curtains at the window. The child blocked her ears. And her nose.

She easily smelled blood, and she easily heard muffled screams.

Maybe they should have made the curtains thicker.

The child was left to conjure up ideas of what went on among the adults in her home. Having being kept from the facts, she created her own reasons. They were reasons of childhood horror tales, melded with childhood fairytales into a frightening explanation.

The child finally found sleep, marveling at how her mother, the doctor, never failed to keep her beautiful chiffon saris pinned so firmly and secure. Despite it all.

The child kept cheap bars of rose-scented soap under her pillow, and throughout the night, awakened to moaning sounds, and quickly placed the rose scent under her nose. The smell lulled the restless child into a restless sleep.

CHAPTER FIVE

SATHIE WALKED AWAY from the doctor and her daughter, two women breathing sparks at each other. He took the long route to his rented room in town, a building behind a big house halfway between a Hindu temple and a mosque. Well placed. When he entered his neat room, he immediately fell onto the piano standing dark and beautiful against the only window. His fingers tingled with anticipation, he stroked out some bars of music he had tried to forget. But then he thought of the one tiny glance cast at him from the doctor's daughter, and he wanted to play long ballads again.

Oh, I did not notice it then but I notice it now. This woman is a goddess. A beautiful piece of the moon in that perfect place where all women someday find themselves. That magical age, when awkward youth is a discarded skin and sagging skin is an awkward garment. The best time of a woman, that ending of spring, so softly leaving, dropping crushed flowers at the feet of lovers, knowing that autumn will arrive and bring deeper colors. But it has not arrived just yet. She is still a blazing flower garden, the dew still drips from her petals, but they drip with knowledge.

She knows her own power now, in this season of her world, she throws aside all fear with a wave and a nod. She knows so much. She has known first love, she has known first stabs, she has tasted deep lust, she has coveted, she has flaunted, she has asked, she has pleaded; she has finished her allocation of tears. She has stopped hating her lumpy, bumpy soul. This is the season in which she should be picked. Pick her. This is when she tastes the sweetest.

I am a man who loves women. They have burned their bosoms into my chest. Followed my body, back to when I was a lithe, naughty child who hid behind Father Timothy's piano at the posh Catholic school, learning by his pumping feet about the power of music. Not his hands. His feet.

Back to my beginnings.

I take you to a perfectly vegetarian household, the most uppity-up Brahmin family living most uppity-up-up in the penthouse of an apartment on Beatrice Street, Durban. What is this boy supposed to do all day, surrounded by praying women? His men have died, and their pyres have been pure. This pure boy, this high-born, priestly caste, handsome little male issue where there have only been disappointing female issue, let us send him to school.

His grandfather was a barrister, London trained. His father too. Pity they had to go and die. It is agreed, he will learn his Vedic mantras and fulfill the karmic obligations of this high-caste family. Come now, the child is bored sitting and watching us women churn ghee.

I refuse.

M'lord.

I refuse.

My high-caste grandson will not go to that filthy coolie school filled with the stinking bottoms of cane cutters' children, mingling with beef bottoms of Mohammedans, but if I recall, I do love the Catholic boys, so clean, so neat, such sweet singing-singing darlings. St. Anthony's Catholic School. Nice place. Let him go. Never mind the Christ Holy Ghost boys; he must always keep his sacred thread tied around his chest, and when they start their singing, he must say our Vedic scriptures inside his head.

Father Timothy with the missing teeth feels his toes are itching, Durban so hot, too hot. Festering ground for itches and toe sores. Dearest Father stops pumping his feet on an organ, reaches down to scratch a toe and scratches my head instead.

Oh, have my toes grown hairs? Is it not supposed to be the palms rather? Oh my, oh my.

Boy, what is the meaning of sitting at my feet? We Catholics don't do things like that, you know. You Hindus and your feet touching. No need, boy. No need.

Father, I am in angelic beatification of the heavenly beauty of your organ.

Oh, look now, boy, I know we seem to have gotten some reputation about these things but no no no no, not me, we don't encourage that sort of thing here. I don't care what you have heard.

Father. What I'm saying is I love your piano.

Right. Oh, yes. Indeed. My thoughts exactly.

I lie to the pure women, my grandmother and aunties, who line the walls and floors of the penthouse on Beatrice Street, panting and puffing with worry, wondering if I had perhaps run off to play cricket with beef eaters or if I was perhaps learning to play fah-fee with laborer Indians.

But I am Indian, Grandmother.

Spit! You spit now. You wash that mouth. You are a Brahmin boy, from the proudest Brahmin family in Tamil Nadu. You spit now. Never call yourself Indian, you hear me? Here in this Durban, that is like calling yourself the excreta of donkey monkey dog frog.

Spit.

Where do you go to after school, beautiful boy-child?

Oh, aunties and grannies. What to say? Father Timothy says I must learn to say the proper English. You see, these H's have become a bit of h-an hinconvenience. If I want to be a barrister one day and h-all.

Oh, of course my child. H-elocution is so important in this world. You take all the time in the world. We fully support a

Tamil boy who is learning where and when to pick and drop his hetches.

Now who would have ever thought that our devoted son of the Church, dearest Father Timothy, nurtured a supreme love and skill for the music called jazz?

Who knew?

You want piano. Sit. Sit, Brahmin boy. Now I show you real music.

I sucked it all up, like marrow from bones. Jazz tunes. The greats. Here, Brahmin boy, come listen to this. Scratchy gramophone record, smuggled into this town. This, dear boy, is music.

Well, said the fat man, the owner of the Jazz Lounge, who happened to be strolling through the Catholic school on his annual donation run, where he expended large sums of his money on scholarhips for the bright, young boys of his community. He stopped dead in his tracks, hearing the strains of the piano deftly played by Sathie's young hands, accompanying the boy's voice that rang out as if he had been born crooning, and he could not believe his ears. Here, in this dowdy Catholic school, lay a talent such as this. The owner of the Jazz Lounge knew music and he knew skill, and it wouldn't take long to train that voice and musical flair, good enough for the stage. God darn it, Father, where have you been hiding this talent? This boy can sing. Voice like satin.

Get on that stage, Satin Boy. And for hell's sake, remove that darn string from around your chest. You're a grown man now, open up that shirt and show them your sweat, the women are going to lose their minds.

Ladies and Gentleman, may I present the latest singing sensation, from our very own streets, the handsome, the debonair, the Voice!

Satin is born. Sathie is gone.

Watch the ladies, they lose their senses, how they fall to the floor as Satin croons. During the day, they wear no gloves; their hands are filthy from sewing-machine oil, their hair matted from baking flour, their skin sallow dark from vegetable selling. At night, they enter Satin's dreams, skirts and stockings, beauties they become.

They were nothing girls until Satin opened his mouth. Now, they faint away, they knock little pretty knocks in white gloves on secret doors—naked in his presence, but they never take the gloves away. Lest he hate their working-girl hands.

I love women. I adore them. I worship them as the deities, these Kalis, these Sarasvatis, these gold-laden Lakshmis. I croon their names; they forget their men, who work in fields, shops, and factories. I carry their broken little Durban dreams into the very stars of the night. Beneath me, even a cabbage seller is a queen.

Zenzi.

Royal African goddess.

By day, you cover your regal head with a dirty headscarf; the knees that I kiss are rough. You spend all your time on them, wiping the floors of rich houses. Did they ever know, Zenzi, that it was you those nights, who transformed into the sultry siren of their dreams, poured into your butter yellow sheath of a frock? You let out all that wild hair and in the halo of the backlit stage, all they saw was a crown. They did not see your face. They cried when you sang, they died when you pulled a note high up into the skies. Oh, and they desired every part of you when you growled a low note. But, by day, they tramped on your hands, and walked over your head, not seeing that they were walking on treasure.

"Hey, Tombi. Yes, you, girl. You missed a spot, Maid."

I loved you, Zenzi. Your voice rumbling out a refrain. My voice, smoothing out your edges. We sang our songs like one monster, each of us a complement to the other, and a compliment too. We broke too many hearts. I did not know our desire was a burning flag, so evident and apparent that everyone could see we were lovers. I did not know that the jealous women would tell their tales to the ever-present secret police who would come for you in the end.

"What? Our Satin. Our man. With a Black. Never. Why doesn't he want us Indian girls? We'll show the Black what happens when she crosses the Divide."

"Well, look. The N'tombi has to learn her place. Leave our men alone. Go dig in your own garden, washer girl."

The show that night was an intoxicating drug. We both stuck that heady needle in our arms. We sang like nothing anyone had ever heard. That night, I was Satin in the spotlight; she remained the Voice in the back. But still, she shone and stole the show. I didn't care; she deserved it.

And after she had sung and roared that voice into a crescendo that awakened angels and devils alike, she stepped out of her backlit place. In full spotlight, where she had been instructed not to show her face, because Blacks were not allowed to sing on that stage. But she walked into my spot of light and fell exhausted into my arms. Something told us this was a swan song. The dancers stopped their trots. Grown men cried. Swan song Zenzi. Swan song, my Queen.

I dragged you into that car. I craved your body even more than you craved mine. We had defied something, and when you act against the bars that jail you, erotic madness courses in your blood. Suddenly, your rebellion all makes sense, and you want to rip the very souls off each other.

"No, Sats. Not here." Her protests were feeble. Zenzi ached for me, on fire from the thunder on the stage, where she had tilted her head up, thrown the floor-wiping maid to the floor, stood fully lit in the applause she deserved. Not everyone applauded. Not everyone was happy for her.

I wanted to ravage her right then, because maybe her bravery would somehow drip into me, and I could imbibe something of her strength.

"Zenzi, we were on fire tonight, baby. I gotta have you, baby. It's dark, baby. It's Tony's car. No one will see us. Baby."

Large, angry hands grab Sathie and pry him away from Zenzi's embrace. They throw him to the hot asphalt, pushing his face into the stinking tar. Looking up toward Tony's car, Sathie sees shadows of men, of the white policemen as they grope and fondle and take his Zenzi. As he is held down, he writhes and tries to escape, but he cannot. He cannot save her from being violated by the very men who think her skin color is filth but take her body anyway. What a man can see when pushed to stinking tarmac, looking up at a window of steam, is nothing that a man should ever see.

The policemen exchange places; the one who had been holding him down picks him up like a rag doll and throws him forward toward the one who had been raping Zenzi with a ham fist clamped over her mouth. Sathie had only heard her muffled screams and seen the hot steam rise onto the windows of Tony's Chevrolet. Now, the policeman who holds him down smells of Zenzi, and Sathie cannot help but retch at the thought of it all. They take their turns with her, and soon she doesn't even bother to make muffled screams, she just becomes mute. But the steamy windows and the moving shadows in the car tell her story. Sathie hates himself for not trying to save her, for not being strong enough to act with bravado, fighting like a street gangster with the policemen. He hates himself for thinking first about the scandal this would cause his singing career. He hates himself for saying and doing nothing. Nothing but lying on the street, the heavy foot of the policeman at his throat, telling him over and over again:

"Hey, Coolie! You banging a native, eh? Can't stick it in your own curry, eh? Ja, your own kind wants you back, brownie."

Zenzi, I am a coward. I failed you.

"This Black is a hot jungle girl, eh? Let's see. Let's feel. Come here, let me try. Hey, Coolie … who is she to you?"

The policemen finish, they throw Zenzi out of Tony's car into the alley. They bear down on Sathie, cowering in the gutter. Suddenly Sathie can see it splashed over every newspaper in Durban, this affair he is trying so hard to hide. Suddenly he can see the patronage of all the rich Indian women go flying out the door, turning him into a nobody. He had his music, his voice, and his good looks. He had his security in his place in the lavish world that he surreptitiously enjoyed, his little married secrets strewn all over the large mansions of the city who plied him with the expensive things he had grown accustomed to. He hated himself, because he knew that he could never give that glittery world up, not even for Zenzi. In a split second, Sathie knew who he was. And he was a coward.

What a man can deny standing away from a window of five-fingered steam is what a man eventually becomes. A coward. It surprises him how easily he denies Zenzi, all for the fragile protection of his manicured life as a crooning heartbreaker. It was Zenzi's heart that he broke after all.

"Who is she to you, Coolie? This black woman?"

"She is nobody, fellas. Just a girl. You know how these shows get; they throw themselves at me, these unknown women ..."

I love women.

I always will.

❧

Afroze. Afroze. You clean, pure column of light. You stood up today like a rising phoenix, and maybe your bravery will somehow leak into me.

CHAPTER SIX

SHE AGREED. AFROZE said yes. She had spent too many long nights and holidays drowning herself in work at the architecture firm, so surely she could just take as much time away from work as she needed. It surprised Afroze how she didn't really care what happened at the firm, yet just a few days ago, every waking moment had been consumed with the place.

"I'll stay. Just for a little while longer. Because you asked me to, and because I want to see that building destroyed."

The khaya held too many lace-curtain ghosts for her; she could not resist.

She imagined the beautiful catharsis of taking a lead hammer to its rotten walls, swinging at its foundations with every cell of strength. She itched almost immediately to smash the decaying horror to pieces. The image of her body covered in filthy dust and the powder of mortar, bleeding from her knuckles and fingerbeds, crushing every particle of that two-roomed artifact, smoldered into her dreams that night. And in those dreams, here she was again, trying to bite off pieces of wall, breaking teeth, tasting salt. She would relish this particular destruction. Because when Afroze was visited that night by an apparition of her six-year-old self, she realized that it was the derelict tin-roofed building that had stolen everything away from her. It was the voice of the khaya that she had heard whispering a roar into the party-line telephone.

"Take her. I won't keep her. Come tomorrow. Take her now."

Of course, such angers and such vitriolic memories always fade with sun. They linger in deeper, more silent places. But what wrapped her limbs in the sweat of sheets in a dark night was greeted with insipid reality when she rose and splashed cold water on her face. And put on lipstick. Always. Put on lipstick.

Kindle fire, tinder wood. Her eyes were new this bright morning.

She sat across from her mother; this disgusting old nobody-woman in a stupid wig and a ruffled burgundy morning gown. Abrasive lace caressed her sagging old-old throat and reached toward her eyes with a mock.

"So, you want to build a school, do you? One with your name on the door?"

"Rosie, your sarcasm is very unbecoming. I know that I did not give birth to a bitch."

"Ah, Mother, you are correct. But then, what did you give birth to?"

A knife is required. One that can cut through the cloying fat of tension. Ever efficient, Halaima appeared, handing a butter knife to Sylvie.

"Doctor, your toast will get cold. And you know how much you hate that."

Sylvie felt the spell break. She looked away from Afroze's challenging eyes, and calmly began to butter her bread.

Sathie sat silently eating. He began to wonder if he had created a situation that was just a bit too much for him to handle. He had settled very comfortably in this household of the doctor.

He knew that her illness had softened her—she allowed him into her deepest world because her vulnerability seemed to grow faster than the tumors that ate her. He was lucky. He knew how, like a stray dog, he had sneaked into this house, hoping that he would go unnoticed until the time when he was loved so much that noticing him would mean nothing at all.

Now, maybe his comfort had been shattered by his own hand. These two warring women might just shoot him in the crossfire. Perhaps he should not have persuaded Afroze to stay. He looked across the table. Afroze sat in a pool of sunlight. Red and copper brushstrokes appeared in that mane of hair. The slight plumpness of 42 softened a face that had once been too angular. She was beautiful. She did not merely glow; she blazed. Sathie swallowed a lump of poorly chewed egg. How possible was it for a man of his age to fall in love? Women would be his ruin, yet again in his life. Mother and daughter.

"Well, Mother. There is no point in arguing. I personally think that what you plan to do is very noble, and building a school here for the community is certainly going to uplift this entire town. From what I can see, this old town needs a face-lift."

"I'm doing it for Bee," Sylvie replied and flashed a wonderfully soft smile to the little girl.

"Bee … of course. Our Bibi." Afroze muttered.

"Shall we go and look at the state of this khaya?" Afroze stood up and dusted her hands. All too ready to begin.

Sathie sprang up, ready to follow Afroze, who was marching with a determined chin, jutted out in the direction of the piece of hell-history she was about to destroy.

"Sathie," Sylvie growled low, an almost inaudible approach of thunder.

He turned around, the change of face remarkable. The masklike smile again applied in thick paste where just a second ago were licked lips and eyes aglow. Rehearsed in body, Sathie elicited his little kowtow.

"Yes, my beloved," he said with exaggeration.

"Come help me to the front room, Sathie. You promised you would read the newspaper to me. I am finished with breakfast."

Sathie made a cartoon of swiveling his head back and forth.

War goddess daughter, in her fetching pair of jeans, marching to battle concrete-and-brick history. Crone-goddess mother, in her outstretched painted nails, watching his face with the expression of a woman who knows when her man looks toward another. Clever old minx.

"Of course, of course, Sylvie. My sweet, lovely Sylvie. Come, Halaima, take the doctor to the front room. I will join her in a tick."

Afroze turned around. Her eyes asked him, "Coming?"

Halaima picked up a teacup and rooted her feet to the ground. "I have to clear the table," she announced and mocked Sathie with her clever eyes. And although she would normally bustle and flutter at her tasks, she stood with just one teacup in her hand, throwing a challenge.

Sathie realized where he was in the game of queens; he pawned his immediate desires.

"Come, darling Sylvie. Let me help you up. And off to the news of the day we shall go."

The pair of them tottered slowly away. Sylvie rested her wigged head on his strong shoulder. They murmured little familiar stories to each other. Sathie had heard them so many times, he sometimes heard them in his sleep.

"Yes, Sylvie, yes, I remember. Yes, Sylvie, of course it was a very bad time for you. Yes, Sylvie, you told me about the rats. Yes, Sylvie, no one will ever forget. Yes, Sylvie …"

That proud woman, that majestic teacup holder with eyes that held a world of seens and unseens, stood frozen in a pose. She looked directly at her rival in the doorframe.

The other proud woman. Blazing flames of hair. Not a filly any longer, not a pasture mare just yet.

"Well, clear up the table then," Afroze said.

"I'll do it later," Halaima answered, and sank down on a stool near the kitchen door, making a show of examining her nails.

CHAPTER SEVEN

WHERE IS IT written that one who has suffered has to be long suffering? Sylvie, reaching her seventies, had hidden the greatest secret of all from her own child.

Sylvie, not just a cruel, evil witch-mother. Sylvie, who began as a reluctant activist, morphed with the hard years into a rampant activist of the anti-apartheid struggle in a land that was running with blood. Now, she lies silent in a dry town, and no cares what she threw away so that she could be a warrior. Who made the rules that silenced the activist? Sometimes, when the fight has been fought and the day has been won, all the fighter would like is for someone to immortalize their struggle. A book would be nice. A plaque, perhaps. A street name would be just first prize. A bust or bust.

Oh, look, books are written about famous freedom fighters now. Memoirs filled with stories told by people who knew people, sometimes written by gnarled old hands that had pulled triggers or detonated bombs, mouths filled with speeches, those jailed days, those broken rocks, those pins pulled from grenades. Because now, after it all ended, the struggle had become glamorous. And women of the struggle, rampant female banshees who stared apartheid in the face and spat, had become fashionable to know. Especially the ones who were still alive. Of them there were few. Back then, when politicians were raping and imprisoning them, frightened grannies warned their girls never to turn out like them.

What you want to go to high school for, girl? You stay at home and learn to cook or you'll end up in jail like a black woman. What you think, Nelson going to find you a husband after you done shaking your ass at black rallies? In your dreams.

Doctor Sylvie became notorious for dreams. She had them and she lived them. And when it all was over, and the country was one, she just never made it into the hall of fame. In a book of a thousand pictures, where was this one?

Why had this face lost the privilege of becoming another black-and-white portrait of the Resistance in an overpriced coffee-table book to be bought by patriotic expats? One needed to ask these questions. Heroes only became their archetypes when the smoke had cleared, when someone decided to shadow them around asking the right questions. How did you and why did you and when did you and now what will you and …

Oh, Sylvie, the writers have not come knocking at your bright green door. The photographers, the biographers, the chronographers, oh, Sylvie, purrty Sylvie … you are not even a footnote. Forgotten you, they have.

Quite a slap in the face. Even when the ones who you fought for never saw your face, and the soldiers who you stitched together with rough twine died before they opened their eyes, and the place where they finally took you was so dark that even when you were allowed into the light with the moles who ratted you out, they were too blind to view your face, you hoped for a day when your story would be made into song.

Not every fighter in that war selflessly and coyly declined medals. A medal in a glass cabinet would do nicely. Thank you very much.

A declaration of who you are and how large a role you played in the struggle would be a good thing. Someone had to know it all. It was not just the final nod of a medal, a ministership or even a government struggle-hero pension plan. Someone had to finally care, to sit and listen to your tales of your prison days.

Sylvie.

When I get out of here. If. If. When. If …

When I get out of here I will wear lipstick. Red, bright red. The brightest red to be found. Red like the color I cannot see.

Red I can feel.

Blue I can smell.

Green I can taste.

Orange, purple. Are there more? I know there are more. A spectrum of others. Shades and hues, tints and tinges and tones and myriads and many. I know they are out there. I saw them once. I see them in words. I see them in memories. I catch them. They fall on me. A shawl of colors. Find them. Keep them. They are there. They were there once.

Inside the jail cell all you see is gray. Stark, bleak gray. The walls are the same color as the floors. You lie suspended not knowing if your feet are in the air. Windowless cube. A naked bulb buzzes, and you will never know if the sun has risen or the sun has set. The filthy clothes are gray. The rough blankets are gray. Gray exudes from your pores into gray buckets. Food tastes of gray. Ashen. Maybe your hair is gray now.

Sounds become sights. Women play one-two, tappity-tap. One woman has seen a ray of daylight through a crack in her cell. She tells us. One tappity-tap, soft like her inner thigh, and one tappity-tap spreads like gossip from cell to cell. So soft, you hear it because you have been trained to hear what the guards and matrons have been trained not to hear, and you mark the passage of one day.

Someone sees dark night through a drafty hole. Two tappity-taps. How else would you know that time has passed? How else would you know there was life beyond your gray? Others marking walls, others marking time, pacing in bare feet. Four women-sized paces this way, five women-sized paces that way. And stop.

We are sisters. All inside this mother's gray womb. We all scream when one of us is dragged by her hair, for they have figured out the tappity-tap. We may never see her again. But watch … her sister starts up the tappity-tap. Glorious music, sister camaraderie. We will not stop our tappity-tap. It is our language and our only salvation. When one goes, one immediately takes up where she left off. Because this is how we have been trained.

Is it not the most natural thing in the world for a prisoner in a solitary cell box to spend the endless hours reflecting on the life they have lived? Up until that fateful moment when you become a prisoner, your life is never a reflection, it is a reel of ever-present moments that you don't take the time to watch. When you are alone, and all you hear is the scratching of rats, and you are grateful for the sound of the scratching rats, you begin to play the movie reel, projecting it onto the bare walls of your cell.

But the movie never fully plays out in sequence; it lurches, time traveling from childhood laughter into hot nights of lovemaking, careening into the childbirth that split your body into halves. The walls have scrawled writing of women that have been there before you. Scratches into the gray paint that they could never wash off when they hose down the cell after its inhabitant has gone. She has not been freed; she has just vanished. You only know that they walked the Earth because they made it a point of digging into wall paint: "I have been here, I was here. I lived."

When you stare at the lurching story of your life as it plays itself out again and again on the walls, their words become the captions. The silent movie of your life bears a monologue; it bears the whispered words of all the women that have been there before you. You know that their words are the same as your words, the cartoon bubbles of a hundred silent women become just one story; there is no difference between every single one of them and you.

That you love lipstick, the redder the better. That you smoke cigarettes on a public street, and men write letters in complaint about you. Smoking doctor. Woman. Indeed! That you wear your hair just so, that she enjoys caramels, that she loved sex, that she lost her nerve in the end and that she and she and she …

She is who you are. She is the you, who I have become. Sylvie Pillay, prisoner number 1434/80. Prisoners in a country where the murdering is not confined to the incarcerated.

I spread a rank mat on the floor. Somebody once told me that one must place a forehead on the ground to pray. I try it and it does not work. I am not connected to this Earth in any way. This prison may very well not be on this Earth; it has traveled through space and time and left the beautiful soft, sexual soil behind and landed on an arid planet. I do not feel her, this mother of saline ocean sons and fertile, undulating daughters. Even my Earth has left me. All I have is this memory, this reel on constant. And now, the celluloid is burning with holes too. Even this memory is leaving my side.

There is a daughter. She is somewhere left behind. I watched her walk away from me, those legs of no shape, no discernible ankle, no flesh of thigh. But she is my flesh. I remember how she broke me into pieces. Birthing her was the easy part. They stitched up the cuts when she was born. I sent her away, that watchful child. Sending her away from my breathing space left me with no air.

She looked at me with hate. I had not known before that children can hate very deeply. I pulled ever so lightly on that silvery cord that I thought would always connect us, even though I never knew how to be with this daughter. I had faith that this cord would send messages along its pulsating length. She swung those insect legs into a car, and the cord began to fracture, bisections along its thin girth. I was losing my child. And she fed herself on hate because it was better than being hungry. The car drove my child away. It was the fault of the car. It was the machine. I will hate that metal kidnapper. It was not me, it was not me. It was the fault of that car. I want to blame that car. I place this on record, Brigadier. It was not me.

One rap on your metal door. This means cold, uncooked porridge has been thrown like trash at your feet. I eat.

CHAPTER EIGHT

I AM A poor girl. I was born into a world of cheap. *Food that is picked from the fields outside your door is the tastiest food you will ever eat. Grandmothers who massage coconut oil into your hair at night are the most expensive gifts you will ever receive.* But I knew, even when I was a young girl, that some people are born for things that they can never be prepared for. Larger things that come with double edges. If a call against injustice comes to you in the early hours of a poor morning, you may hide under your blankets and shiver, saying in your sweat, "Go away, go away. Go to someone else," but the call will never go away to someone else because it has chosen you. Even when your mind and your body are not prepared for what you will do in your life, you wrestle. And then you give in. You resign, and it is then that you feel most free.

They said it was a disgusting thing, a young girl wanting bigger things. They did not understand all my wants.

"So pretty you are, girl. What is this studying you want to do? Better you marry a nice boy, have a nice house, give nice children. Wasting such a pretty face."

My father was a carpenter. The wood spoke to him when no one else would. In the hours that he spent chiseling and chipping away at blocks of nothing, arriving sometime in the middle of a day at the most beautiful cabinets and tables, he communed with worlds that spoke more than the dissonant world in which he walked. His five sons did not look into his eyes.

They resented the rough hands that brought scraps to a mahogany table. An intricately carved table, inlaid with the little chips of oak, a pattern created from a place that he could never name, his daughter could see. I could see.

I was the only daughter. Born last. Born because one day, while carving and sanding and fondling wood, he asked for a believer. He demanded an old soul who would stand in silence next to his workbench and speak without words. I came to him, and I knew him.

He knew that one day, this daughter would leave him and walk into an abyss. But he was glad that he had brought her here. He knew I would suffer. But he was glad that I would.

Despite all the hands that pulled at his pretty girl, my father pushed me far away. To a safe place where I did not have to hide my brain underneath a pile of dirty laundry. He sent my boat out into the world, and he said a silent prayer that it would not sink.

"Selvarani, you go. Go to the medical college."

"Appa, I will make you proud."

"I don't want you to make me proud. I want you to make me satisfied."

"Appa, I do not understand."

"Selvie, you came to me because I asked Goddess Lakshmi for a way to change this world."

"Appa, I will make you proud."

"Selvie. Go. Just go away now."

"Appa, I will."

The medical college was called Natal Medical School. It had never admitted nonwhites, and it had never admitted women. But the world was changing. It was in 1964, when defiance was bubbling inside the bellies of townships and spilling over into the hub of cities paved with gold, that I entered the medical college as one of the first nonwhite women to gain admittance. I joined three other women. The others that joined the black section of the same university were all men. We were told we were lucky to have even been considered.

There was the outspoken young princess, the pampered daughter of the Motala family, a tight-knit unit of Gujarati-speaking Muslims who had set up most of the booming businesses in Durban. Their Fatima would not hear of marriage and veiled decorum. She hissed and spat and threatened her way into allowance. Medical college was, for her, an act of rebellion in a world where rebellion was so strongly frowned upon. Especially for girls.

And then there was Gladys, a silent Zulu woman from a place where we knew she had seen horrors we could never imagine. Gladys walked into the college like a royal combatant, telling everyone that her traditional name was not the mouth-hiss prefixed Gladys. But her true and real Zulu name will be known to no one, for as long as she was forced to study in the arms of a white man's paradise, she would answer to the name he had given her. She vowed that on the day that freedom for all came to our land, she would answer to her true Zulu name.

Gladys became my closest and most vocal of companions, for we shared a room. The loud-mouthed Fatima could not tantrum her way into living at the college dormitories, although she deeply desired it. She was driven to college daily in a beautiful car, which she exited with distaste, sometimes kicking its tires before her driver sped away. She believed that her privilege was her deepest shame. Yet she never found comfort in our crammed dormitory either. On her visits to us, her nose would twitch at the smell of cabbage, and sometimes she wore soft, suede gloves.

Mpho was the last of the women admitted that year. She was known for her sweetness. Underneath a bookish beauty lay a heart of pure treasure, a place where we girls would go to hide. Under the soft eaves of her glance we could find comfort when our little brown hearts were broken by unsuitable boys. Hers were the lovely cushioned cheeks we rested our foreheads against when the professors told us to learn how to scrub pots and fold laundry as we huddled over strong chloroform-smelling cadavers.

Learning the pathways of blood vessels, slicing into muscles long dead, we tried to make as little noise as possible. We knew our place was a treacherous one. And when we cried to Mpho, or watched

Fatima scream rhetoric and Marxist quotes from atop a bed, watched eternally by the sullen Gladys, we did not realize the large noise we were making by simply being there. By passing our exams and tests, by dodging pathology professors' wandering hands, and by pretending to be more stupid than our male colleagues we slipped like stowaways through the system. They treated us like anomalies, silly girls who, if briefly indulged, would soon go away. Most of our professors—and almost all of our fellow students—were convinced that we were there simply to snag a doctor to marry.

Medicine is for men. And the black and Indian men that had finally been allowed to study it in that hallowed place felt that their special world had been somehow commandeered by four tiny women. Within them there lay revolutionaries who could see the ugliness of segregation by color of skin, but who could not bring themselves to see how they kept women in boxes. They read Trotsky, they quoted Marx, but in their hearts they wished we would just go home to cook dinner.

Four silent women, we trod with light steps. We passed every one of our exams, but we had to follow the rules of the game. We worked very hard not to pass too well. We made sure we never took first place. In the bedroom I shared with Gladys, in that substandard hole in the ground that we were given, we gathered by day and spoke of our suffragette hearts. And in the nice building across the street where there was running water and maybe a painted room, the nonwhite men who had gained their place at the black section of the Natal Medical College eyed us for signs of rebellion. They believed that rebellion belonged to them, the men.

They held meetings, speaking deep into the night in secret coding, using medical and anatomical words to describe how the people needed to change their consciousness first, and act on their rejection of apartheid later. Their leader was a handsome man, standing noble and grand in his Blackness, but we did not know that he was listening carefully for news about us women and our own political discussions which we spoke about on our own. This leader was not blind to us; he had been secretly talking with Gladys, who told him everything.

It was Fatima who fell first. None of us imagined she would. Somehow, somewhere in the middle of a world filled with women who veiled their beauty behind the gauziness of black and tinkled their bangles behind embroidered curtains as they learned the way to a man's heart, Fatima had stepped lightly but in wavy lines around the stones that surrounded her. She straddled the world she came from, the pampered world where a young woman such as she was discouraged from politics, and constantly harassed subtly and not so subtly to get her medical degree and open a shiny private practice as far away from ugliness and poverty as her world was from it now. But she spent the nights with secret books that expounded freedom, democracy, and the ugliest of words to her people—Communism.

Fatima held the reins for as long as she could, but one day she lost herself in the chains of her schizophrenic world. She could not amalgamate these pampered offerings—the hand of the richest merchant, the ideology that there is no such thing as religion and God that all was one and one was all. She ran off in the middle of her final year, and all we heard was news of the lavishness of her wedding party. Gladys lifted an eyebrow and sullenly said to us two remaining, "I always knew it."

I looked to Mpho, who smiled in her way, a warm golden ray that made everything better again.

"May she be happy."

And she was. I hope she was.

One morning, shortly after Fatima left medical school to her wedded life, Gladys arrived at my side. She was still fuming from how rapidly Fatima had walked away, after being given such a golden chance to study, to become a doctor, and to serve the community and the struggle. I was preparing to go on the much-feared surgical ward rounds with Professor Andrews. I knew that I had to ensure I stood far enough back so as not to be envied by my fellows, but not back enough to be noticed for doing so. I remembered how my aunts used to say that the way to rule a husband was to never let him know that you were doing it.

Gladys pushed a piece of paper into my hand. I was too sweaty and nervous to look because I knew what it contained. It happened that way. The leader, although also a medical student, kept away from almost all of us. He had forged ties with a few people who he felt were key players, and they were his voice and his eyes. It was too dangerous for him to be seen in public—he avoided many lectures and tutorials because he knew that he was being watched and soon a day would come when he would have to run or risk being picked up by the Special Branch. Gladys was one of the people whom he had allowed into his inner circle. In awe I would often ask her to tell me about him, and to speak about his ideals of Black Consciousness, and late into many nights she would whisper all the theories and plans to me. I became hungry to include myself in the work, and one day I admitted it to her.

"Sylvie, I am no fool," Gladys said. "I have watched you, and I have listened to the things that you say to me. Your words have power. But I am afraid to call you into our world."

"Why? Gladys, I want this. You know I want this."

"But look at Fatima. We listened to her speeches, we were seduced by her talks and lofty ideas. And just when we included her into our secrets, she turned and walked away, carrying these secrets with her, and throwing our choice in our face. How do we know you won't do the same?"

"Gladys, I want this. I want the chance to fight for our equality. You have seen me flare up in my tiny talks with you. I have so much more in me, so much more. I want this chance."

Gladys had simply nodded and rolled over to fall asleep with ease. I on the other hand could not sleep; I paced the room, wondering if she would awaken or was aware of my restlessness. It was true, I wanted this. I wanted to launch myself headfirst into the world of activism. I was tired of subversively scribbling in journals. Every part of me ached to join in, to do good work, to meet our leader and to make him see how committed I was.

I shook Gladys awake. No moment could be lost now that my hunger was awakened.

"Gladdy, listen. Wake up. I … want this. I want to join you. I want to meet him, to work with your group. Don't leave me out when you go for your meetings. I will not desert the struggle."

Gladys sighed, not from sleep, but a deeper sigh, one of awareness and slight apprehension. She seemed exhausted. "Sylvie, it is not easy. It is not the glamorous world you picture in your head. You should know ... the men don't welcome us in their group easily. They believe this fight is theirs. How will you handle that?"

"We've been handling that since we got here, haven't we, Gladdy? They didn't want us to become doctors either. They pushed us to the back of the lecture halls, the laboratories, and the wards. So we stayed in the back, but we still learned as well as them. We are still as good as them in this medical world. I know in my heart that this is what I want."

"Go to sleep, Sylvie. I will think about it," she replied, but from her tone I knew she would agree to take me to meet her comrades. It was only a matter of time.

I was filled with fear. This was the only real bold step I had taken since I had defied my old aunts and grannies and listened to my father's voice telling me to go to university. Now, his voice came into my head again like a distant echo, and I heard myself reply:

"I will make you proud, Appa."

Despite the fear, I waited. And like a virgin who knows the night will come when she would become a woman, I held fear and apprehension at bay with excitement and deep desire. I had been awaiting this moment that I had known would come, the moment when the leader would call me to his chamber. Among us black students at the medical school, we knew that political work and the activism of the Black Consciousness Movement had its roots in our very own backyard. Some chose to avoid it and look away. I chose to dig down. In my own way, I had coveted a life that was larger than myself, and I always hoped the day would come when I would be given a chance to openly show my inner thoughts.

My father had always spoken of justice. In his uneducated, carpenter's mind, he understood human beings and politics better than many schooled academics. And the reason for this was because he believed in right and wrong. He did not know the big words to describe what was right and what was wrong, but in simple peasant language he stoked the furnace of a burning mind. I read voraciously, I devoured thoughts, and I began wanting change so salaciously that I became a harlot on the pages of my journals, writing out my deepest secretive ideas and philosophies of how the world should be, rather than the ugly place it was.

At medical school I kept writing. My reading in the dark hours had taken me into the deepest heart of the Resistance, into the most delicious taste of a democracy. In a bound-up journal, peeling at its corners, my words danced out desire as I channeled the great words of those who had come before me. I filled the thin, blue lines of the pages with written words because I would not and could not speak them out loud. I wrote like a revolutionary, but I wrote in secret. I did not know that Gladys was reading my words and talking about them to the movement that she had joined.

It was a night in winter when Gladys came to our room, sniffing and holding a thick shawl around her. She was not well, I could see it. She had been spending hours away from us women, and away from the lecture halls and wards of the hospital. I knew where she spent most of her time. It was with him, Steve Biko, the leader of the South African Students Organization, a man schooling himself in Black Consciousness from the literature he voraciously read and disseminated from the great philosophers like Marx and the great American activists of the Black Panthers.

Gladys flopped down on the thin mattress next to me. She glared at me with large, unreadable eyes.

"Sylvie, do you know who this singer called Donny Hathaway is?" she suddenly asked.

"Of course. I love Donny Hathaway. He is a jazz and blues singer from Chicago."

"Oh. Shee-car-goh," Gladys exaggerated the name of the city, almost as if she were mocking the way I had said it.

"What's the matter, Gladys?" I asked, seeing something lurking in her eyes that I could barely recognize. She seemed febrile and on the edge.

"Yah, what do us black women know about famous jazz singers from America, huh? We only know our township music."

"Gladys, Donny Hathaway is famous for singing many songs that mean a great deal to the struggle for Black Consciousness," I told her.

Gladys rolled her eyes. "Of course you would know that, hey? Well then, he wasn't wrong about you after all, Sylvie."

"Who? What are you talking about, Gladys?"

She rolled over onto her stomach, cradling her chin in her hands, her eyes straying to the dark tiny window above us.

"Get some clothes on Sylvie. Steve wants to meet you. Now."

I jumped up, scattering the book and papers that were in my lap, explaining the convoluted physiological processes of tuberculosis.

"What? Me … now?" I gushed like a little girl about to meet a hero.

"Yah, now. He read all that stuff you write about in that journal of yours. I gave it to him."

"What?" I shouted and began to scramble around in my tin trunk near my bed for my journal. It was not there.

"How could you, Gladys? That is my private property. I write so much of my personal things in that journal. It is private!"

She smirked and stood up. She swayed slightly, probably the effects of her terrible cold and fatigue.

"Ey, don't act like you didn't want this. I know you. Secretly, you have been dying to meet Comrade Biko for a long time. Don't think I haven't heard the longing in your voice when I talk about him. Anyway, I did you a favor by showing him that book."

"What do you mean … favor?" I asked and this time I did not hide my anger from a woman who I frequently was in awe of. Her strength and singleminded sense of purpose impressed me, made me want to be brave like her.

"Well, you know so many things. You and Steve, you both read the same books, both have the same ideas. Why would he not want to meet you? It was bound to happen."

"So, you don't have the same thoughts as him, then?"

"Agh Sylvie … don't start that on me. I listen to Comrade Steve and his theories on psychological emancipation of the black man before we can achieve physical emancipation. Although he makes sense, I think our struggle needs more force. We can't be spending time giving books and pamphlets filled with song words by American jazz singers to mothers whose sons are being murdered."

"Gladys, I know the people are suffering. Believe me, I see it in the wards everyday. But I think Comrade Biko is right. Unless we can look at ourselves with pride and know that we deserve basic human rights, how can we expect the white man to take us seriously?"

Gladys stared at me for a while, and then threw a shawl at me. "See, you even talk just like him. Put that on. He is waiting."

He stood next to a dirty window, and I immediately knew that the window was deliberate in its filth. It made things murky, it lent secrecy to its occupant. No one would care to look at him hiding there, because they'd believe that nothing important could come from such filth. But in the gloom, he glowed. He glowed like a man possessed with the knowledge that he could change the world in which he had been thrown. I loved him from the second he called my name and asked me to enter his world, filled with the hidden texts of noughts and dashes hidden inside books of human anatomy and words of disease.

In the dirty room, in his hand, he held my journal. "We have been looking for you," he said, and I ran with abandon into the open arms of his movement. Black Consciousness.

"I have been looking for you," I replied.

And slowly they all filed into the room. Midnight, a time for lovers. They arrived to welcome me into this world, and my free fall into it was the most beautiful and the most heard I have ever felt. My father would have been proud.

Gladys and I were the ones he guarded most closely. He realized that within the masculine fight, a feminine idea could tip the scales. The women, he always said, are the ones who would do the most fighting in this ugly war. His every sinew spoke of seduction, and Gladys and I, who had been starved of belonging in a world of men, we welcomed his seduction like true concubines.

In this era, in the stronghold of apartheid, we were not allowed to mix. Indian and black and white were forced into a separation that was clever. Some were given more, and some were given nothing. We were not allowed to hold gatherings, so we snuck into the murky room like rats, holding medical textbooks as if they were armored shields. Within them we held our plans and dreams for the future. The traditional and orthodox women of my family knew, but they could not stop the tide on which I was being carried. They wrung their washerwoman hands. But their daughter belonged to the struggle now. She did not exist any longer.

I completed my internship at the largest hospital in Durban. The one that overlooked the mighty Indian Ocean. Right on the sea-sand doorstep. Here, I was given the work that no one wanted. The professors, the surgeons, and the physicians did not hide their disdain that they were forced to allow an Indian girl into their wards. I treated tuberculosis and the worst forms of cancers. I forced my gloved hands onto white bodies who would rather have died than take pills from me into their mouths. The wives of white white-collar men, who came writhing in labor pains, would scream out their vexation—they would rather be torn in half than allow the coolie to pull their babies out of their wombs. They sometimes insisted the pills be washed before they took them into their mouths; the water melted the powdery tablets into a bitter mush, but they preferred that to my hands.

I continued my work with the Black Consciousness Movement, and soon we had organized ourselves enough to join with the early members of the United Democratic Front. Slowly, from within a tiny apartment on Victoria Street, we began planning a series of marches and speeches that would begin to spread the word—Resistance was coming, and coming fast. I took on the task of writing. I had a gift for it, and I didn't hold back. I spent my nights writing frantically, powerful words about Black Consciousness, quoting famous freedom fighters from Gandhi to Martin Luther King, Jr. I used simple, yet strong language about how we had to elevate our education and consciousness first before we even dreamed of advancing on the apartheid government. In the apartment, we had an archaic typesetting machine, which any one or the other of us would painstakingly use to set my words into thick inky blocks. And when the room filled up with stacks and stacks of yellow pamphlets filled with quoted speeches and dates for meetings, a few of the members would take them—hidden inside black garbage bags—to the tops of buildings in universities, colleges, factories, and even in the heart of the city itself. Here they would throw sheaves of paper wildly out to the wind. The pamphlet bomb. Do it fast enough to get as many pages out as the wind could carry, and then run as fast as you could as the Special Branch chased your heels.

Many in our group began to get impatient. They could not quell their angry blood and took to the streets at night, spraying walls in the elite white part of the city center with graffiti. "Free Mandela," the black ugly graffiti blared out. Everywhere, those words scrawled across shop fronts and office buildings.

I was alone in the apartment one morning, just arriving from a night shift in the emergency room when I heard hushed voices from the stairwell. Too exhausted to care, I glared at the stacks of papers near the typesetter, waiting for me to begin the ardous task of printing. The voices became louder, and when I heard shouting and a scuffle, I threw open the door to find two of our men throwing wild punches at each other on the stair landing. Ben and Sizwe. They had recently begun coming over to the apartment to join in any discussions, or to assist in any way. I had regarded them with suspicion, wondering if they were perhaps informants to the Special Branch, but my Comrades convinced me that they were serious members from Johannesburg, who had recognized that Durban was now becoming the hub of activity in the struggle.

Ben had Sizwe pinned against the wall, holding him by the neck. Sizwe clutched a brown package close to his chest, gripping it so tightly that he would not even let it go to protect himself from Ben's tight grip.

"Give it to me or I swear I will kill you right here," Ben shouted.

Both hadn't noticed me at the open door, and I was thankful that most of the tenants on our floor were out at work.

"Ay wena, you don't know me, Ben. I will kill you first. Let me go," Sizwe said through gritted teeth. I could see the dark intent in his bulging eyes.

"Fokoff you, Sizwe. Give it to me. We had a plan."

"You changed our plans, you coward," Sizwe spluttered. The pressure of Ben's hands at his throat made him wheeze with forced-out words.

Ben released his grip on Sizwe's throat, perhaps afraid he could actually suffocate the friend who had been close to him for years. But he had released his grip just so that he could lunge for the package, wrapped in brown paper that Sizwe held tight to.

"I'm no coward, you hear? It's the wrong time," Ben said and pulled the parcel forcefully.

"What the fuck is wrong with you? Stupid. This has explosives, you fool," Sizwe said, and hearing this, I gasped loudly, suddenly realizing what the brown paper package really was. A parcel bomb.

I had been hearing some talk among some of the more militant men about taking the struggle beyond just words into action. I had dismissed it as simply the bravado talk of desperate men aching for our activities to move to a new level. Many felt that violence and rage was our only way forward. They balked at our pamphlets and poetry, calling those efforts mild and cowardly.

My loud gasp startled both men, and they stopped scuffling. They saw me standing at the door with my hands to my mouth in shock.

"You, woman ... shut that door and get away from here. Men are talking," Sizwe said menacingly. My feet were rooted to the spot. Something terrible was going to happen, and I knew I was the only one there to stop these two men from either harming each other in the stairwell, or harming innocent people with that bomb.

"Stop it. Both of you. What the heck do you think you're doing?" I shoutd down to them.

"My sister, get the fuck out of here. This is men's business," Ben said, forgetting his fight with Sizwe and turning on me.

"Bullshit. Men's business? You hotheads don't you realize this is all of our business. That's a bloody bomb, for hell's sake. It could go off right there and blow us all to pieces, not forgetting the innocent people on this block."

Something about what I said seemed to create a small window of reprieve, and both men visibly relaxed their tense bodies.

"Listen, Sizwe, this is crazy. I told you. Now is not the time. The time will come. So just give it to me, you hear?" Ben said, his voice calming and placating.

The slight release in Ben's grip was all Sizwe needed. He glared first at me, then at his friend, and faster than we both could react, he dashed down the stairs, zipping the parcel bomb in his jacket.

"Oh, bloody hell. Now look what you've done, woman," Ben said and ran down the stairs.

I panicked.

Where was Sizwe planning to detonate that bomb? I knew that most parcel bombs were homemade, filled with fine-pounded commonly used chemicals in an amalgam that would detonate with a depressed switch that would be released once the package was opened. Clearly, this bomb that Sizwe was carrying was intended to harm someone; it was not just meant to blow up an empty building or even a postal box. Someone had to open it to detonate it. Someone, maybe many people, would be hurt.

I ran after Ben, shouting after him, "Tell me where? Tell me."

I was frantic, wildly chasing Ben down the lane, knowing I had to inform someone in our leadership immediately.

Ben turned around, and hesitated for just a fraction of a second. He knew it was too far gone now.

"Beachfront," he shouted to me, and sped away.

My heart racing, I rushed back to the apartment, wondering who I could contact and how. Nothing could be done fast enough. The Durban beachfront was a lavish, sprawling esplanade where only white people were allowed to frequent the beautiful open-air restaurants and bars. I couldn't think why, on a weekday morning, Sizwe would want to detonate a bomb, when most of the places would be almost deserted.

And then it dawned on me.

I had read in the newspaper a few days ago that the mayor of the city was planning a special birthday breakfast for his wife at one of the best restaurants on the beachfront. Sizwe was heading there. And the distance from our street to the beachfront would not take him long. What might delay him would be that people of color could not simply walk along the promenade near the restaurants. Many of our people had been arrested for simply standing nearby to look at the sea or the carnival rides with their little children. No one dared walk openly there. Sizwe would have to skulk behind alleys and the back of the restaurants, hiding behind the many decorative palm groves that lined the seafront. As I bolted, panting into the apartment, I prayed that Ben had gotten to him in time. Of course I knew the seriousness and desperation of the comrades in our struggle. We had been achieving nothing real by passively disseminating literature and giving heated speeches. But I still clung to the ideology that Steve taught me, and to the passive resistance words of Mahatma Gandhi. We did not have to take this struggle to violence. We could win with our sheer numbers, and our elevated consciousness, using intellect and not force to gain equality. Perhaps I was naive. Perhaps I was.

When I barged into the apartment, I almost collapsed with relief to see that two of the men who also held firm to the idea of nonviolence had also returned from their jobs, to grab a bite to eat from a pot on the stove that we women ensured was always full.

Panting and barely able to get my words out, I doubled over breathlessly, the words coming out in staccato bits and pieces. All they heard was "letter bomb" and "beachfront," and both were out the door.

I collapsed on the floor. There was nothing further I could do now. If Sizwe planned to deliver the parcel disguised as a birthday gift for the mayor's wife, in whichever way he had planned, it was probably too late.

But it was not too late. Sizwe had been delayed from entering the esplanade by a strong and increased police presence. In his volatile rage, he hadn't thought clearly. He only wanted bloodshed; he wanted the attention of the press and the authorities so much that he had been blinded by his hatred.

I remained seated on the floor simply staring into space, my ears cocked for any sound, anything that would give me a clue to what was happening. A few people filed into the apartment, probably to get a decent meal before they went off to their jobs or their tiny, shared homes. My apartment was noted for being the one place people could come to for food and comfort, or even to bed down if they were stranded. I said nothing.

A few of the women who regularly stayed the night with me if they passed the curfew time, when people of color were not allowed to walk on the streets, came in and saw me in my state, numbly staring without my usual smiles and greetings. Most of them assumed I had seen some terrible cases at the hospital and asked no questions. And I was glad for it.

Finally, after what seemed like hours but probably was just barely even one hour, Ben came back with the other two men. Sizwe was nowhere to be seen. The men walked in with defeated, hunched shoulders.

"Sister." Ben shook me out of my daze and crouched down next to me, his hand on my shoulder.

"Sizwe … the bomb … what …?" I murmured.

"They got him, Sylvie."

I slumped forward, knowing that we would never see Sizwe again. He was probably dead already. Dead and thrown into an overcrowded morgue, where no one would bother to ask questions about cause of death. He would just disappear and remain yet another nameless casualty of our frustrating struggle. If there ever was a time when I wanted to lose all my composure and scream to the wind, it was that day.

I held onto Ben, sobbing. "Stupid man. Stupid, stupid man."

"Agh, Sylvie, you know that they grabbed Sizwe's nephew a week ago? He was a good boy, just walking home from work, maybe a little after curfew. They grabbed him, and now he is dead. They tell the family he fell and hit his head. Fell from what? He was walking on the bloody street for fuck's sake … fell from what? Sizwe went crazy after that, Sylvie. He couldn't leave it. He had to go and make this bomb. He found out that the mayor was having this birthday breakfast at that restaurant, and he convinced one of the waiters to deliver the parcel to him. I tried to stop him … I tried to …"

Ben collapsed in a fit of rare tears and cried in my arms.

I felt so tired. Defeated, angry, sad. But mostly, I was tired.

Sizwe's disappearance sparked off a wave of dissent. We had been fools to think we could ever have contained our fight to a peaceful, intellectual one. The wave spread, mainly among the youth. News of Sizwe's and his nephew's plight moved like wildfire, and soon even our best orators and writers could not contain the rage of the youth. They began to throw stones, they began to get careless in their rage, openly walking around after curfew, or defying their white bosses.

It all seemed like a wild, crazy game at first. But when graffiti slogans made way for bricks thrown through windows by overexuberant and raging members of the Movement, we knew that the days of pamphlets and words were coming to an end. I held firm to my job at the hospital, using the time to keep my ears peeled for any bits of information that filtered among the white doctors, who ignored me, and the ever-looming police, who watched me carefully. Any information I could find I wrote in code in my journal, and then copied and passed along to one of my comrades, who would undertake the complicated steps to get the information to the leaders of both the Black Consciousness Movement and the newly forming United Democratic Front. In this way, we found little clues of where the Special Branch would be raiding next, ensuring our apartment was always kept clean of any signs of political activity. We hid things well. Any policeman who came would just find a group of layabouts reading fashion magazines. It was illegal then for a gathering of people to occur in one place, but that was confined to outdoor spaces. In the apartment, we hid so many people when the police paid a visit, I often wondered if you shook the apartment as in an earthquake, how many people would fall out of the cracks.

Gladys had been sent away to finish her internship in a township, in a black hospital. Obviously, to the white man, an Indian feeding you pills was slightly better than a Black.

❧

There is something very profound about belief. It carries you across the dark days. It makes you trust that somewhere inside the nebulous clouds of doubt and a never-ending struggle that there will be a day when truth will be realized. And recognized. We all wanted both: truth and recognition. It didn't really matter which came first. But when you are part of a struggle that strips you of an identity, that turns you into a piece of a dangerous machine, every tiny aspect of individuality struggles and strains to burst out of confined quarters.

We learned first that we were nothing. We learned early that we were less, that our place in the land was as small as the specks of dust that never left the soles of our feet. And suddenly, all the loneliness and all that subservient kowtowing began to take a shape that made us belong. We had a tribe. And our tribe understood. Our tribe had a purpose that was larger than personal suffering.

It was time to forget who we once were. Indian was not Indian anymore. Beautiful meant new things. Clever took on the best of monikers. Fighters. Warriors. Finally our worlds began to make sense. Sylverani, the Indian girl with hair in thick ropelike plaits from a township where only Indians were allowed to live, died then. Sylvie was born. A nonwoman, yet a strong female; a non-Indian, a nonperson. Only a cogwheel. And a willing one. When we struggle, when we fight injustice, there is no I and there is no *you*. There is only *us*. And we shall overcome.

And yet equality does not always extend a generous hand. Men talked of it, they wrote of it, and they claimed they fought for it. But they were men. They owned the struggle. Our leader always spoke highly and fervently about the power of women, and how their role in the struggle was so necessary, but sometimes when he allowed the men to push us women into corners or to silence us midsentence, I wondered about men, and whether they would truly accept the power of a woman. Deep within their fighter bones, they had no place for a full form of equality. I joined them, a woman in the room. But I was never their equal. They understood egalitarian words and waxed eloquently on high-minded theory. In the real world, they believed that equality belonged only to their kind.

The divide between men and women in the struggle made us unhappy in our conjoined twinness. It became a silent code. Yet another code that we had to learn. Not a code of dashes and zeros, not a language of identifying informants and allies. But a lovely little code of us and them. Our bodies and their bodies bore bruises of sameness, the uniformity of beatings did not distinguish between the body of a man and the body of a woman. But men were the self-proclaimed owners of the struggle.

In other words, the struggle was sexist.

CHAPTER NINE

IN 1971, DURBAN had begun to shine with a patina of politics. It was the Durban Moment, and the frustrating labyrinthine streets and alleys thronged with angry activists who kept their documents, registers of active members, and pages and pages of manifestos and banned articles written by the founding fathers who were now imprisoned, close to their chests. Speeches and marches flooded the humid streets, and chasing the headiness of ego, men stood on podiums and enjoyed the sounds of their own voices. They paraded their resistance, and allowed testosterone-laden war cries to ring out in the squares. They grew drunk on the power of the audience. The drug was rich and spicy, and they imbibed.

Preening, the males had much to say—peacocks are so much more beautiful than their drab female halves. It is a powerful thing to rebel, to be a renegade. Sex came so freely offered to the man on the podium. Danger was the aphrodisiac; it made the blood rise and swell. Indeed, the struggle was real, the struggle was fatal, but it also brought its gifts. In the reckless times, when young blood rushed with a cocktail of defiance and knowledge, we reached out for each other in throes. Lovemaking was dangerous, and that is why it was so sweet.

Men and women who were denied one another's bodies found that they responded so rapturously when forbidden.

We were the silent sisters of the struggle, we women. We understood it well enough.

The deeper into the heart of activism I delved by attending meetings and rallies, by listening to the passionate speeches made by young men tasked to become leaders, the more involved I became, eventually officially placing my name on the register as an active member of the African National Congress. Now, all the splintered movements and groups began to unify, and although it was a process where many egos were ruffled as each leader of each group had to give up his control, they understood, after many meetings, that a combined, solid effort was what would win. The unified groups then melded their members into the large body of the African National Congress, with one leader and one charter. I willingly fused my writing work as a member of the Congress, and I began to join in the effort to produce and print activism literature, plays and poetry that spoke the rhetoric that our jailed leaders could never speak. Still a firm believer that violence was not needed to win this battle, I contained my work to solitary writings. And once I was in the ANC, I knew that I would never leave.

The men and women of the Congress were given an equal chance to vent their minds. But in life as in activism, men's speeches and their tirades were given more weight. Perhaps they felt women's words held too much emotion. Or perhaps they felt that our words had their place.

There was no romance in the struggle. Our leader was in a jail; our leader was probably dead. But we sensed him, pushing us onward. And as strongly as many members pushed themselves into the arts of warfare, preparing their military practices for the day when they would have to take up arms, so strongly did we grab and touch and feel one another. Because one another was all we had.

When comrades who were willing and passionate were given their orders to flee to the secret training camps abroad to learn hard combat skills and weaponry training, they did not hesitate to take up the call. But on the nights before they were preparing to leave, they clung to each other just for warmth and comfort.

Young boys and girls who had barely held a knife were sent to the training camps to be taught how to assemble and disassemble AK-47 rifles in the Soviet Union, and to pack and smuggle them into South Africa via Angola. Grenades sometimes went off in untrained hands, and some as young as 16 would arrive back in Durban with hands blown off, miserable and ashamed that they had failed our struggle. I received them, the ones that actually survived the bush training, and the rough bush surgery, often their limbs gangrenous or so mauled that activities such as brushing their teeth was an impossibility. I found ways to smuggle them into our hospital late at night, watching their feverish eyes, and often watching these youth die before they got there. I swore never to touch a weapon in my life. I held on for nonviolence. Little did I realize that the day when I would ask for a gun was soon upon me.

❧

It had been one of those Saturday nights at the hospital. I found myself swinging like an exhausted pendulum between doing actual work and consoling distraught night-shift nurses who had been given double-barrel shifts in Accident and Emergency—the worst place to be on a Saturday night. The dog-tired women swarmed around me, teary eyed, moaning of having been on their feet for over 24 hours, complaining of drunken students retching and hitting out with huge arms and legs at the nearest human target, using words no one wanted to hear. The hospital in the city center served a population that still harbored the deepest racism. It sent white patients into wild rages when they encountered a person of color who had an education, a good English accent, and a position of power over their sick bodies.

I always hobbled away from nights like this, my mind churning with the desperation of nurses and doctors of color, who had no one to speak for them. Only once had I tried to collect their grievances and taken them to the stern hospital manager, Mr. McNamara, a man who would not look ill-placed behind a huge, high platform wielding a gavel. He had not even allowed me to continue my plea. I showed him the pages and pages of grievances.

"Mr. McNamara, I really think that if we allow a union to form, this Union of Medical and Health Workers would work together with management to make things better for everyone."

He threw the pages toward me, I hadn't even sat down and the leaves of paper fell on the carpeted floor at my feet. He looked at me with a bland, dry look and spoke. "So, Doctor Pillay, do you enjoy being called 'Doctor'?"

I nodded.

"Yes, you ... you I have seen running around the wards, trying to push yourself forward, overpleasing, showing off. You know this English term—'upstart'?"

"I'm not!" I said sharply, and with his raised eyebrow, I tempered my speech. "I mean, I know the term, but I can assure you, sir, I don't show off or anything. I just do my job as best as I can."

The old man still regarded me with ice blue eyes. "Well, I have heard little whispers, my dear doctor. Whispers that you have long been involved in some activities, joining a bunch of rebels and communists, having your big mouth flapping at meetings. I have heard ... but I suppose I choose to not say anything. Unless ..."

I was shocked. I had been very discreet about my political involvements. Was there someone among us who was an informant? I could not lose my job now; I would be lost. Thoughts swirled around my wearied brain like the swirls of smoke from the cigar that the manager had lit and pulled on deeply.

"No ... I ... I haven't. I mean, I promise you, sir, I am not involved in things like this. I ... I just do my work, and then I go home to my parents' apartment and remain there. We are a conservative family."

He dragged again on the cigar, and looked toward the window. After a long silence, when I shuffled from aching foot to aching foot, he sat staring out at the beautiful Indian Ocean, which crashed in warm, angry waves onto the shore near the hospital.

"Doctor. Take my advice. Find a husband, go and do all those Indian fire rituals you people do at your weddings, and then keep his bed warm. I can see that the places you are going is going to cause you, and me, much trouble. So forget any grand union ideas. Or else forget even being allowed to practice this degree called medicine that we so kindly put in your lap. Understood?"

I lingered for perhaps a second too long, instead of jumping to his words and scuttling away, mouthing *sorry* and *yes sir, absolutely sir, thank you, sir, never again, sir …*

His eyebrows shot up at my delay. Suddenly, he banged hard on his dark, wooden desk, and the sound echoed through the room and bounced off the door that was tightly shut. I jumped in shock and suddenly saw the menace in his eyes.

Quickly, I hastened to pick up a few pages of my neatly written list of grievances, each one followed by a stupid color-coded suggestion of how to address it.

I don't think I was able to grab even half the papers, before he banged the desk again, harder this time. I ran out of his office.

My breath came in short, harsh bursts as I ran down the flights and flights of stairs to exit the hospital. Even as doctors on call, we nonwhites were not allowed to use the elevators, no matter the emergency. The stairs it was, and the stairs it always would be. As I exited the main doors, my lungs gulped in salty air, thought to be a tonic for the patients when the hospital was first built. Now, the salt burned my eyes and my chest.

"Haai, Dokotela! Ini?" Hey, Doctor! What?

I looked to find one of my favorite security guards arrive for his shift. He almost reached out to hug my shaking body, and then we both stopped ourselves. The white security police from the Special Branch, who always posted themselves all over the hospital, looked in our direction.

"Nothing. It's nothing, Cedric … I'm just tired." I muttered and walked away. I didn't stop trembling until I had walked all the way down the Beachfront Esplanade, my practiced footsteps only allowing myself to walk on the tiny footpath that people of color were allowed to walk on. The early-morning workers, street cleaners, and domestic servants walked on the path too. The silence was palpable, only the raging sea created a soundtrack to raging hearts and minds. And on that day, mine was one of them.

The sun had risen as I went up the two flights of stairs into the apartment that I shared, the one that always seemed to house a hundred bodies, men and women losing decorum, and sleeping in each other's arms, strewn all over the floors and furniture. My job brought me to this home at odd hours, and I would often find a couple in the undulating throes of lovemaking, wedged behind couches, or under kitchen tables. By day, they were stern and serious cadres, organizing and planning, writing pamphlets and speeches. But when night crept to indigo dawn, they just reached for each other's bodies, and even the married forgot their vows. All they needed was comfort.

As I crept into the apartment, dreading meeting anyone in my distraught state, all I needed was comfort too. I did not find it.

I found one of our regular visitors, one who seemed to always have his fair share of behind-couch comforting, and who always ate more than his ration of food that the women activists were always tasked to cook, no matter how busy or clever they were … when it was time to eat, all eyes would stray to a woman.

"Oh, Nathan," I said, startled from my own thoughts, to find the lanky general secretary of a fast-flourishing mineworker's union seated at the kitchen table, sipping tea. He looked up at me, his eyes dark and hooded, some sort of vitriol lurking inside them. Nathan had always been a shadowy figure to me. He never spoke much, but when he did, his words were violent, often filled with rhetoric that could inflame and incite. I had watched him seduce an angry mob of construction workers wielding large machetes and sticks, boiling to kill the foreman because their wages had not been paid for weeks. The foreman, a tiny, wiry Indian man, hid shaking and mewling. He had locked himself inside a crane control box.

It was Nathan, and only Nathan, who could quell this bloodthirst. The workers were strong, and they were hungry. It had been a potent combination that would have seen at least one man dead. As the crowd bayed, Nathan used flowery rhetoric, the almost pastorlike preaching at a crane pulpit. In trickles, the murderous mob had stood down, keeping their ire in a locked box, waiting for the day they would attack the white boss as he slept beside his lily-white wife.

The calming effect of Nathan's words reached the highest ranks, and soon he received orders to prepare to join the world of unions, where the true politics lay. It was sweat that made the men's skin boil. It was not, as most thought, a boiling of blood.

I always treated Comrade Nathan with a mixture of awe and apprehension. The air around him buzzed with something unstable and dangerous. His eyes never really met yours when he spoke, unless you were part of a clapping, roaring crowd. And today, after my draining night shift and my encounter with the hospital manager, Nathan was the last person I needed to encounter. I backed away from the kitchen door, hoping he was too lost in thoughts to bother with me. But Nathan had seen me, and he called out loudly.

"Aha, it is our doctor. What … don't run away like that, Doc. Come, sit, have a cuppa with me."

He dragged a chair next to him backward and it made a horrible screeching sound as metal scraped on cold concrete.

Reluctantly I took a seat, and my foot felt something hard yet pliable under the table. Someone had bedded down there for the night.

"Oh, don't worry. It's only Freddie. Needed a place, you know. They've been looking for him ever since he was caught at the Westville campus, rallying up a storm with the student council in broad daylight, shouting out his Marxist speeches. Stupid idiot."

I barely knew the man he was talking about, but I rapidly pulled my foot away as I felt fingers begin stroking my ankle, advancing upward. Nathan saw it and chuckled. He pointed to the teapot on the stove.

"So, make me some tea, Doctor. Nice and sweet."

I glared at him. Again his head nodded toward the old enamel jug we used as a teapot. It was the largest cooking vessel in the kitchen, and tea had to always be available.

"Nathan, I am really tired. I've just come off the trauma room night shift, okay?" I said, hoping my tone was placatory, and then wondering why I was so trained to make my tone appeasing, even when talking to a man who was clearly my intellectual inferior. I realized, with a sudden berating squeeze of my heart, that no matter how much I had to say, I always dropped my eyes and spoke in softer tones when the men in the room could summon devils with their voices.

Nathan looked at me intently, then smiled a conciliatory smile. He held both his hands up, his rough palms facing me. Would he leave me alone now? So easily? I had spent too much time with men like Nathan, my own comrades, who hid their sinister poison behind false smiles.

"Okay … okay, Doc. No need to fret. Relax. Let me show you how I make tea. I'll even make you a cup."

He reached into his jacket pocket and pulled out something wrapped in a dirty floral cloth that looked like a pillowcase from my bed. He set the shrouded object down on the table, and it was heavy enough to make a dull thud. Slowly, Nathan began peeling away the cloth, and then I knew for certain, it was one of my pillowcases. Just as he had peeled away layers of many willing and unwilling women's undergarments, he revealed beneath the dirty cloth, a gun.

I lurched backward. I had seen so many guns. The men and women at our meetings carried their weaponry with pride, only relinquishing them to a huge, metal trunk hidden in a false-bottomed cupboard when the messages spread that we were going to be raided. The gun did not frighten me. And yet although I had helped to hide many weapons, I had never really been able to use one, or even to hold it for longer than the seconds it took to drop it into the metal trunk.

"Touch it," Nathan said, slowly in a calm, soft voice.

I shook my head and stood up. "Nathan, I am really tired. I need to sleep."

His sinister voice stopped me from moving. "Doc. I said … touch it."

"I don't want to," I said, my voice rising.

His voice remained even and measured. "Doc … oh, our lovely Doc, with the hands that heal the white man and his white whores. I am beginning to think that behind all that glassy, stiff facade of yours, you actually desire the white colonial master. You know, ravage you, and all that … You know …?"

"Please, Nathan," I huffed out in a whisper, "please stop this now. I'm going."

"You are going nowhere. Sit!"

He lunged forward and grabbed my arm, pulling me back to the chair. This time, my foot hit hard against the sleeping Freddie, who was not sleeping because he began stroking my ankle again, his fingers lurking on the skin beneath my trousers, where my sock ended. They advanced up my calf, and I felt like insects of every variety had crawled from the Earth's bowels and onto my skin.

Nathan placed my trembling hand on his gun. I recognized the gun. It was a heavy prize for any of the men to attain, newly arrived in a complicated bootleg network from Angola, one of the places where the military wing of the Congress was training our soldiers in preparation for the day when we might have to make a peaceful struggle into an armed one. Like a steady stream of cigars and whiskey, weapons arrived in Durban; and in a complex network of secrecy, they were distributed among the comrades. I had always declined a gun, despite many of the women telling me that I should keep a loaded gun near me. They knew things I did not. Yet.

"Sylvie, sometime you might need it, not to shoot the colonial bastard, but to shoot the bastard who walks arm-in-arm with you as we march."

I had never really understood those words. Now I clearly did.

I touched the metal. It was warm from its cozy home within Nathan's jacket pocket. He took my fingers and made me stroke the barrel, and crooned a poem softly.

"She walks in beauty like the night. Like … blah blah blah, and blah … what's the words, Doc?"

I stared, dumbfounded. Too shocked to say anything. Nathan laughed. I heard Freddie chuckle too.

"So, Doc … you want to be a revolutionary, hey? Well, let us have a lesson. We'll call it … Lessons in Weaponry 101. Okay, brave Doctor Sylvie … show teacher your equality. Pick up the gun and shoot me!"

I pulled against his vice grip. I was embarrassed to feel tears starting to spring from my burning eyes. He saw the start of misty tears in my eyes, and pushed even further, his voice rising.

"Shoot! Stupid woman, I said pick up the fucking gun, and shoot! Here, let teacher show you …"

He yanked the gun with my hands still wrapped around it, and in a manic moment, pointed it at my head. I heard a distinct *click*. He had released the catch. I started shaking uncontrollably.

"So … you see, Doc. Can you see? You shake like a leaf inside a kitchen, yet you and your girls want to join us in the war? We don't want you girls. This one is for the men, you hear? You learn, and you learn fast. Keep to the kitchen, lie in our beds, and make us some nice brown children. That's all. Are we clear?"

In my steaming tears, the cocked gun at my forehead, held by my own hand, I knew that I had to get power back from this menacing man. We women had always spoken very hastily about the sexist and often appalling behavior of many of our own. We had never really sat together and spoke it out in full, gory detail. Each woman came up against it, but each woman quietly looked away and dealt with the worst things, crying alone into pillows. It would be weakness. Even our ideas and plans were taken by them, presented by them to satisfied leaders, high up and far, far away. But we still held on. We still pushed our way into meetings and marches.

I sat at the table with a gun about to go off, and I saw it clearly. Many of our men were sick. They were so steeped in hatred and years of racist violence meted out on them that the abused became the abuser. And we women were soft targets. Misogyny that hid inside veins of men who spoke of equality came out to dance when the alcohol flowed, or the night had been rough. They turned on us.

I looked up, glaring at Nathan; I nearly crossed my eyes looking toward the gun imprinting my forehead. But still, I glared.

"Put it away!" I said through clenched teeth.

Nathan didn't move.

"Put the fucking gun away, Nathan. If something happens here, you are out in the cold. Even filthy Freddie wouldn't be able to lie to get you out."

His fingers slowly released the grip, and the painful metal point released its dark push into my forehead. Nathan reclicked the catch and calmly placed the gun back onto the dirty cloth. He looked away, his eyes searching for anything to focus on, anything but my crazy eyes burning holes in him. His vision settled on the enamel teapot.

"Relax, Doc. All I wanted was a cup of tea …" he muttered.

"Make your own fucking tea. And don't come near me again. Understood?"

He kept his gaze away, and I bolted out of the kitchen to the sound of Freddie loudly chuckling.

"'Ey, Nates man. That wildcat got you good and solid. Watch out for that one … she's not like the other chickies."

My muscles were like rigid rods as I collapsed into my bed. It took a long time for my body and mind to uncoil and relax, and I never slept. Later that day, I sought out one of the women who sporadically came to stay at the apartment, a scary tanklike woman called Lulu.

"Get me a gun," I told her. And she understood me.

"Good, my sister. This struggle is not peaceful. More than anything, we women have to watch out for ourselves and each other. Our enemies can be the ones sleeping in our own beds," she said and handed me a 9mm semi-automatic.

"Maybe it is time we asked our cell leader to send you for training in Angola. You need to toughen up, Sylvie." She looked into my eyes.

My emotions flared with a combination of exhilaration and fear, and I nodded at her. I had seen many men and women receive their orders to get military training, and I had seen the wild look in their eyes.

And indeed, in the tangled emotions of danger and death, of fervent desire for freedom, passion played out among our own members. Willing women, sometimes unwilling women—it did not matter in the heat of that city. A rolling, tangled body of one, making love to itself, satiating itself in the doom of a tomorrow that might never come. *Touch me now. I may not be here tomorrow.*

I shook with fear at each approaching moment when I anticipated being called up to go for military training. I learned how to use the pistol, but strong fear gripped me, thinking of life in the field. I had seen too many mauled bodies of friends and comrades to even desire the day when I would be called up. I wanted to be brave. I wanted to stand in the face of it when the day came, but the day never came. My vacillating was answered the day I lost all my nerve, and suddenly I just wanted to be comforted like any frightened young woman.

Ismail.

Anger sat so well on that man. It was created for his face. He came to us, we were the only place he could go to to hide out. He had been beaten to a pulp. He had started a fight in a restaurant on the beachfront. He was a waiter there, and he had only been one for a week before he could stand it no longer.

He was the second son of a family of poor people. And like his namesake, and like all middle children, his name was forgotten in the writing of history. There was an Isaak in the great Book, but no Ismail, and this little ablation, the surgical removal of the illegitimate son, the one borne of the servant Hajra who inspired wars and gospels from the time of Abraham had the fire of the disregarded raging in his blood. There were those who bowed to the East and sang out their calls to prayer in a mournful muezzin's voice who demanded the right given to Ismail, that Ismail was the one Abraham, the one they called Ibrahim, almost chopped up to honor God's rather gruesome request. But the argument for Ismail the lamb, the forgotten child, wound itself into families. Every Muslim family had a firstborn, Muhammad, and always a second born, an Ismail who was almost always their forgotten one.

This Ismail was born causing turmoil from his first breath in this world.

Ismail was conceived in rage, and was born to rage. Created with a hungry belly that never felt satiated. He wanted everything. Every sight, every sound, every conversation, every corner of this world, Ismail craved to devour.

I, who had been searching for someone or something to subdue my fear, found the strangest attraction to this wild man who had arrived on my doorstep, bleeding but laughing like a rebellious vanquisher.

"Doctor Sylvie. This boy is beaten up very badly. The Special Branch are on his tail. We can't send him to a hospital."

"Why do the Special Branch want him? What did he do?"

I had been spending my nights at the apartment of a comrade in the chattels of Fountain Lane. This simply furnished apartment had become a hub of secretive activity; people came and went at every hour of the day or night. There was always food bubbling on the old stove, lest a hungry revolutionary come tumbling in. The camaraderie was heady; we felt as if we were perched on the edge of the world.

By day I worked in the white man's hospital. By nights, we comrades skulked into one another's homes. Any home would do. We read our journals by candlelight.

We spent hours discussing Gandhi. We read smuggled verses and banned books. And we spent hours teaching one another the coded language of our Congress. When they brought the bloody mess of a man into the room, everyone looked to me. Doctor.

Ismail. Beaten like a dog because the steak he had served a sugar baron's daughter had too much salt. He had grabbed the steak from the lily-white hands, and in plain view of the tittering lunch ladies, had licked the steak with his tongue across its girth.

"Not salty now, Madam."

I peeled off pieces of his shredded skin. He laughed. Throughout his painful treatment, of stitching and cutting, he continued to look into my face, chuckling in amusement.

"Pretty bloody thing, aren't you, Doc?" he said, staring at me, and did not flinch when I lanced his wounded shoulder. I did not give him a painkiller.

"Well, we have gin, but you are obviously forbidden," I remarked as he rolled in agony at my feet, chuckling madly, and trying to grab my breasts.

"Lovely doctor … my mother told me how I had devoured into her breasts with such force and rage when I was born that with my newborn toothless gums I drew blood. She has hated me since. I like your breasts, Doc."

"Shut up while I stitch your face."

The angry Ismail. He did not leave. He was a troublemaker, that I knew. But I felt like a woman when he wrapped me in turmoil. A bush warrior, a vigilante hard on his luck but with the charm of a Lothario, and the rakishness of a man who knew how much his anger attracted women. In this upside-down world of belonging to a struggle but belonging to no one at all, a lover comes to you with many trump cards. A woman may have all the intelligence in the world; she may marry her mind to a distant dream of truth, purpose, and the fight for larger things. But maybe the men were right when they kept us away from the limelight. They knew that our weak hearts would betray all the strong words in the world.

In the stupidity that grabs you in late-night trysts, you feel grateful for the wildest of forbidden kisses. Suddenly you are a giggling girl. Suddenly what you say is not important, and you begin to dream of other things. He only knows that he must grab you quickly, for if he did it tenderly, you might just start remembering the purpose you were placed on this Earth to fulfill. What a deep disappointment to the true face of a struggle hero, the day a woman loses her heart.

"Comrade, I am sorry. I am sorry, but I love this man."

"You stupid woman. You bloody stupid woman. You will throw away years of training, years of our hard work to land in a man's bed? I thought I knew you, Sylvie."

"Comrade, I am sorry."

"We are so close, Sylvie. We have mobilized. Our struggle against this apartheid bastard has now become the struggle of this world. Sylvie, the world is listening now. Our cells are placed all over this world, they are strong. We are ready. Now is our moment, now, Sylvie."

"Comrade, I am sorry."

"Stupid woman. Stupid. Go! Go follow your man. Like the Indian doormat you were born to become."

"My comrade. I am sorry."

The sour taste of disillusionment lies heavily at the back of your tongue until it becomes so familiar that you don't recognize that every day you are swallowing gall. Mad passion can easily be transferred. Once you are passionate about people and fighting for justice. Your heart constricts and forces out the blood of an oppressed sufferer, you see the black and you see the white. Then you change. And you change because it has to be this way.

Now you become selfish; you can only see a narrow road, and on this narrow road walks you and walks a child that is yet to be born. Now is the moment when you choose.

Gladys Mabaso. I hadn't seen her since we both were flung into working at different hospitals. Sometimes I heard news of her, news that she had run away from her work in the hospital in a predominantly black township, and had fled willingly to Angola to receive military training. When she appeared at my window, sent by her cell leader to recruit me, I could clearly see the ravages and rage of this military training on her face and body. She moved like a dangerous cat, and an equally dangerous soldier who thirsted for blood.

Like a thief, always sulky, she rapped twice on my night window. The sleeping man did not stir. The baby inside the stretched skin sensed that there was something more important than sleep, and became the only eavesdropper. The witness to how I had fallen.

"What is this? I see that the rumors are true, Sylvie," Gladys whispered. She looked at my large, pregnant belly like someone would regard rubbish at a roadside. She prowled like a lioness in a kitchen that she hated. She peeped through a window; she could not settle. Her boots threatened to awaken the sleeping man.

"I am sorry, Comrade."

"Bullshit, Sylvie. You don't lie to me, you hear? You are not happy like this."

"I am."

"You are throwing us away. We had a mission, a purpose. Shit, you're an idiot."

"And this baby, Gladys?"

"Oh bloody hell, Sylvie. We all had babies. I left a daughter and a son in their beds when my handler called me. We were on the path, Sylvie. So close. So close."

"Are you happy with your choices?"

"I am useful. Happiness is not a word."

"I think I want to find that word."

"Disappointment." Gladys spat on the floor.

My hand flew to my round belly. She smirked. She paced. As she lurked, her energy sucked the life and breath from my straining lungs. She looked thin and exhausted. She looked like she was on fire. I suddenly felt envy surge through my bladder, and then water flowed down my legs, onto the floor.

"Bloody hell, Sylvie. Clean yourself up. That baby is coming."

The belly heaved high. She realized what was happening and swore loudly. The snoring, snuffling noises of the man in the bedroom stopped. Ismail called out my name in a muffled groan. I stared in shock and panic at the wet patch at my feet.

He called again. Closer now. Gladys sprang like a street cat toward the window. She turned to look again at me, holding my low-lying tummy in both hands, my hair unkempt, my thick socks stained wet.

"Sylvie! Sylvie!" Ismail shouted as he approached, "I told you I don't like noise when I'm sleeping. You don't bloody ever listen, you woman."

Gladys, both legs out of the window now, her sneering face poked back to face mine. *Is this what you wanted?*

"Is this what you wanted? Go. Go to your man. I thought you were different." She shook her head and whispered, "I will see you, my comrade. You know too much already. This is not over."

Gladys was gone. And the baby came, breaking my bones, tearing me in half, arriving into my world on the day I realized I did not want this new life. I wanted the old one.

But Afroze, you were here. You looked like you would never have any flesh. You were so thin you looked like a baby bird that was dropped out of a nest. I could not look at you; I was afraid to touch you. I could have broken you. Ismail named you. He said it was the name of an Indian film actress that he loves. I thought it was too large a name for its small body to carry. Ismail said you would grow into the name. I think he meant me.

We could not stay in Durban. Ismail could not settle anywhere. He fought and screamed at the wind. Gangsters, police, and angry employers walked the streets looking for him. He had to run. People he hustled, swindled, they sniff everywhere for clues. They learned that he lived in a run-down outbuilding with a baby and a woman. They came to our door with threats and guns.

"You, Doctor. You are rich. You pay us what he owes."

"We have nothing," I whispered and it was true. Ismail raged and stole us into poverty; all my earnings are gone.

We escaped like fugitives in the middle of the night to the town where he was born. The baby screamed throughout our midnight drive. And we arrived in Brighton long before dawn.

This cottage. An old woman opened the door and sucked in her breath almost in terror when she saw Ismail.

"Nahi … nahi … Jaaa. Tu Jaayaha thi …" Not you. Go. Go away from here.

"Bibi Foi. Thamaro Ismail aawi gyoh." Aunt, your Ismail has come back.

"Nahi. Nahi." Not you. Not you.

She pushed the door shut. He stopped it with a foot. Foot in the door.

"Open it," he said through angry, clenched teeth.

Her myopic, cloudy eyes saw me. She saw the baby stirring and wriggling in my arms. She opened the door.

Ismail the troublemaker. Not even welcome in his birth home. Very quickly, he became unhappy, restless. That place was stifling him. That devastating rakishness, that scoundrel so handsome, he knew all he could do was run away again. He ranted at everything.

That place was suffocating him. I was suffocating him, asking him to find a job somewhere. We couldn't keep relying on his old aunt for money. I couldn't work at the clinic. Too many questions would have been asked, and people he hid from, even here in this tiny town, must never know we were there.

We both were angry, seething at what our life had come down to. He was allowed to give vent to his rage. I had to be silent, calm, and soothing. For the child's sake.

He could not touch me. He could not touch the baby. He hated from everywhere inside his cells. The old aunt simply nodded her head. She knew this rascal from the early days. She remembered the time when, as a toddler, Ismail had simply stood up. Never crawling, Ismail the baby went from lying flat on his back to standing up like a lightning rod. And then all he did was run. There was no stumbling block in the path of that relentless child. The old woman could only pity the girl with a baby, the girl who hid many secrets behind her large, almond eyes. All Ismail knew was running. The girl would soon be bereft. It was inevitable, and the old woman knew that all that would ever come to pass had been written in books on the day that you are born.

The day he decided to run away became the day when I tasted sourness. I had cast in my lot with a loser, a scoundrel man. It was, of course, too damn late. He came to me as I was watching Afroze roll onto her back and suck her little toes. He caught me in a smile.

"I am leaving. I can't stay in this coffin here. I am done."

The old woman saw him saunter away, tossing a cigarette onto the parched Earth. Her eyes told me stories. *See, I knew this would happen.* She died soon after. He didn't even come for her funeral.

CHAPTER TEN

UP UNTIL THE day Ismail left, I was a lightweight. Just a caricature of what it meant to flirt with fighting. A woman of insipid behavior, a wastrel of talents. A loser of the voice. Words left me. All those years of sitting in dark rooms, hearing the spoken word about oppression and suffering, lying on floors lined with the songs of men who were great and men who had struggled and all the voices of the men who had taken me firmly in hand and told me who I was and what I could say and when. But they could never tell me why.

Rage can bubble insidiously in the witch's cauldron; notice the way a crone is the female and the wise wizard is the male.

I was in that frustrating, suffocating house, the absent snore of that man echoed through walls that refused to be beaten down with a broomstick. He got to just get up and walk away.

I had ideas. I had dreams and I had words that were purely my own. I did not need the baritone voices of men who had gone before me instructing me why I had freedom in my blood and a talent for words inside my flesh. I had lost myself, but I knew why I had been given this art, like the air that I breathed. Healing bodies, and weaving words—I was bestowed the Graces. The

Graces became angry when I threw them away for something as insignificant as love.

And suddenly, alone in a town that slept through every important event in world history, I knew my purpose. It was a shot-up drug. It was a desire to be seen and heard, it was the need to finally make a stain on the pure, white fabric and perhaps use fingernails to rip it to shreds.

I had been a willing automaton, sitting in a librarian skirt, taking notes at the most important meeting in my own life. But I changed. I threw off the shackles of quiet domesticity and shocked even my own self in how swiftly I began to take strength. Time to roar. But it came at a price. And the price for passion is loss of softness. When you are so hungry for your voice to be heard, you cut throats. You sever ties that bind you to this lonely nothingness. Sometimes, a little child cannot realize why you are too frantic in your quest, that you might forget their birthdays.

It didn't matter now. My time had come, and my youth was at its peak, my brain was at its sharpest. I apologized to the child, but I apologized in silence. There was no time for soft words. It was time to mobilize, Comrade. You have been given birth. And the second coming is so much sweeter than the first. The velleity with which I had once worked for our struggle against white domination would now end. Now I would throw myself headfirst into it, and I would bear the losses inside my heart. I grabbed that baby, this girl-child who had been thrust into this lap, and I looked the baby in her soft eyes and howled. The baby howled. She howled because her mother was being born. She howled because babies, like feral animals, can smell danger, they can smell hunger.

I suckled that child. She suddenly felt ferocious at my breast.

"That's it girl," I said and pulled her from the hard, cracked nipple when she had filled herself so much she looked like she would soon vomit it all up.

"No more. I hope you enjoyed that one," I held her up and her head lolled with the satiety of a mother's sweet milk.

"Stay awake, stay awake," I shouted, but babies can sleep through storms. "Your mother is going to work, my girl."

And in a silvery cord connection, this satellite-born sent an imaginary message to the base, the mothership. *My beloved Congress. Comrades, I am back. I want in. I have returned. Take me, because this angry struggle is all I have in this world. And I am good at it.*

When the howl is howled, the pack will come.

"Come, Comrade. Join us," Gladys said.

She took my soft hand and showed me that I had somewhere I belonged.

"That baby is hungry," she remarked, standing in my country kitchen, arriving at the exact moment when she was supposed to have arrived. That moment when I grabbed my destiny with both hands.

Yes, it is true. My comrades in the Congress had been keeping close tabs on everyone that had ever worked with them, and although I had disappeared into barren Brighton, they had been watching me. Anyone who had ever been privy to their secrets never escaped into obscurity. They had eyes in every corner of this blue Earth.

"Comrade, I knew you would see your place in our fight eventually. We have a special place for you and the medical work that you do. I gave up practicing medicine; my fight is now a physical armed struggle, but you will play a role behind this thick veil of secrecy in this town. Once the struggle takes your cells, you are never the same again. Feed your child," Gladys said. She had tracked me down in Brighton, and brought with her the call to come back.

"She'll be fine." I pushed a cold bottle to the fussy baby. She fussed even more. But hunger makes the believer out of the philistine, and soon enough hunger wins the day. She held the bottle with her feet, and sucked noisily at a teat that I had not even bothered to clean.

"Strange thing that baby does. Uses her feet but keeps her hands locked tightly into fists."

I ignored the endearing anomaly. Afroze: the baby was like that and like that she would remain. A girl who would always do the most difficult things to prevent herself from doing the most obvious things. I did not know this growing child. But I knew that did not matter anymore. I knew her with my flesh and, for now, that was enough.

"So, after my work in Brighton, when do I return to Durban?" I asked Gladys, almost tasting the tang of the salt air, and the drug of the Revolution.

"You don't. You stay here in this hole in the ground, Comrade," Gladys said and peeped out the window to see the arid winter stare her in the face.

No No No. I want out. I want in. I cannot remain in this ghost town one second longer. Brighton. The place where dreams come to die.

CHAPTER ELEVEN

THIS BRIGHTON, SO cold and ugly, forgotten by God, not even rain or sleet made her innermost core wet; she remained dry. She was an old hag. Every branch of every tree crackled with an angry, unforgiving static. No one in that town knew anyone else. Everyone had their holes, and business was business as usual.

Such a pained past, this Brighton. Nobody had cared about the Englishman who built this town, the fraudulent Lord Pomeroy. Most people concerned themselves with his wife, Lady Charlotte. There still stands in Brighton a little plaque that is well hidden by an umbrella of dark green ivy. On it her name thrived, while his name had seen the effects of the burning sun and faded away.

He was forgotten. She never would be. Lady Charlotte Bruce, a Scottish bride, tossed about on the Cape of Storms, following a man she was given to. Like the commodities he was accustomed to, she was packed onto a ship and never told her where he was taking her.

Once she was docile, but when they arrived at a salty, fetid port called Durban and he had piled her into an ox wagon and lumbered her body to this godforsaken place, her fire began to rage. Her hot blood, her fury at this waste of a life in a craggy world, where all she saw every day and every night were rocks and burned black backs digging trenches, she raged and lost her mind.

She paced the length of the road that was being dug, the one and only road the town would ever boast, and remained in her thick, starchy crinoline petticoats despite the terrible heat. Her mind roamed the recesses of a beloved that she had left behind, a young soldier she had met on the beaches of Brighton, England, during a vacation when she was but 15. It had not been a romance—a fleeting glance and perhaps the soldier had touched her gloved hand. But stranded here in the worst of hells, chained to an unloving lord, the affair began to swell and grow in her mind until she was convinced that the greatest of romances had taken place. And like all great romances, the heartache was what she endured.

In a frenzy, one night, when her husband tried to take her, his rough hands so inept, the caresses driving her wild not with desire but with gall, Lady Charlotte threatened the lord with a knife to his throat. She threatened to slit it clean should he not name this ugly, barren town Brighton where he had imprisoned her.

She sent a pitiful letter to authorities in England and explained in painful words how she suffered in this hot African world, and all she ever yearned for to ease her mania was a simple piece of cloth. A piece of cloth would cool her heart, and she begged and pleaded to be given this prize. One colonial lord of the East India Company, whose ships came with regularity around Cape Horn, bearing trunks filled to the brim with brown sauce, fish paste, and lavender soap to service the intrepid travelers who had come to conquer Africa, felt a flutter in his otherwise cool heart. He acquired the piece of canvas fabric that the desperate lady craved, wrapped it with his own soft hands, and with pity in his soul had it brought onto his ship, so that one December day when the sun in Africa's Brighton was at its most vicious, a package arrived for Lady Charlotte.

The town gathered as the parcel changed hands and as the package found its way to the lady's bedroom, her husband kept a wide berth, knowing full well the sting of his fiery wife's hands on his skin.

Lady Charlotte had dressed in her finest that day. She sat in the one cool place in her home—under the brown eaves of her attic—and ripped the package open. She emerged from her inner sanctum bearing in her hands a piece of blue and white striped canvas, a piece of fabric that had once been part of an awning of a wooden vacation hut on a beach in Brighton. Lady Charlotte gave a loud sob, and yelled out equally loud orders that this piece of fabric would stand as the flag of this town. And a merry group of Norwegian missionaries, who had come to bring the word of the one true God to the infidels of this African wasteland, accepted Lady Charlotte's treasure, and strung it up with dignity on a flag pole made of wood outside their mission hall. They rang the mission bell fifteen times, in honor of the fifteen horrible months that the unfortunate lady had endured in the town as the lord's wife.

And the following morning there came a throng of local people, who marched in their dark brown masses to stand under Lady Charlotte's window, and sing the only hymn that the Norwegians had taught them. Their white teeth glittered in the warm shine of their dark brown faces, and their chief, who had been the first to convert to Christianity, demanded that the lord name the one main street after his real lady.

The fake lord was flabbergasted, offended, stung. But the chief and his masses remained standing outside his wife's bedroom window, repeatedly singing the hymn. Lady Charlotte slept that night with a large knife tucked under her pillow and glared at him, showing with bared teeth her intent to use it should he fail to comply. And finally Lord Pomeroy relented, giving up his grand dream of naming the street after himself. He had lost the war for the name of the town. The battle for the naming of the street was futile.

Almost immediately at the Norwegian mission, a place the raving lady had taken to spending most of her days, listening to the civilization of children, wandering the dry grounds and muttering to herself, two plaques were forged out of thick alloys, with deep etchings: lady charlotte road. These two tiny plaques were set into large pieces of concrete where the road entered and exited Brighton. Two plaques—honoring the suffering of a lady that the people just seemed to love, because they noticed the suffering in her wild eyes—stood a kilometer apart, guarding the one street like bookends.

And at the far end the Norwegian mission, where the first plaque remained under the wooden flagpole, grew large its congregation of converts. The nuns and one priest were devoted to their singing masses, which picked up psalms and hymns with rapidity, and also picked up a Norwegian accent as they sang songs to the civilized God.

The striped flag of fair England's blue and white, the canvas awning from the beach of Brighton, waved lethargically in the rare, heated wind, because thick canvas is not meant to float like a flag. It just hung there, looking flaccid and convoluted upon itself, until Lady Charlotte could bear it no longer and took herself to the local medicine woman who lived in the hills that surrounded thc fast-burgeoning village.

The lady procured for herself a thoroughly African solution to her problems and drank a hefty portion of a local potion, squeezed from the mash of a rare root that only grew in Zululand, and finally the lady found peace. With a face that had turned purple, and lips that swelled so much that they had looked like they would burst, she lay in her coffin. The Norwegian missionaries and their flock sang her funeral songs in thickly accented English.

They buried Lady Charlotte far away, in a proper cemetery in Dundee, because the town of Brighton was too rocky to dig graves, and over her coffindraped the striped awning, which when the burial was done, was sent folded back to the missionaries, who placed it in a glass cabinet nearest the entrance to the mission, where they protected it like a treasure.

"Well, Comrade, that is a pretty story but it means nothing now. All it means to the struggle is that you are here, and no one knows this small town even exists," Gladys muttered as she sipped her diluted tea. "So he left you here. Well, the child will just have to come along for the ride. You stay here, Comrade. Listen. I am telling you that these orders come from a high place. You stay here."

"No, Gladys." Again the howl began, but Gladys silenced me in her own rich growl.

"Listen, Sylvie. Stay here. This is where we need you the most. We need a safe house. A place that the Special Branch would never even suspect existed. Look at the perfection of all that has come to pass. The struggle is strong, Comrade. We don't exist, Sylvie. It is only our fight that is the real human being. We are just the vessels."

"Much like a mother, right, Gladys? Just the vessel."

"Yes. A mother, very much like a mother. The quiet force behind the barkings of a man. The woman lies silent and the woman does the work."

"I need to come back to Durban, Comrade. I hate this soundless crypt. I need to hear voices, I need to listen to the words of the wise. I am dying inside this perfect cottage. Gladys, things are happening in Durban. I hear things."

"Forget Durban. It is just a stage. A stupid, hot stage that allows the loud sounds that mean nothing. They stand on squares, and they hold their rallies. They are our smokescreen. The deep heart of the struggle lies in the most nondescript of places, where we can hide our comrades away until we send them for training to Lesotho, and from there to our military camp in the Soviet Union. But these dark, deep places are where the real work is done. Durban is the foil, my comrade. My sister. No one looks anywhere else because we shine the brightest light on that port."

"What must I do? What? What?"

"Stay here. We need this house. Make arrangements. We will be sending our best to you. Keep them here inside your unsuspicious fairy tale. And, good that you're a doctor, Sylvie, because they will come to you beaten and in shreds."

I nodded. Somewhere in the bedroom the baby mewled. I did not move my body from the hard-backed chair I had slumped in, listening to Gladys talk, listening to the sound of my own voice, heard again after such a long time of silence.

"I'll arrange for a nursemaid. Someone we all know and trust. You have important things to do."

It began immediately. In the rasping loud quiet of my shuffling slippers on the polished, wooden floors, I heard myself say time and time again: "Well, you did ask for a greater life. Well, you did ask."

Beatrice arrived. Beatrice was not her real name. She took the baby away from my body, and I felt greater relief than I have ever felt. And inside my relief I hated myself for feeling it. But there was no moment for it. The baby was tended to. That would do.

Would she know I am her mother?

It does not matter now.

Just work fast, Comrade. Work fast. Our good people are breaking their bones and shattering their skins for something greater than all this, you see. The time is soon coming.

Beatrice was a trained soldier in the guise of a maternal nanny. She knew intelligence skills, which I was soon to learn. In her feeding and burping and tying of pink ribbons in the child's hair lurked a sense of purpose that I would soon come to reprise as my own. Her strong limp, that listing to the left, the one deaf ear, told me that Beatrice, who sang songs to the baby, had lived another more sinister incarnation. We never spoke of it. When the baby slept, she taught me all she knew. She taught me the coded language of the military wing of the Congress; she taught me stern protocol within a rebellious army, where the world imagined a gaggle of rowdy terrorists.

Yet they were the deepest thinkers and philosophers of their time. Forced to study in bushes, they learned fast, and so did I. My house began its preparations. The strands of my place in the large black, yellow, and green fabric of the African National Congress became woven and they glowed like the most beautiful sun. A free sun, under whose rays everyone was equal.

My home became a safe house. And a bush hospital. I was terrified. But there was no time for fear.

The first arrived so soon. In a beautiful woven web of messages that held no words, it became my legacy: this house, this town. The place where they brought the broken ones.

I followed instructions sent to me in a code that took me days to decipher. Beatrice eventually tutted and pushed me aside from my huddled place at my mahogany desk that smelled so much like my father—the linseed oil and the lavender oil polish scent never quite covered it up. She spoke with her eyes, nodding as I learned the code. I had forgotten it so quickly, but it soon flooded back, much like love. I never really forgot how to do it. Much like love, chased it away from my memories and I beat it away with a stick, but it was me. I was it. The training came back.

The cottage had to remain, for any eye to see, a pretty little home for a young doctor and her child. The more feminine, garish, and lacy the better. *Act in this play, my comrade. No one must know that in the back there is a little house, a khaya, where there are supposed to be broken tools and discarded baby toys lies a haven.*

A dark home, a safe home, a place for those to collect their thoughts before being taken away for training or to hide away permanently. Inside the dirty two-roomed outbuilding with crumbling walls, a full operating theater mushroomed out of need and pain.

Slowly I began accumulating supplies smuggled to me. In my baby's packs of diapers, in bundles of noisy toys, and in sets of dotty little dresses lay vials of morphine. In that surgery, pain was the largest dragon we would ever slay.

In their moments of intense raw pain, even the best of soldiers, men who had vowed to bare their bodies to a hailstorm of bullets for the sake of freedom, became weak and begged to be set free. Their bodies lay open, but they wore their hearts on their sleeves as they were roughly carried in at midnight, gritting their teeth, biting their very tongues and holding onto my hands as I pushed brandy down their throats and rationed their beautiful morphine dreams.

In my hurried sutures, there lay sewn-together secrets. Only I would know that in their deepest searing pain, most men would have renounced their activism. Only I knew how they cried that freedom for all was not worth this. But I would never tell their secrets, and I would always know that what happens between two people in the throes of the most burning pleasure and pain becomes very watery when the dawn comes in.

Stitched up, hobbling, they always awoke from their fevers craving to fight for our cause again. With hooded eyes they watched me, hoping I would never tell that in our dance together the night before, they had screamed otherwise. When they left me again after their days of battling demons, I would always reassure them with a light touch on their shoulders before they were huddled onto the floor of rusty vehicles, covered with burlap bags.

"Go well, Comrade," I would say.

"Amandla!" they would whisper.

Within a thick dirty sack, a pumped fist would show through, the way a baby's balled-up fist sometimes shows from within a womb, an imprint on a mother's stretched skin.

CHAPTER TWELVE

MOTHERHOOD DOES NOT need the mother. This daughter grew beautifully despite me. Despite the fact that I never smothered her mornings with kisses because I was too exhausted from a long night of holding down a thrashing man, taking his superhuman beatings when I refused to stick a needle into his skin and take the pain away. The ration of morphine was small. But those in pain pay no heed to this. All they see is their own suffering, and they are killers in their souls. Their strength surprises even themselves when they lunge at me from their blood-stained cots, and through gritted teeth and eyes of menace tell me they would easily strangle me with bare hands if their pain was not quelled.

I became strong too. I handled them with all the force and anger I could muster, pushing their sewn-up bodies back to supine weakness, where I could stand over them and hold their faces close to my own, their hot breaths mingled with mine, and tell them that this was it. This was all they were going to get. I once held a man at his throat, pushing down hard. He had shattered a femur after jumping from a three-story building, hiding precious documents inside his clothes. I had no morphine to give him, but I hit him clear across his head with a rough plank. I muffled his mouth with a rag soaked in brandy and, as Beatrice held him down, I took advantage of his daze and pulled with brute force at his ankle. The bone cracked into a set. He bit so hard on that brandy-soaked cloth that he broke teeth. He had enough strength in him to hit me clear across the room.

The next morning I stumbled from his delirious bedside and into the kitchen, looking like a casualty. My daughter was seated at the kitchen table, a plump toddler of three. She was dreaming lazily and giggling at the dust motes. She looked up from her cold porridge and saw me stagger like a drunken woman into the room. My ear still rang from the blow on the side of my head. The child's jaw dropped open, seeing me. As the years passed, I avoided the child, though I always knew where she was. Her giggles and little words fell like feathers in a house that was hard and unrelenting.

I managed to always slip from her gaze, leaving a room if she tottered in dragging a toy, or not looking up from the most mundane of tasks when she wandered around me.

But I looked at this morning child, her curly hair tousled from sleep, those little mewing sounds that exasperated me in all their benign innocence. How she found the beauty in the ugliness and managed to live in innocence made me envious. I wondered if this girl would ever know how to stab at the heart of hurt.

I wondered if something so fragile inside her little chest would one day break into pieces, leaving behind shrapnel that would become a part of her flesh. I knew that she would suffer much, because I knew her. And I knew me. She was too trusting. I was too remote.

She, like all children, did not know the bane of hate. They loved. I had once watched her put her entire soft arm into the jaws of our ferocious guard dog. A brute of an animal. A Brutus. She did not doubt even for a second that the massive, salivating jaws would ever betray her and clamp down onto her sweet flesh. And the dog did not close his jaws. He only growled a warning, which she threw off in a child's laugh. She withdrew the hand and kissed the dog on his head.

Seated at the kitchen table, her wide eyes stared at the bruise on my face. And as she had once kissed a mad dog, she smiled at me in unintentional affection.

"Ma," the word spouted out of her fat lips, and she shocked herself by saying it.

I knew that she was of my own flesh, that she had never been much for movement when she lay dormant inside my body, that the moment she was born and handed to me, she would not close her eyes, and lay there staring unnervingly, deeply into me until I could stand it no longer and placed her on the bed beside me. But she had never shut her eyes, which were large and luminous like twin candles, and I had quickly turned out the lights so that I would not have to look at them. They burned even in the darkness.

"Beatrice," I rasped, realizing that a rising panic had fluttered into me, not knowing how to stem a threatening tide of something I did not recognize. It felt like a magical pull, a rope that made me want to glide effortlessly into this baby embrace. It frightened me. It shook the hard resolve that I guarded with a brittle, shaking hand.

She lifted her hand from her porridge bowl and reached it to me, opening and closing the fist. "Twinkie twinkie witt-will star, how I wand-wer what you ARE ..." She sang, lisping and accentuating the last word with a porridge-covered smile, and something in me started to scream.

The child was trying to comfort me with her lisped nursery rhyme.

"Bea ... Bea ... Beatrice ..." I whispered. I backed away. From my own singing child. From my own sleepy girl. She was destroying me.

"Take ... Take... her away. Take her away," I gasped as the woman who did all the things for my child that I never had done, lunged past me and scooped the bewildered baby away.

"Mommy sick ..." I heard the child say.

"Yes, Mommy sick."

I rushed to the sink and splashed water on my face and sank down onto the kitchen floor. The navy blue sari that I wore splayed over the tiles and I gathered up the fabric and bunched it underneath me, fingering and troubling the soft chiffon until I pulled a misshapen hole in it. I could hear the child squealing in delight on the little swing set that had been set up for her in the dingy yard. My breaths slowly centered downward from that high and dangerous place that I had been sucked into. But inside this vortex the most horrible feeling in the world had taken hold of every part of me. An ache that was as sweet as it was searing, an invisible-visible weight on my soul. I felt it inside my womb. *I have wronged this child.*

I heard her laugh again. Another woman swung my child in the air. Another woman caught her. Another woman held her close and breathed in the buttery scents of her, murmuring in a voice that I could never have owned, the soft nothings that a child is reared on. I hated that she thrived, so firm and rosy and like a blooming tree. I hated that she did this despite me. Without me. But my hatred was for me. I had done this, and I had to run through the gamut of my own choices. That child would always thrive.

"Where Mommy?" I heard her say.

"Come to me. Mommy's here," another woman replied. Mommy is here.

Afroze stopped looking for me when she was four. She did not wander the house trying to catch me in corners. That early morning after her sixth birthday when I ran wildly around the house stuffing her clothes and toys and books into plastic bags because we had no time to look for suitcases, I refused to look at her. I knew she watched me in my frenzy and I knew that she did not understand any of it. When I pushed her body away from mine toward a car spewing fumes into the clear air, I finally looked at her and she was looking at me with the final look of desperation. *Stop all this now, Mommy, and take me into your arms.*

"Please, please take the child. Take her now. Anywhere, just drive her away from this house. Take her to the Seedat family across town. Now. Do it. Please. Here, a note. Take it. Tell them to phone her father. Now, please take her away. Now."

Afroze heard only part of the conversation. It was the worst part.

Did she see me standing at the window watching her go? Did she hear my words, whispered over and over again as she was driven away?

"My daughter. My child. Always remember my name."

The Special Branch came for me an hour later. Secrets were always exposed, and I had waited for this day. So many men and women, soldiers of the struggle, had passed through my home. I had bathed and fed them, I had stitched them up and sent them back into the world, I had poured medicines down their throats, I had bandaged their gaping wounds with stringy compresses that had been washed too many times.

Their names and their records lay hidden in flimsy files, locked up in the khaya. When the police looked, all they saw were rats, dirty cloths, broken implements. We hid them so well, the only records indicating that any of those people ever existed, or that they had fought for our freedom. The stink of that old building gave us a helping hand. The police wanted answers, but they were too disgusted by rats and filth to go digging for them. The piles of papers remained there, underneath debris. They were my true children. Not Afroze. Them.

They had sworn at me, professed love to me, beat me, and kissed my hands. But the game was up. As I always knew it would be.

"Run, Doctor, you still have time. I'll tell someone to bring a car."

"No. I will stay. Let them take me."

"But you will go to prison, Doctor."

"I will join my comrades then."

Doctor Sylvie Pillay was arrested on October 26, 1977, under Terrorism Act No. 83 of 1967. She was detained without trial at the Pretoria State Prison in solitary confinement, along with several other female comrades, for a period of 57 days and nights. After severe interrogation and torture, almost all of it undocumented, she refused to provide the Special Branch of the South African Police with any information on her patients or their whereabouts. She was offered opportunities to give up her comrades who were in safe houses across the land, or to divulge the location of her meticulous medical notes and files. She did not resist arrest and spent much of her time in silence. She was denied access to any reading material, and only received a Bible to read after intervention from her lawyer. This was the only real help her figurehead lawyer ever gave her.

Her mind eventually fractured, after days of torture and threats to her child's life. She became suicidal and severely depressed, suffering hallucinations and episodes of self-injurious behavior. She was released, without trial, without record of arrest, and returned to her home under a constant and ever-looming police presence. She remained watched and harassed, all her activities and correspondence closely monitored. After a long period of dormant recovery, she was allowed to see patients again but had to confine her practice to nonwhite tuberculosis patients. She silently and reclusively spent her decades this way, and when the news of freedom came one day, she found out only accidentally. No one remembered her name.

PART THREE

IT WILL BE KNOWN

CHAPTER ONE

WHEN A TOWN sleeps, drugged on the potion of secrets, there comes a moment when oblivious slumber betrays itself. Anything in a cage will at some time stand up and snarl. The nature of dormant life is that somehow, even for a fraction of a moment, consciousness rises from underneath layers of mud and rears its head.

Brighton chose the weekend of Easter, every year, to open the gates and unlock the chains, letting itself loose. And then after it has spent itself, it returns to its drowse for yet another year. On the weekend that Christ was crucified, all the gods in the sky agree, just once, to a truce of festival. It is on the day of the crucifixion, a Good-Enough Friday, that the people of Brighton, in their diverse calls to the heavens, put on displays and shows that amaze, beautify, fortify, and satisfy. Good enough to last an entire year to come.

Dawn finds Mass being held at the otherwise useless Norwegian Mission Chapel, in the midst of angels singing hymns and overenthusiastic evangelist pastors expounding loud sermons in an accent that veers strangely toward an American twang.

Waiting their turn, like patient but irascible children, the Hindu devotees of the Shiva temple across town begin meticulous ritual preparations for a festival in honor of the harvest goddess, Amman, and Muruga, the son of Lord Shiva, who is a prince of war and mountains. The brother to the amiable, jolly elephant-headed Lord Ganesha, Muruga governs force, where Ganesha presides over the softer things in life, like art and the writing of letters.

The festival, the Kavady Festival, has devotees design and decorate large chariots to be pulled with fervor and small wooden ones to be borne on the shoulders like a burden that is placed at the feet of the gods.

During this auspicious Friday, it also being a Friday, stirring their pots of meaty broths, eager Muslim brothers await the late-night call to prayer. Their adept musicians end the night with their instruments and voices in a night of Qawali singing—rapturous poems of trancelike devotion, sung in honor and praise to the Sufi saint Khwaja.

Afroze awakened with abrupt wide eyes. "Oh, I am still here."

She had been dreaming vividly of sitting in Moomi's kitchen, listening to the loud clinking noises of Moomi's metal spoon clattering against the tin pot of stew bubbling on the stove, rapidly mixing her own blend of spices and chopped tomatoes in a cacophonous din, the sounds an unhappy woman creates in her kitchen.

When Afroze's eyes sprang open, she almost exclaimed out loud, "Moomi, why so much noise?" But she quickly realized that she was lying in her childhood bed, in her mother's house, and the sound of metal was coming from the ringing of the bells at the temple nearby. Even though she had left Brighton a six-year-old child, the memory of the Good Friday festivals remained embedded in her brain. They had been her happiest times, being carried on the shoulders of one of her mother's lovers, or held tightly by her nanny, watching her favorite festival in all its grandeur. The Hindu festival of Kavady.

The colors, sounds, and smells of one of the largest Kavady Festivals in the Southern Hemisphere would excite her imagination for days before and after. It is true, the town was a silent, slumberous one, but when it came to festivals, it held nothing back. Going large, extraordinary, and over the top was Brighton's way of staging its own rebellion.

And the Kavady Festival was the favorite child. It attracted hordes; it even attracted documentary filmmakers from chilly European countries who swarmed around every ritual, their camera lenses reflecting their amazement at the sheer force of something so exotic.

Afroze stood up, wondering how the burdens of her past had somehow slowed her body down into an achy fatigue. No amount of sleep could place a balm on the unnatural malaise of her muscles. She remembered her activities of the day before, wondering if her attempts at kicking down the door of the khaya had exerted her body too much. Her mother had refused to give her the key, and she remained sitting in her bedroom with Sathie petting and cajoling her at her bedside.

Every part of Afroze ached, yet she felt strangely exhilarated. Perhaps because the horrid building at the back of her mother's house was all hers now, to destroy. To conquer.

She thought of Sathie, the man calling himself her mother's lover, and she could not explain, even in her own secret reflections, why she quickly batted aside any thoughts of him. Somewhere in the middle of her restless night, she thought she smelled him nearby, that heady combination of leather, wood, and minty breath. And the scent that only a man can give off and only a woman can smell.

Afroze knew that despite her best efforts, the smell of him, lingering as a nebulous notion over her sleeping form, had calmed her through the night. She tried to summon up any emotion to banish her thoughts, and she settled on the rampant anger that flew toward the room where her mother lay, clearly dying but hanging on with bravado.

She heard someone move around the kitchen, and the smell of breakfast cooking assailed her. She pictured a plate of fried sausages and had to place her hand over her mouth to swallow hard on a rising nausea. The wave passed. Afroze needed desperately to get out of that house. And she knew where she would go: to the fragrant fires of the temple. The Kavady Festival had always given her some comfort.

This festival was the culmination of a month of rigorous fasting, where no meat or fish or fowl was eaten, alcohol and drugs were forbidden, and no bedroom activities were allowed. Just for one month. The salivating devotees would hearken to the loud songs of Lord Muruga and Goddess Amman, aiming their cleansed bodies toward the bearing of wooden chariots on their shoulders.

The largest chariots were festooned with flowers and colored with a rainbow of powders—whose origins were somewhat dubious, as there always seemed to be a terrible asthma outbreak after festivals—would be carried by these dazed and crazed devotees up the main street, a snaky one-way with the strange moniker of Petrol Road. Of course, in official terms, the main road of Brighton carried the name of the love-crazed wife of the English lord, but now only two tarnished plaques on either end of the street bore her name. The locals, not particularly caring for the history of Lady Charlotte, had christened the street Petrol in honor of the two fuel-filling stations that sat across the street from each other.

Two fuel stations in a town with more bicycles than cars seemed incongruous and unnecessary, until you heard the story of the two warring brothers who both wanted to be "Lord of the Gas." In the inexplicable tales that dotted the history of this town, Afroze and her parable of mother hatred fit in perfectly.

And it was just the thought of hatred that spurred Afroze's slow body toward the field where all the devotees stood with their festooned chariots at their sides. They had taken vows and come in from towns and cities dotted all over rural Zululand to carry their burdens, such as crosses and heavy wooden structures laden with flowers and fruit, and continue onward toward the thin snake river. Here, they begged their final pleas for healings, riches, babies, husbands, and everything in between that made a life worth living.

Crying, beseeching, in deep trances, they waited for the sun to be directly above their bodies. The announcement of noon needed no expensive watches. Into the overburdened river, hundreds of altars would be immersed. The river was weak; it could not contain flotsam and jetsam iconography: flowers, fruits, photographs, and dreams. The altars were never borne away but remained bobbing in shallow water for days.

Silently, the pragmatic temple officials would eventually send surreptitious cleaners who, by cover of a darkened sky, would clear away the debris. The vows and yearnings of hundreds would have to be carried away in trash bags. Some believed that the temple priests took these offerings personally in a fancy, clean truck to be immersed in the sea in nearby Durban. Most knew that their desires, in their physical incarnations of wood and dead flowers, ended up in nearby landfills. It was best to be sensible, and not think too hard about things like prayers. And where these prayers went.

Afroze found strange joy in watching the preparations for the main ritual, a grand, loud ceremony where a very large chariot would be pulled with strong ropes by the very devoted. The main chariot was the protected home of the effigies of Goddess Amman and Lord Muruga, that forgotten son of Lord Shiva. Everyone knew the jolly face and the waving trunk of the beloved elephant lord, Ganesha—Shiva's preferred and pampered son. But Muruga seemed to have been forgotten in Ismail-like fashion in the pages of lore. The Kavady Festival brought him out to shine.

Perhaps the desperate and pleading devotees, who had fasted and prayed for miracles, realized that it was not always the popular one that came to their rescue. The unsung hero may sometimes answer your call more profoundly than the fat-cat favorite, the one that gleams in the daily sun. There came times when it was best to beseech the underdog.

The preparation for pulling the heavy chariot up the hill that was Petrol Road was calculatedly arduous. They could pull with their hands. God would answer their call. But if they pulled with their pain, God would reward them with so much more than they had asked for.

Pain was coveted in the form of piercings. Young men with shiny bare backs would drink copious amounts of milk mixed, possibly, with the paste of marijuana to send them into a trance so deep that they never felt the metal fishing hooks piercing their skins, hooks laden with huge limes that pulled their dark skin downward. The most devoted, in a rolled-eyed turbulent trance that they never remembered afterward, would attach the ropes to the hooks, and pull their weight in flesh. They danced in their devotions, their tongues pierced too with fanned-out pins. They preened and showed their piercings with aplomb. Certainly, they had to put their sacrifices and pain on show. For all to see.

Blood somehow was never drawn. Or blood was rapidly wiped clean away with rough towels. If blood *was* drawn it would show that the devotee hadn't been altogether sincere in his fasting in preparation for his pulling of the chariot, and perhaps had enjoyed a piece of fried fish hiding in some Christian friends' house—or even worse, a piece of beef while skulking in the home of a Muslim.

And of the Christian and Muslim people of the town, they watched the chariot parade in a jumble of awe and disgust. But they watched anyway. The Christian flock, fresh from their praise singing on Good Friday, left the mission chapel, tapering their songs and ministrations to a delicate act of timing, ensuring that they flowed onto the street in time to see the chariots being pulled. Timid ladies wearing Easter hats held embroidered handkerchiefs to their mouths, afraid of fainting at the sight of it all. The converted ones, the ones who had been brought into the flock from Hinduism and been dunked clean of their pagan practices, were the first to shake their heads at the barbarism of it all.

Inside the catacombs of their born-again hearts, they tried not to think too much of the barbarism of a crown of thorns and the bleeding hands and feet of nails in wood. But still, they could not look away. No one could. Later, they ate roasted lamb and raisin bread at tables decorated with stuffed bunny toys and sunflowers, cocking their ears for the raucous songs that spurred the chariot pullers onward and forward.

Within the perfumed coolness of their domes and minarets, the Muslim men padded to the windows in clean, bare feet. They too did not want to miss the fantastic spectacle. The old men muttered about how the Sufi saint Khwaja also enjoyed a parading chariot, a green-and-gold one that did not ask to be borne by pierced skin.

In all their differences, on the Goodest Friday of Fridays, the collective soul of all Brighton throbbed to many beats. The soft hymns, the frenetic chanting, the raptured Sufi songs—all cried out together. Pray for us all.

CHAPTER TWO

AFROZE FOUND SAFETY and solace in a cluster of women. It was something she missed greatly in her life, a female tribe. Somehow, women never really liked the pretty puzzle that was Afroze Bhana. She struggled through school days in Cape Town, never quite making a close girlfriend with whom she could giggle. In university, she took architecture and found that, in this vocation, which celebrated feminine curves and flowing lines, women were a scarcity.

But women can be cruel creatures. They know themselves in each other's eyes. They stamp validation of all their little acts and rites only by viewing everything through the eyes of a sister. Clothing became beautiful only when appraised by another. Love became real only when the bits and pieces of it were shared and spoken about to each other. Heartbreak somehow lived up to its name once recognized by the words of a sister-woman. Loving each other, hating each other, copying each other, and never fully able to see without the others' eyes is the language only women speak. And a shy, scared tomboy who cannot find words is an easy limb to sever.

Afroze spent much time looking for the friendship of a circle of the feminine. She found comfort in Moomi. But as she grew into a young woman, there were things she could not tell her stepmother. She yearned for a sister or a best friend, but she was never lucky enough. In her Cape Town society avatar, she did the expected dance, the air kissing, the playact of having women friends. But they were not really friends at the end of the day. They just clung together in a fashionable cluster, skimming the surface of closeness in short, sharp chats about fashion.

Suddenly, here in Brighton, Afroze the refugee felt a deep craving for feminine energy. She desperately wanted to belong to a kin of women. The Kavady Festival that she so enjoyed was a celebration of feminine energy, the bounty of harvest from a female Earth.

As she edged her body into a group of laughing girls, almond-eyed maidens with long, plaited hair and adorned with an array of magenta bougainvillaea, sudden unexpected elation ran like a current through her body. She laughed along with them, and it was the sweetest of sounds.

The beautiful maidens stood close enough to see that sometimes through a threadbare, cotton loincloth, a devotee's devotion went too far, but they knew well enough to keep away when the throngs went mad. There had been one a time long ago, when the Kavady Festival was at its height of popularity, a time often spoken of by yellow-toothed old men, that a group of the town's most beautiful maidens had stood too close to the lustful animal thrust of a devotee in trance, and as he danced on one limb with hooks and spikes in his dark flesh, he had swept like a wild simoom into the little petals held by the simpering bunch of sweet virgins. Nine months later, all the virgins who had been present gave birth to dark-skinned baby boys with strange holes in their backs and palates, and a penchant for playing with the gourd vegetable called monkey balls because no one knew what they were really called. Brown babies with cleft palates and holes in their backs became big men with cleft palates and holes in their backs and the purity of the virgins was never questioned. Lord Muruga was a mischievous chicken. He had just played a trick.

But just to be safe, the parading of the virgins at the height of the Kavady's frenzy was always very closely guarded by a very fat woman in a red sari and wild disheveled hair, who patrolled the group of virginal charges and didn't need much to scare the men away.

The men, freshly pierced and in a frenzy, were urged on by the increasing tempo of the devotional songs and loud drumming of a percussion instrument never seen outside the festival, but whose stretched top skin somehow defied the strict vegetarian fast of the devotees who dared not even carry around leather wallets.

Of course, could men who normally wore formal business suits or skinny jeans store a fat wallet in a loincloth? They took their chances, hoping that when they reached the heights of their frenzy that the tightly wound cloth wouldn't betray their dignity. There were those who hoped for a loincloth to fall to the dusty ground. Those were ones who needn't ask the lords for blessings after all.

As Afroze melded into the fragrant gaggle of pretty, young girls, feeling free and happy for the first time in a long time, she joined them in their playful taunting of a young man who came rushing forward baring his chest, pierced in many places. As he fixed his sharp eyes on the flirt of the group, he came up into her face and stuck out his tongue and wiggled it naughtily. The gleaming, metal spike that pierced his tongue looked dangerously sexual. Clearly, he knew his role well. The flirty girl, standing next to Afroze, blew him a kiss. And all hell broke loose.

The guardian of chastity, the fat woman in the red sari wound too tightly, hair wild and unkempt, came rushing forward at this tryst.

"Shame on you. Shame on you. Disgusting behavior, acting like a whore to tempt our devotee away from his trance. Witch woman, loose elastic on your panties, I'll show you what Goddess Amman does to flirty-flirty kissy-kissy girls!"

She dived into the throng of bodies, arriving back out of the mass by pushing and shoving those bodies aside. In her hands she carried a large, stained bucket; and before anyone could move, she threw the entire bucket of brightred colored water toward the girl. The girl was agile. Afroze suddenly felt sluggishly slow once again, with almost no reflexes.

The entire bucket of red water splashed Afroze full in the face and drenched her white blouse. She crossed her arms over her chest, realizing too late that she had worn a white, cotton blouse and no bra. In this dry-bone climate, her bra had become a chafing irritation and seemed to have shrunk in Halaima's boiling washtub. She had relinquished wearing one for days now.

Afroze gasped and screamed, reeling backward with force. She was about to hit the ground in a stumbling, clumsy fall when she felt a strong, steady hand grab her waist and whip her around quickly, shielding her wet white shirt in a tight embrace. She breathed in deeply. The smell of leather and wood and minty breath.

Sathie.

"Come, come with me, Rosie. Get out of this crowd. Things are getting quite out of hand today."

She was grateful for his supportive arm; her legs felt like they belonged to a rag doll, and she leaned on Sathie as he guided her out of the crowd, keeping his large frame in front of her to protect her wet modesty.

"My house is just here, near the end of the field. It's too far for you to walk back to Sylvie's house. Not like this; the streets are thronging."

Afroze nodded. And she knew exactly why she had nodded her head. Warmth and a dizzy, drugged haze settled over her. She followed Sathie numbly, but not dumbly. She enjoyed his strength and direction. It made her feel like a warrior-woman. And not a meek cast-away little waif, come home to seek a semblance of love.

Sathie led her to a tiny building behind a larger house, unashamed to take her into the hovel that he slept in. It was small, but it was clean. Just a room, with a neat bed, a beautiful piano against a sunny wall, a writing desk, and an old wardrobe that smelled of sandalwood. Now Afroze knew why he smelled that way—the quality of old wood, the scent of delicately carved patterns in sandalwood and teak inlays. Afroze appreciated design in all its forms, and she fell in love with beautifully crafted pieces. Her affection for wood and expert carpentry had seeped into her veins from her mother's carpenter father, but she never knew this at all.

She stepped bravely into Sathie's room. There was a natural ease now. Not a doubt, not a moment of hesitation shivered thought her mind, but strong sensual anticipation shivered through her skin. Sathie walked over to his cupboard and pulled out a sandalwood-smelling towel. He stood away from Afroze and handed it to her, unable to take his eyes off her at all.

She knew now. She had not remained behind because of an old, ugly building or her reputation as an architect. She had lingered here because she had seen something in Sathie's eyes that made her want to stay. She had no shyness with this man. Everything with him seemed natural, her way seemed clearer than she had ever known it.

She ignored his offered towel, and staring him in the eyes, she slowly peeled off her wet blouse, standing before him brazen and proud, hiding nothing.

Suddenly, the roles were beautifully reversed. Sathie, the suave master of seduction, the verbose lover, with words caught in his throat. He had never seen something as beautiful as this. Bare breasted, her skin still stained with the streaks of red coloring, gleaming like a goddess in the light. He saw before him the true, flaming Diana. Her youth, her proud stance, sticking out her breasts for him, only him. Wild, moist, dark-brown masses of curls tumbled over her back, into her face; a lock caressed her fleshy lips.

This youth, this supple skin, the almost feral look on a face that usually looked bland and afraid, aroused him more than he ever thought possible. He wanted to drown in the rivers of this woman offering her body to him. She asked with her eyes for him to drink every last drop of this elixir—he knew now, he was given a reprieve, a way to taste the long-forgotten days of Satin. The Lover.

He threw his Panama hat on the floor, shrugged off that frustrating jacket, and crossed the floor. No turning back. Warm, rough hands cupped her full, heavy breasts; she shivered as he brushed his thumb across them gently.

"Did you tell Sylvie yet?" he asked and pained her further by sweeping over her sensitive nipples again. He squeezed her breasts and she winced.

"No. I've told no one," she answered.

"Well, it certainly suits you. You glow and fill out like a true Mother Goddess."

Afroze smirked, catching his eye as he bent over to lick her nipple lightly, maddeningly.

"I thought you said I was insipid."

"Be quiet," he commanded. "You will never be anything but spectacular. Afroze ..."

He whispered her true name into her ear, and drew out its sound with hot breaths. It was the most delicious sound she had ever heard.

The frenzied singers at the Kavady reached fever pitch. The clanging of bells, the banging of tribal, raw-sounding drums, the combined heat and feverish prostrations of hundreds of barebacked devotees, teeth bared, saliva and sweat and blood in the keening of men and women, all rolling together in an undulating dance ... the dance, forbidden, sweet and slick in a tiny room behind a big house. Everything became one. Afroze howled out into the world, and nothing made sense anymore.

The heat of the day had risen to lie in the eaves of heaven. The cool breeze was almost too feather-light to perceive. Afroze lay in tangled sheets, filled with lazy languor, wanting to be nowhere but here. Sathie stood at the window, looking out at nothing in particular. He wore a white vest, his suspenders dangling from the waistband of his trousers. His feet, bare and white, were so beautiful. They looked delicate and fine. He pulled out a cigar and lit it. Suddenly realizing his mistake, he quickly made to put it out in a saucer at the table.

"Oh, Rosie, I'm sorry. I forgot about ..."

The fragrant smoke, an inviting smell of vanilla and toasted almonds, was quick to envelope the tiny room.

"Leave it. Smoke it. I like the smell."

"Don't be silly, Rosie. I'll go outside."

Afroze could sense his anxiety, and it enraged her. She felt like a woman lying in a married man's bed. He had broken the spell, the astounding potion they both had sucked on earlier like thirsty travelers. Now his eyes could not meet hers, and his body had become skittish.

She stood up and began pulling on her clothes. Rapidly and in anger. He watched her but did not stop her. Only when she was fully dressed, in a stained shirt and crumpled trousers, did he make a feeble attempt toward her.

"Stop, Rosie. What's wrong now? Why are you leaving like this?"

She stood at the open door and glared at him. Sathie could not meet her glowing eyes.

"You called me Rosie," she said and walked away.

On the dark street called Petrol, the remains of the day showed signs of the frenzy that had happened while the chariots were being pulled—the festival climax that Afroze had missed. She kicked aside broken pieces of gourds, whole apples, crushed flowers. She arrived at the gate to the fairy cottage and could hear the Qawali singers begin a crooning chorus, ten men together in perfect synchrony, telling the poems of Sufi saints that once walked the Earth. She caught the words of a familiar song.

In poetic Urdu, the song spoke to her across fields and minarets: "The one with lusty gazes must fear only God."

She could not help but laugh out loud as she walked into her mother's house. A madness had gripped her, and this was a dangerous insanity. It cared nothing for consequence.

Her mother's door was wide open. And the old woman, as if having received predictions of times to come from a djinn who slid down moonbeams, called out, "Rosie! I wondered where you were."

"Out, Mother. Kavady...."

Her mother stared at her with eyes that missed nothing. With her bald head, draped in her red, satin gown, she appeared bizarre, but astutely so. "I see. I see, Rosie. Hmmm, I wonder what time Sathie will arrive for breakfast tomorrow morning."

She put her painted fingers to her lips, stroking them in deep concentration, looking deeply at her daughter.

Afroze turned abruptly away, and in her bedroom fell asleep immediately in her red-stained blouse.

The Qawali singers had now moved on to a beautiful rendition.

Your veil has fallen forward, dear one. Now I see your gaze is drunk.

CHAPTER THREE

IT IS SURPRISINGLY easy to allow your actions in a dream to galvanize the actions of a day. It is wonderfully simple to make a dream your guiding light. Does not a murderer dream of blood on his hands and, upon waking in a cold sweat, he finds his hands are clean? Much is told in lore and in life about the dark grimoire of sleep and the places it takes you when you want nothing in your world to appear voluntary.

It is as if a dream sweeps its hand, clad in a black velvet glove, toward a screen, giving you permission to see what your mind hides away. But if this is what a dream does, if its purpose inside your neuronal fireworks display is to gate all your secrets, then a dream is not a good thing at all. Veils, in all shapes and sizes, in their black and their gauzy white, are dangerous things. For they are such easy things to blame.

Er … I blocked it out, and er … it haunted me in my dreams, and … er, I guess I didn't know it was wrong …

There were no dreams for somnolent Afroze this time. Soundless, deep, and almost-dead sleep took her pleasured body into a shelter of nothing. There is a first time for everything.

Like a chrysalis she lay curled up, a ball of worm. Creepy crawly into the house after a very naughty deed indeed. But, naughty turned a little whispering mite into a butterfly with sticky wings. Tomorrow, she would unfurl her new pair of purple passion wings, outward and outward. They would never stop at doorways or gates, they would push with force, breaking walls with their delicate strength.

Look, it was funny, very funny, that an afternoon of sex with a man twenty years older than her—the rather incongruous pungent virility of this aging masculine coupled with her ripe-age feminine—would have been so pleasurable. But it was very pleasurable, and it was not the act itself that made it so. It was all that surrounded it that made it so much more than it actually was. It could have been the trances and dances of the devotees, their bare skin glistening in rapture. It could have been the songs and hymns, the fervor of a day that screamed passion up to heaven.

It could have been all the things that one might imagine it to be. Like the usual suspects of a little reverse Oedipal Electra or the analysis of archetype. Crone vs. harlot. Simply put, daughter takes her mother's lover.

And it was all of those things. It was also more. Afroze bedding the older Sathie turned out to be the best way forward, the means and methods that allowed a woman to soar. And of course, to soar is so much better than to crawl.

Afroze had had lovers, a fair number of good ones. She had fallen in love and lust many times over. Cape Town was a city that made it impossible not to fall in love a hundred times a day. Everything about the city made every bah-humbug careen into a melted moment. Romance hung in the air. Sweeping views of movie-style sunsets from Chapman's Peak made one want to sit on a bench and kiss someone. Oceanside cafés flooded with availability; blue and silver color schemes and artfully chosen lounge music made one decide early on in the evening who one would be taking home for the night.

And that mountain. That mountain throbbed sexual energy into one's pores. It had tiny magnetic fields within it that pulled polar opposites together, to attract and to crash into each other like bodies of moths. The streets thronged with love and lovers. Kissing couples of every variety. Just like that. Stop and kiss in the middle of traffic. Quite cosmopolitan.

Afroze had broken some hearts, and had hers broken by some. She had sneaked out of beds at dawn carrying shoes and stockings in her fists. She had waited in bed, pretending to be asleep, when takeout coffee and cornershop croissants were brought to her in grand expectation of her awakened surprise. She had even taken walks in flower gardens and accepted daisies into her long hair. Been there, done that, Afroze.

Sathie, in his trousers and tucked-in vest, those old-school suspenders hanging at his sides, those feminine pretty feet and those satin, soft lips—nothing amazing and nothing new. But she liked him. Despite and notwithstanding all the deeper reasons why an abandoned girl would steal her mother's lover, despite it all, she liked him. She really did. Revenge was secondary.

"Mama, where is Uncle Sathie?"

Bibi was pouting. And pouting with force. She looked dolefully at the seat next to her, the one that her sweet, sweet benefactor always occupied. She genuinely liked him too. Sweets were secondary.

"I do not know; now eat your breakfast, Bibi. And say your *dua* before eating." Halaima chastised the girl, placing a plateful of crisp bacon on the table, making certain to keep the plate as far away from Afroze as she could.

"Not hungry this morning, Rosie?" Sylvie said, and flitted a quick glance at the empty chair before settling her strong, unblinking gaze on Afroze.

Afroze shifted a little in her chair. The ache in her lower back, a dull throb threatened to divulge all her secrets. She resolved to maintain the qualities that had seeped into her body with yesterday's bravado.

"No, Mother. I am starving," she replied, and to prove her ravenous appetite, she shoveled huge forkfuls of fried eggs onto her plate and almost immediately into her mouth. She gulped noisily on her sweet tea. Determined to provoke. Her mother looked at her with keen acuity. Afroze felt fortified, strong, and a woman anew. She looked back, wanting to appear straightfaced, cool, yet some acid leaked out of her eyelashes and dripped onto her lips, which curled upward.

Despite her unbending stare, Sylvie's stare back held little malice. Ignore the painted mouth, the dark black-lined eyes. Ignore the skewed wig. Witches often do not look like such parodies, and mothers often do not look like obvious mothers. Ignore the obvious uneasiness of a primal place, a place that responds badly to long, unblinking stares. See that in the eyes of this undeserving mother crept a whisper of worry. A whisper so soft that it became the butterfly wings that beat a spreading, concentric ring.

But Afroze did ignore. She was too steeped in her own version of the way things had been, she could barely see the way things were now. She wanted to recapture a moment when she was a petulant teenager with raging hormones, rebelling against a mother who told her not to date the boy with the motorcycle. Sylvie had sent her away when she was six. That number never left her brain. And her teenage-girl angst had been meted out on another woman.

Another woman had handed her a sanitary pad through a bathroom door, opened just enough for a little 11-year-old wrist to slip through. Sylvie had not had a rock-music-blaring, purple-haired-gum-chewing, spotty-faced angry young pubescent to manage. Sylvie had been spared. Afroze wanted to spare her nothing more. She wanted to throw things in her mother's face. Sylvie knew all this, with one trained glance at her child. She may not have reared her, but she knew this girl. Sylvie thought it best to indulge her.

"Quite an appetite you've worked up, Rosie. Maybe this place is growing on you," Sylvie said dryly.

Afroze felt game for a fight. She did not let her mother's manipulative attempts at being droll in conversation while bubbling in underlying venom bat her off her path.

"Yes, this town is growing on me, Mother. I'm thinking of staying on longer. That's if you don't have me kicked out and sent away, of course."

She muttered the word "again" and was certain Sylvie heard it.

"Stay. Stay for as long as you like. Who am I to prevent a consenting adult?"

Afroze, betraying her cool facade, glanced at the empty chair next to Bibi, the empty space that would have held the kindle to her rapidly growing fire. Her glance did not pass unnoticed.

"He won't come," Sylvie said with casual finality and continued chewing her toast.

The possibility that her mother might be right, that the chair might always remain empty, caught in Afroze's throat. Disappointment turned bitter gall into biting pangs that twisted her stomach, now full and slightly queasy. It was not only the rising thought that her mother might be right that constricted Afroze's gut with anxiety and hate. It was that her mother had to be the one to tell her.

She imagined a laughing, manic witch telling a simpering Snow White, "Someday your prince will not come."

Did it have to be Sylvie who bore the crown of disappointment and rejection down onto her bowed head? And why must she bow that head, after all? She had transcended now. She had evolved and morphed in just one night. One act of harried, secret passion had given her the right to lance wounds. The time had come.

Of course all this bubbled inside Afroze. The morning was quiet and peaceful. Autumnal mornings are so civilized. They never assault you, throwing your body around to heights and troughs of heat or cold. They sip tea with you, making light banter, so refined and subtle. Preferring beige to bright red. Here, Afroze sat, an aching back niggling at her memory, scratching deeply and vigorously at the beige, waiting to find the red. Demanding to draw blood. She was spoiling for a fight.

"My dear, your face is flaming. Do have a sip of water," Sylvie said and chuckled. Was it mocking? Was it?

"I ... I ... my face is fine. I don't want water," Afroze spat out a toddler tantrum. She suddenly sounded squeaky and was fast losing composure. The brittle, little self-possession she had erred in thinking she was now a custodian of began to fissure.

Pretty silly to think that it took a day to dilute rage into equanimity, when it took a lifetime to create it.

"All right then, my dear, if you insist you're okay. I was hoping that while you're here, now that you have decided to stay, you would put that university education of yours to good use."

In a state of distraction, her mind lingering on Sathie, Afroze stared blankly at her mother. Sylvie shook her head in annoyance and continued.

"Well, I want to convert this house and that wretched building at the back into a school, as you have been so well informed by our Sathie." The words "our Sathie" boomed out like a clap of unlikely thunder.

Afroze choked on the water that she had claimed not to want, coughing messily, bringing loud giggles from Bibi, whose large eyes had been flitting back and forth between both women in their trapeze of balance.

Before Afroze could speak, displaying by her expression that a massive tempest was about to be unleashed, a stupid tell-all revelation downpour that would more than likely leave her exposed and ashamed, Sylvie held back the black clouds.

"I want to build on this land. Such a shame to waste this large piece of land on a stupid cottage. I'm certainly not going to live here much longer. I want a place where I can put a plaque with my name on the door."

Stupid nature. It will persist. If a storm brews fierce and threatening, and the clouds have collected enough watery tears, if a drop of tear against a drop of tear creates enough friction to cause lightning bolts of savage intent, nothing will quell it.

It has been said that there are two things that can never be stopped: fire and water. And here, in this place, in this moment, in this town, at this table, in this house there was an angry abundance of both.

Afroze threw a napkin onto the table, knocking over a tiny jug of milk. She stood up abruptly. Fury finally came to breakfast. It shocked with its eruption.

"A plaque with your name on the door? A gold plaque? A bronze plaque? What kind of plaque do you want, dear doctor? Maybe a colossal plaque made of the years and years that I lay sobbing, wondering why my mother had sent me away. Will that plaque do you proud? Maybe a plaque of your cold heart, a plaque of your selfishness?

"A plaque of loss? Yes, I agree, Mother. I will gladly design a building for you. One deserving of your name on the door. And I will call it a mausoleum, a crypt. Grave! Because that is where your old, self-centered bones are going to rot."

Halaima pounced like an agile panther, pinning Afroze against her hard frame, holding the leaf-shaking seething body in a strange sort of hug. Afroze panted, having spat out the words, spittle lingering at her lip corners. Heaving and railing, she could not be stopped. She writhed her body, a bag of angry snakes, and tried to twist out of Halaima's vicelike embrace.

In her ear, she heard Halaima whisper, "That is enough. Enough. You are being cruel. The doctor is very ill."

"She is not ill, the witch. She will outlive us all. Because she has fed herself and forgotten her child. Thrown away, like a shoe she no longer liked the look of."

Sylvie sat unmoving. It was an ancient sort of wisdom that held her body in a different sort of hug, telling her that this tirade must not be stopped. It was vitally necessary. The poison had to be allowed to leak and then pour out of the wound that had been covered over with an imperfect scab for so many years. There could be no other way.

Sylvie shook her head at Halaima, but all Afroze saw was a shamed mother, shaking her head as if in denial of all her sins.

"Deny. Go ahead, you mistress of lies. Deny me again. I'm waiting. I want to hear you say it, Mother. I want to hear the words again. 'Take her away. Please, take her away. Now. Now.' Say it again, Mother. But this time, I am not a helpless child; I am a woman, a good, strong woman. What does he call you? Ah, yes … his Diana. His Artemis. Oh, Mother, look at you. Look at your sagging body, your stupid red lipstick on that failing mouth, that wig. You are bald. Bald, Doctor Sylvie. Bald and old and ugly and dying. Finished. Done for. No one will remember you, Doctor Madam. You don't deserve a plaque with your name on it anywhere but buried in the ground."

"Are you done, Rosie?"

Afroze looked away. She twisted off the ropes of Halaima's hands, and crossed her arms over her breasts. Her rib cage ached with the effort of all the vehement vitriol she had spouted. The only sound that could be heard was her hard, raspy breath coming thick and rapid like a train about to derail.

Slowly, Sylvie stood up. She leaned on her walking stick and began to drag her body away from the table, making for her bedroom with great effort. Halaima again pounced. This time, like a protective mother lioness, reaching out to help the hobbling woman negotiate the tiny space between where she ate and where she slept.

Sylvie put up her hand and, in a motion, told Halaima to let her be. She knew she could reach her bed. The drag-drag-depression sound of her walking cane on tile lingered long after her body had found its bed.

After she had left, Halaima turned to face Afroze, rage in her taut body. This time she was an eagle, a sharp-eyed eagle, yellow eyes blazing, seeing all. Even the tiny burrowing creatures that were blind to light.

"I hope that this outburst is the last one. The doctor is very sick, and I hope you finally have it out of your system."

"Oh, please. Stop being so self-righteous. Yes, she is sick. She's still a kicking and screaming banshee. And she feels no remorse."

"She feels remorse," Halaima said simply.

"What do you know?" Afroze said, tears that had been manacled now began to prick into the corners of her eyes.

"I know that there are many things about your mother that you don't know."

Afroze turned and looked at Halaima. Tears began to flow freely now, and Afroze made no attempt at stopping or hiding them. They fell in splashes onto the brick red–painted veranda floor.

"I'm going out," she said.

"He is not going to be there. He is gone," Halaima said, and a softening of her gaze said so many things: the knowledge of a sister-woman who knew of rejection and of lovers who disappeared into the air of it-never-happened.

Afroze ignored Halaima and almost ran the distance across the field where the chariots had stood, the ground still bearing evidence of the rituals that had happened there. She stepped over dried flowers, she crushed pieces of fruit, she kicked aside burned-out coals in her march. And she knew before she arrived to knock at the door of the tiny outbuilding at the back of a big house that he was gone.

His door was open, as if he had just fled having heard her footsteps. The room looked sterile, cleaned well of their combined scent. The only lingering smell was of the lovely, fragrant cupboard that stood empty with its doors gaping, mocking her. Nothing here, sweetie. That man sure is gone.

A woman came to stand next to Afroze, possibly the owner of the big house. She looked at Afroze staring at the empty room, and sighed a *tsk-tsk* she had done many times before.

"He left his piano," Afroze murmured.

"That piano was never his," the woman said.

CHAPTER FOUR

THE QAWALI SINGERS are going home to rest. They have sung their praises deep into the night. All the way across the world, in the city of Ajmer, India, there are Qawali singers who have sat on pure, white daises, fervently putting ancient poetry to song, in praise of the Saint Kwaja Gareeb-un-Nawaaz at the mazaar, on the anniversary of his death.

It is the sixth day of the festival, its deepest heart, and commemoration belongs to where his remains lie, in the ancient city in Rajasthan. The desert echoes with the concluding *badhaawa*, a passionate recitation by thousands of pilgrims, a poem sung out loud with no musical accompaniment. The ever-present percussion instrument, the femininely round tabla, is slumbering here—it had been only the beating of it that had driven the souls of men to look inside, look outside, look everywhere for their beloved. As the evening becomes dawn, and the festival draws to a close, the most burning desires of faithful lovers need no percussion, they need nothing of strings or chords to pull their hearts toward God.

In the small gathering of the Brighton mosque, a band of brothers bearing just their voices wrap their beloved tablas in white calico.

They will store them away for a night when they will beat their drums to prayer again. There is always a time for praise and there is never a time when drums fail to drive faith into any heart, even the heart of the most faithless one.

Afroze left the tiny room that converted her heart from a tiny, whispering speck into a roaring, angry wail. She did not know which way her footsteps would take her. The road to the Norwegian Christian mission was a meandering one, and it would take her directly to their creaking door. There, she knew that the door would open to reveal dusty halls, walls covered in tapestries by the tiny patient hands of the Savior's brides, lovers who have never known the touches of a mortal man. Inside the filigree of ivy walls, she knew she could easily disappear and live forever on tonic, angelic voices.

In the Shiva temple, floors were being swept with a long, grass broom, the *swish-swish* sounds turning a once-sandy floor into the polished marble of pride and joy. Inside its fragrant, open courtyard, she knew she could sit and lean her aching back against a cool pillar, and she knew the tinkling sounds of bells would soothe her. She knew that the smell of burning, fragrant fires would anesthetize her to the world, and she would forget all space and time.

The tall minarets of the little mosque, now scented with rosewater, would allow her to lie flat on floors of lush green carpets in the section where ladies sat last night, behind carved, latticed panels of soft rosewood, equally in love with the mystical beauty of the poetry and song. Here, she could allow a soft, black veil to hush away all her cries.

It was so easy. So easy to find places that would take a wandering traveler. Safe houses of the Gods that would shelter her away from the world, soothe her and calm her and give her a place to belong.

Afroze remained frozen, standing on a street of noise and bustle. She did not know if she should go left. She did not know if she should go right. Maybe she should just stand in a space, frozen like a statue of a Botticelli Venus. She felt her body swell, her breasts engorged, her hips filled out in the most beautiful roundness, the authority only a woman can possess.

It was not nice vacillating between God's houses that each call out to you, offering separate but equal solace. Which house of which

God to go to when you were a refugee in someone else's land? It was not nice not knowing where to go, being a parvenu. Being rootless in a ruthless world.

The choices were presented, each with a most pleasing allure. But when there were choices, the troubled soul sometimes chose none but the place from where it came. Afroze chose to go home. To her mother.

❧

Sylvie lay down flat on a silky coverlet, hating every fiber of comforting silk that caressed her old skin. She hated the color burgundy, and she hated the fakery of painted-on peonies in a country where no one had actually seen a real peony. How perfectly restful she would have felt if she lay on a sack of rough-hewn brown cloth, its fibers twisted and warped by the many bodies that had flung their nightmares helter-skelter in the few precious moments when the stark lightbulb seemed to not exist anymore. Her true sisters. Comrades. How they lay in those cells. Four steps across. Four steps down. And they were done. This was just number one of the thousand more rounds and rounds she would do in that cell.

Please. Please turn out the light. Just for five minutes. Please. So we can sleep.

But the lightbulb in its relentless wattage hisses.

I will burn. And I will burn bright. And I will never stop burning.

Somewhere inside the lightbulb moments, the bloodied sack moments, and the moments when she regretted not taking the easy way out, there was a moment that the sleep-deprived began to imagine that sleep must mean death. And that death must mean peace.

And yes, the struggle was strong, the training was good, the comrades tapped their urges to her with a spoon on a concrete floor, egging you to hold on, just hold on, my sister. But somewhere, the womb of her began to ache for what it had left behind, long girl-legs with no ankles, just sticks rapidly drawn into the backseat of a stranger's car.

Activists were mothers and they were fathers too. The struggle for a free society was her illegitimate child, while her real one flew away from her, to distant places. And they would hate her forever, because they do not understand. And yes, she did think of suicide. Often.

After all was said and done, after trials and after beatings, after the world howled at the same moon and, like a magician's rabbit, the freedom and democracy that she had been fighting for was granted by fearful presidents, after her comrades gained high places in a building that once sentenced them to death, and she a piece of forgotten history, she accepted the burgundy silk coverlets and garish curtains because maybe someone believed that you finally deserved opulence and grandeur. At least someone wanted to coddle her, and laud her with soft furnishings. Still, the best moments and the worst moments she had ever known had been when she lay on dirt.

Sylvie dozed, but this was not uncommon. The cancer had become a tenant of a body that was too weak to manage evictions. Inside the secrecy of tumors lay the times when she had hoped something would come and take her life. And now something had. At a most inappropriate time. A time she looked into the firebrand eyes of the girl she left behind, and something called "mine" swelled up, pushing tumors and failed organs into the back seat.

I have so much to tell you, my child. Daughter of mine. I have so many things to teach you. I have so many moments I want to ask you to walk through with me.

Do you know that I love pears? Do you know that they taste best when left on a warm windowsill for a while, imbibing the sun until their cells burst with juice? Do you know that I have a favorite color? Do you know that I sing popular Indian movie songs sometimes?

Do you know that I prefer afternoons to mornings? Do you know that I wore saris because, in a world where we had to give away our unique Indian identity and become African, this stupid, uncomfortable, very impractical garment was my only connection to where I came from? Do you know that I saved my best silk sari for you to wear one day? And that I kept my ugliest one for you to dress me in when I go?

Do you know that I love you enough to make my heart burst?

And do you know that I don't know how to tell you?

Afroze.

CHAPTER FIVE

THE BANGING ON the door was relentless. At first, fast and unbridled. And when there came no answer and fatigue set upon a fist, slow and almost melancholic. Thud-pause-pause-pause-THUD-pause …

This tired pounding, chiding the occupants of the doctor's house to answer wordless pleas. When no one stirred and the sound was left unanswered, a voice took over the pleading.

"Doctor! Please, Doctor! I need the doctor. Please, someone come. Please."

Afroze heard the sound, but she ignored it. In her knowing-unknowing malaise, she could not lift her body off the chair in the veranda to stir, to move toward the frantic calls. Someone else would do it. She did not care.

But no one did it. No one rushed to the door. And the frenetic banging and crying did not go away. More than worry, it was irritation that coursed through her. Now what?

It had suddenly become difficult for her to spring up and bolt. Something shared her blood and her life force, and it was not a generous sharer. But she stood up and walked with heavy steps toward the passageway. Her mother's door was open, and on the bed Sylvie lay asleep, oblivious to the loud calls.

Afroze stood at the bedroom door.

"Mother. Mother!" she called out loudly, and Sylvie awoke with a start. It seemed somehow strange that the racket at the door had not woken her, yet the voice of her daughter made her start up to full awareness. This day had been long, and it had been difficult. Some sort of torpid draft had swept through the house, drugging the women inside into a haze of disinterest. *Let the world fall to pieces. I have nothing left to give.*

After seeing the ugly emptiness of Sathie's room, Afroze had arrived home and fallen into the rattan chair on the veranda, unmoving. Staring with unblinking eyes into a frightened, distant place, fear and anger leaving her unable to do anything but breathe slowly in and out. Sylvie had heard Afroze arrive, knowing the waning moon of shame and disappointment that haunted the woman's body, not because she had loved, or that she would miss the lover. But because she hated herself for being so exposed.

Sylvie knew this shameful dance well enough.

Dusk, an ugly part of any day, found both women in a state of inertia, wanting to move toward each other but totally incapable of doing so. Sylvie's sleep had come restlessly but had metamorphosed into a deep one.

She started up in an anxious jump when she heard Afroze calling her, and then she heard the feverish banging and calls at the front door.

"What is it? Who is that at the door?"

"I don't know, Mother. Tell Halaima to send them away."

"Halaima is not here. She left earlier to take Bibi to visit her father."

Both women looked at each other with deepening worry. Not just the anxiety that the banging on the front door brought, but also, the more frightening apprehension that finally they were alone together.

"Send them away, Rosie. I don't want to see anyone."

Sylvie's voice was tired and unusually soft. She sounded like one defeated.

Afroze went to the door and swung it open, glad for the thick wrought-iron gate that protected her safety. In the past, doors could be opened to allow people in. But now, so much danger lurked in all corners of this country that doors had become just wooden icons that decorated the thick, iron gates with many, many locks.

A young man stood at the door. His face was streaked with tears. Some sort of black kohl that he had used to line his eyes beautifully had run in tracks down his cheeks, making him look like a ridiculous teenage girl who had been crying over her first love. He was dressed in a long, white robe, one worn by devout Muslims at prayer, and his white, crocheted skullcap was clutched in his hand. The hand that he had been using to pound on the green door.

Afroze caught him midmotion. A last half-hearted attempt to bash his tired fist onto the wood. He looked defeated, but when he saw Afroze in the half-light standing there, he puffed out a sigh of relief.

"Oh, thank you. *Shukran Allah.* Someone is here. Please. The doctor … I need the doctor …"

"She … doesn't see patients anymore … she is asleep," Afroze said, and hated lying to the frantic teenager.

"Oh God. Please, I beg you. It's my father. In the car … he can't breathe …" the boy stepped aside and Afroze saw a car in the driveway. She could barely make out two dim figures in the back seat, distinguished only by their white cloaks glowing with a milky-white moonlight.

"What's wrong with him?" Afroze suddenly became concerned. She noticed that the boy's face was twisted with distress and fear for his father's life.

"Please, I'm from the mosque … My father, he played last night at the Qawali … he can't breathe. He has asthma. Very bad. He is having an attack."

Afroze hesitated for a second, not knowing what to do. And then she held up her palm to gesture to the boy to wait and she ran to her mother.

"Mother, it's one of the boys from the mosque. His father is having a bad asthma attack. What do I do?"

Sylvie blinked at Afroze. It had been a while since she had seen a patient. She wondered if she even remembered how to.

"Tell them to go to Doctor Ngotho. Across town, near the mission hall."

Afroze ran to the boy, who seemed like he had sprinted to the car quickly and come back to the door, cap still in his sweaty hand.

"She says to take him to Doctor Ngotho. Near the mission hall."

"No. Please. We tried. The doctor is not there. Away for Easter weekend. Please, my father says Doctor Sylvie will help. Please, he is going to die ..."

Afroze left him and sped to her mother, who could hear now the exchange of words and had sat up in her bed. Afroze didn't have to explain.

"But ... I don't have any of my things ..." Sylvie murmured and looked at Afroze with wide eyes, almost like a frightened child, an antithesis of the fast, quick-to-action doctor she once had been.

"Mother, there is no one else. You have to help this man."

Sylvie placed a hand on her chest, tapping it loudly, waking up her heart, knocking courage into it. With unlikely force, she stood up.

"Right, tell them to bring him inside. To the front room. I'm coming now." She quickly threw on a silk dressing gown over her plain, cotton nightdress. In Halaima's absence, Sylvie had put away the frilly, silky nightclothes that seemed to comfort Halaima more than herself.

The boy and another older man, both with faces contorted in worry, carried the old man into the house and lay him on the soft, velour couch. The ugly, leather examining couch had long since disappeared from that room. It was no longer needed.

The old man's skin looked bright purple, deep blue, and scarily pale all at once. As they carried him, Afroze heard the loud, labored breathing struggling from his chest, but as they lay him down, he barely breathed a whisper. Were they too late? The teenage boy, convinced that they were, put a hand over his mouth to stifle a loud sob.

"Papa," he wailed.

Sylvie hobbled into the room, trying to maintain a semblance of dignity in her gait, and on seeing the man lying motionless on her couch, flew to his side. Not caring about her own broken body, she kneeled beside him and, with expert hands wrinkled with age and illness but sure and practiced, she began to palpate his chest and throat. From a pocket of her gown she pulled out a stethoscope, one that Afroze wouldn't have guessed she still kept in her bedside drawer, and listened to the almost motionless chest.

"Adrenaline. Now! He's still breathing, but his airways are in spasm, almost closed."

She looked up at Afroze, who lurked fearfully in the doorway. She had always had a deep dread of illness, always keeping a very wide berth from it even as a child growing up in a house thronging with all forms of it.

"Afroze! Go to the khaya. I have my bag in there. You'll find it easily. It has syringes and glass vials. Bring it here."

Afroze hesitated. Somehow, even in the face of this imminent death, she could not face going into the khaya.

"Afroze! Move! He is going to die," Sylvie's voice was strong and commanding. It hearked back to the old days, when the great Doctor Sylvie would boss and bully everyone around her.

Afroze jumped and was jolted out of her fear and panic. "The keys. Mother … where are the keys to the khaya?"

"In my sari drawer. Now go! Go!"

Afroze ran wildly into the bedroom that she slept in. The large dark-wood wardrobe that contained her mother's saris, the one that she lay awake staring at since she had arrived back in Brighton but dared not open, loomed before her. Again she froze, and she felt hands push her toward it. The teenager had followed her into the room, by his own volition to desperately save his father, or maybe Sylvie had sent him to push Afroze into action. Sylvie seemed to know her daughter well enough. And she seemed to know when her daughter would falter.

"Open it!" the boy shouted, and pushed Afroze with force.

Not stopping to think, Afroze swung the doors open, and the smell of her mother's perfumed saris assaulted her, lingering in the desperate air like a fortifying tonic that sent her into rapid action. That perfume did not haunt her any longer. Something about how it lingered like cobwebs rather than hitting her nostrils like a stone wall made her suddenly love the perfume.

She knew exactly where the keys would be. As a child, she had seen her mother slip them in there a hundred times, but her memories had failed her. In the state of shock seeing the old man gasping for breath, Afroze's mind had gone blank. On the day she had been kicking the door to the khaya after her mother denied her the keys, Afroze only realized later that the childhood memory of her mother slipping something into the cupboard of saris slowly came back to her. It was not that she didn't know how to find them herself. It was that she had enjoyed kicking that door. Running her nimble fingers over the neat piles of folded fabric, she found the one sari her mother kept wrapped in thick plastic. She dug her fingers into the back of the plastic package, and with a jingling sound that sounded very much like a prayer answered, she pulled the keys out. Two large, old-fashioned, thick, iron keys dangled heavily on a big metal ring.

There was no time to hesitate or to muse. The boy again pushed her by her shoulders, not saying anything. Just prowling like a crazed guard, prodding her to fast reactions.

She ran to the back of the house, the boy at her heels. His breaths were rapid, and the sweaty smell of his panic melded with the strong attar cologne that he wore. The heady smell was not unpleasant, but in her current state it made her want to throw up.

At the crumbling yet thick, rough door to the khaya, she forced the first key into the keyhole, which seemed crusted over with age and underuse. It barely moved. She tried the second key. It slid in reluctantly, but she could not turn it, even using her entire body weight as a lever. The boy, his anxiety careening into a heavier, pungent fervor, pushed her rapidly out of the way, and in the dark back yard, she stumbled for a footing. She had to grab onto his strong back to regain her balance.

He tried turning the key with all his brute force, and after what seemed like an eternal wrestling match between metal and wood, the key turned. Both rushed into the khaya, bumping into each other. It was deathly dark. None of them had even thought of a light. The boy pulled a cigarette lighter out of his pocket, and the hissing smell of butane filled the room. The lighter flame was weak, but it was enough. Afroze found the bag filled with what Sylvie had described thrown haphazardly onto the floor. She saw nothing much else in that dreaded room, but as she groped for the bag, her hands grazed a number of oddly shaped things.

"Got it," she huffed, and the boy grabbed it and ran back into the house.

Afroze lingered in the complete darkness for a second. This two-roomed building, this secretive place that swallowed her mother up in its monstrous maw for hours every night, threatened to swallow her up too. She sensed something sinister there—the suffering was palpable, a live, beating thing that cried out in anguish to be acknowledged and let loose. It was as if a hundred voices came resounding from the flaking walls and pockmarked concrete floors, voices that begged for a witness.

Hear us. We were here. Hear our stories.

Afroze shook off the strange eeriness and backed out of the door, the only source of a murky light that fell in a perfect moonlit rectangle on the floor.

In the heart of the indigo-colored rectangle, a sheet of paper lay innocently, obviously dislodged from its brethren by the frantic search for the medicine bag. As she backed away, not wanting to turn her back to that place filled with malefic, childhood imaginations, she grabbed the piece of paper and stuffed it into her pocket. She slammed the old door shut and bolted like a chased fox back into the light and warmth of the house.

She arrived in the front room to an atmosphere that was pregnant with relief. The old man had been given a strong dose of adrenaline. Sylvie had prayed the vial was forgiving in its expiration dates and storage conditions. The patient had begun to breathe with a shred of normalcy. His chest rose and fell weakly, but in a regular rhythm, and almost imperceptibly, the color on his face began to return to normal. Slowly.

Sylvie seemed a new woman. With the body in her hands, she had forgotten her ails, she had forgotten that she had forgotten how to treat patients, and she was deftly setting up a portable machine that would deliver more medication into the man's lungs through a hazy mist of air from an oxygen mask. The dust-covered machine, which was tiny and portable yet ancient in its design, had been lying underneath all the syringes and needles at the bottom of the bag.

"He's bloody lucky," Sylvie growled. "So many things could have gone wrong here."

It seemed that the prayers and praises that the Qawali singer had thrown his lungs at during his time on the stage had gone answered by the God he answered to. The ancient machine worked well enough, despite its veneer of dust. And the doctor who was now avidly listening to his breathing through her beloved black-and-silver stethoscope had come back to life with the life she had saved.

Afroze went into the kitchen and, craving coffee but taking tea instead, found the teenage boy standing at the sink drinking deeply from a glass of cool water. He seemed to relax into a familiarity with the space he occupied. He sipped and regarded her as she put the kettle on and took out a pretty, floral teapot she had never seen before.

"He sang so beautifully tonight," the boy began to talk, not taking his eyes away from Afroze. He had washed the tracks of black kohl off and she could see that he would one day soon be a very handsome man.

"What happened?" Afroze asked him, sensing that he needed to talk.

"My papa is the best Qawali singer in this country," he said with blatant and unreserved pride for the man that he hoped to one day become. "He sang tonight at the festival, the commemoration of the death anniversary of our beloved Khwaja-ji. His dream is to sing at the shrine in Ajmer. And he told me that tonight he will sing at the gravesite of Khwaja-ji. He told me his body will be here, but his voice will be in Ajmer. And I believed him because I have never heard him sing as beautifully as he did tonight. But after he led the final song, he looked upward, he held his palms to the sky, and he fainted, his breath heaving like he was going to leave us. But, the doctor … she brought him home. She brought him back from Ajmer, and she gave him back to us. He brings us blessings from the shrine of Khwaja-ji. We all will be blessed now."

Afroze ignored the whistling kettle. The boy's hypnotic voice, his mystical tale, had entranced her. In her short years in Brighton, she had been surrounded by a mother who did not believe in God or organized religion. In her growing-up years in Cape Town, her stepmother Moomi had been fervently religious, but in a superstitious way—she had been unlearned about the depth of the faith she ritualistically practiced. Afroze had always sought to learn the deeper aspects of everything. Her favorite subject in school, and even at university, had been history. She believed, almost obsessively, that to understand anything, you had to unearth all the secrets of how it came into being. She enjoyed frames of reference, because they soothed her into thinking that she had a place in a larger fabric.

Moomi could answer none of Afroze's deep questions. Her father, Ismail, cared nothing for schooling Afroze in anything, religious or academic, though he spent all his time on his prayer mat. She had blundered around, searching for answers, looking for a world to belong to, and, finding none that spoke to the deepest, most mystical heart of her, she had chosen none. In theory, she practiced the religion of her father because she had lived in his house.

She fasted for the month of Ramadan, she occasionally wore a headscarf, but only to funerals, and she murmured and muttered the traditional words and greetings of Moomi's large extended family during festivals such as Eid. But as she listened to this young boy tell his tale, in her mother's kitchen, a dying man brought back to life in such a beautiful rendition of mysticism, something began resounding deep inside her cells.

"I am going to have a baby," Afroze told the boy.

He looked at her, unblinking for a long second, wondering why this woman was telling him this. It made no sense. And he did not really care to hear it.

But Afroze felt wonderful for saying it. She felt suddenly that this baby that was hiding inside her had now become a person to the world. Saying it out loud, to a boy she knew did not care, who she would probably never see again, made her feel the strongest of bonds with the unborn child. She wanted to shout it out loud. She smiled happily at the confused boy, and told him to go back to check on his father.

Her hands flew to caress her belly. A reflex. A mother's reflex. Suddenly, for the first time in her life, Afroze knew she wanted strong roots, and a place to bring a child home.

CHAPTER SIX

WHEN HALAIMA CAME home from visiting her husband, early the next morning, she sniffed something new in the air of the cottage. She did not know immediately what it could be, and resolved to set about cleaning with extra verve. Maybe strong bleach would chase away this unfamiliar scent. She did not know then, but sensed soon that the house smelled like warmth.

Her night with Rasheed, her husband, had been good. He was a Pakistani native who had come to South Africa after the Taliban had created much instability in Pakistan and it had cost him his entire family and all his possessions. He was young, resourceful, and quiet. And there was always a place for someone like that in any part of the world. Rasheed had been brought to Brighton by one of the feuding brothers of the petrol stations, who had met him in a mosque in Durban and recognized that he was a faithful, reliable man—one that could easily manage one of their many businesses. Rasheed, who had been a teacher in Pakistan, eagerly took on the role of managing a busy Laundromat that sat in a small alley behind the petrol station of the calmer brother.

He had found love in the tall, dark Halaima and admired her for her strength and her religious convictions, and it was a very small affair that saw them marry according to proper Islamic rites.

Rasheed was careful not to send letters of this marriage to the shreds of his family that still lived in Pakistan. There were things some people could never understand. Nor accept.

Halaima and Rasheed lived separately. But both knew this was a temporary thing. Her duty was to the ailing doctor. He had not saved enough money to create a home. Their daughter, the precocious Bibi, flitted between them, a child who knew she was cherished. It was Halaima who began whispering to Rasheed late at night about all that had happened at the doctor's house. Rasheed listened in silence. When Halaima's low voice tapered into silence, spent and exhausted from talking about turmoil, Rasheed whispered to her.

"*Biwi*, my wife. There is a fable of Nasreddin Hodja that my old grandmother used to tell me. And I will tell it to you:

"One day, Nasreddin Hodja sent his beloved son to the fountain to fill up a favorite clay pitcher with water. Nasreddin Hodja handed the pitcher to his son, and then promptly slapped him.

"'Don't break this pitcher,' he said in stern warning to his son, who was shocked and hurt by his father's slap.

"'Effendi Hodja, your son did not break the pitcher, he didn't even leave for the fountain yet. Why did you slap him?' the people scolded.

"'Ah yes, but you see,' the Learned Hodja replied, 'If I slap him after he breaks the pitcher, it will be too late.'"

Halaima stared in mild confusion at the man who she had grown to love and admire.

"Oh, Biwi," Rasheed said mildly, "you see, a parent knows their child. No matter the circumstances, a parent knows the weakness of their own flesh. And sometimes they throw harsh slaps to lovingly protect their child from the child's impending doom."

Halaima sighed. She had grown accustomed now to Rasheed's conversations, highly peppered with fables from the grannies and aunts of his youth in Peshawar. It sometimes took a while to grasp what Rasheed was saying in his style of speech, but often, when she did grasp the essence of his tales, she understood many things better.

"Ey-ey, *Mwamuna*," Halaima clucked, calling Rasheed by the traditional Chichewa word for "husband." It was ill-omened and disrespectful to call a husband by his given name, and even though Halaima had left Malawi years ago and Rasheed would never understand her native village language, she dared not offend God or men.

"I feel very afraid," she continued. "The doctor is very ill. She does not have long in this *duniya*, this world. The daughter, Rosie, is a very angry woman. Maybe she will lose her mind and she will chase us all away from the house. What will happen to Bibi and me?"

"My beautiful woman," Rasheed whispered and drew Halaima close to him, "I am here. We have enough to make our life. This storm between mother and child is not for us to interfere with. Leave it. Allah will provide. He always has."

Leaving Rasheed, Halaima felt comforted, as she always did after seeing him. Bibi was happy, proudly brandishing a box of crayons that her father had presented to her with a flourish.

"What will you draw first for your papa?" Rasheed asked, swinging her thin frame high in the early, dawn air as they prepared to leave him and return to the cottage.

Bibi stuck out her fat, bottom lip and pondered for a long time. "Papa, I will draw Rosie. She is so beautiful."

Halaima clicked an annoyed response. The same response she had shown when this Rosie had appeared at the door some days ago, brash and unafraid, suddenly wanting to enter her mother's life. Halaima had become afraid then. She had heard talk in the markets of this daughter, of how she lived the high life in Cape Town and how she ignored her ailing mother who struggled to survive on a government military pension—the pittance they doled out to all activists of the anti-apartheid struggle. She recalled how furious she had become when Rosie had given Bibi a hundred-rand note. As if she could buy love and affection with all her money. Halaima was just a nursemaid to Doctor Sylvie, but she sometimes thought that she should have been the daughter of this amazing woman.

She bustled into the kitchen, leaving her bags near her room door, not bothering to even enter it and settle before she started to clang about, making the breakfast that the doctor adored. Always the same thing. For the years that she had known Doctor Sylvie, she always ate the very same breakfast—two fried eggs, crisp bacon, sausage, and toast. And she always drank strong, brewed coffee, boiled for hours in a pot, then strained. Even when the cancers began to eat her bones, she never faltered in her appetite. Through the long, arduous journeys to the government hospital five hours away for the poison of chemotherapy, she would arrive home, retching but starving for her breakfast. Sometimes it was all she ate the entire day.

Halaima was at the stove frying bacon when Afroze wandered into the kitchen. She didn't seem to mind the contents of the frying pan. In her hand, she carried a bar of soap, which she smelled often, placing it under her nostrils and inhaling deeply like a drug. That cheap soap seemed to have calmed Afroze down, and she was almost pleasant in her conversation.

"Mother treated a man last night, a singer from the Qawali group at the mosque."

Halaima looked up in consternation. "How did she manage? Is she okay?"

"Don't worry, Halaima, Mother did a fine job. She hasn't forgotten her work, despite her sickness. The man's son blessed Mother for saving his father's life."

Halaima looked at Afroze lingering at the kitchen table in her fluffy dressing gown. She saw Sylvie appear, how the young, beautiful Sylvie must have appeared years long ago. Yes, they did look so much alike.

"I went into the khaya, to fetch her medicine bag," Afroze said lightly.

Halaima, who had said nothing till then, stopped her business and stared at Afroze in fear. Halaima had sneaked into that old building. She knew what was in there. She knew what had happened in there. Would Afroze damage them all, now that she knew?

"So you know?" Halaima whispered.

"Know what?" Afroze answered, her light and airy mood broken by Halaima's serious tone. Afroze's eyes narrowed suspiciously and Halaima realized Afroze knew nothing about the secret of the khaya.

Yet.

But Halaima also realized that the moment for knowing was now upon them all.

CHAPTER SEVEN

THE KETTLE WHISTLED. Mist formed on the windows as steam escaped the pressure cooker inside the boiling vessel. Halaima tried to escape Afroze's sharp stare by pretending to set a tea tray that no one had really called for. She vacillated between speaking and keeping the silence that she had grown accustomed to. Since she had come to work for the doctor, Halaima had become more than just a caregiver. She had sat up through late nights, becoming the doctor's confidante. And although there were times when Halaima would be falling forward in exhaustion, her arms aching from cradling the sleeping Bibi, she would not stir to carry the child to a bed or even to fall into the soft mattress herself. When the doctor began speaking, Halaima respected her words, and she respected that when someone tells you what is in her heart, the last thing you do is move away.

In their sporadic nightly conversations—which were actually monologues, stories upon stories told by the doctor—Halaima invited the confidence by nodding and murmuring approval. She quietly gave the tortured, old woman the gift of a willing ear, because Halaima knew that it was a gift that no one had given before. Many people had come and gone in the doctor's difficult life. Many had spoken to her, spoken at her, spoken about her. No one had stopped to hear her speak.

The doctor's voice rang out with stern commands; it barked medical orders. She had held court over important things, for country and for individuals, but no one had allowed her to speak of the murderous pain that she housed within her heart.

Afroze.

She, this daughter that had been sent away, saw only a corner of the entire painting. She stood there, with her nose pressed so firmly against it all that stepping back and actually looking at it in its entirety was foreign to her. She had come to this home, angry and filled with the burning need to hurt her mother. She saw only a woman who was gruff and angry, and she recalled only the skewed version of how she had been abandoned.

Halaima knew the reality. And being the custodian of this knowledge gave her a grave responsibility. Was it her place? Should she now unravel the truths, end this once and for all? She felt too small and insignificant for a task as colossal as this. Again, she avoided saying a word, hoping that now, today, magic would begin to open knots.

But there is no such thing as magic. Magic requires a magician. Afroze's all-consuming stare frightened her. She worried that if the truths were revealed, debris would be left in their wake. And where would that leave her?

Afroze sensed the anxiety in the always-composed Halaima. She persisted in her intense regard, and stuck her hands into the pockets of her dressing gown, squaring her body for a confrontation.

Magic.

Magic cast by a magician in the sky. We all knew the name of this magician.

Afroze pulled her hand out of her pocket, and in it she grasped a browned, torn page. Magic made her stop looking at Halaima and magic made her cast her eyes at the piece of paper in her hand, the piece of dirty page that she had stuffed into her pocket when she had gone into the khaya to fetch her mother's medicine bag.

Prisoner Number 1434/80: Sylverani Pillay, Medical Doctor
Arrested: October 26, 1977
Solitary Confinement: 55 days
Depressed, delusional, suicidal.
Charge: Treason, Terrorism, Harboring of Dangerous Criminals
Under the maintenance of law and order to be detained for a 60-day period wihout trial on the authority of a senior police officer.
By Order: Special Branch of the South African Police Services

Look.

Look now how the hands of a daughter who hated with such poisonous rage begin to shiver and shake. Look now, how she reels forward into the arms of a foreign refugee. She is looking here, and she is looking there, and her eyes are wild as they dart about, opening to truths that have been hidden from her for so many years. See her. She cannot stand. She cannot sit. She cannot bear. She cannot cry.

What is this? What?

She grabs the hands of her mother's caregiver, her only confidante in the world, and she digs her fingers into the smooth, dark arm, imploring and begging, unable to speak. *Tell me. Please tell me everything. I fear that I have known nothing at all. I fear that this castle I have built from the time I came into this world is one that was built on misunderstanding and hatred. Take me down from my tower. And show me the truth. Why now? Why, when it is too damn late, must I find this truth? Why?*

Magic. That's why.

Halaima made Afroze drink a glass of iced water. She watched the slow calming of her breaths, and waited until Afroze's eyes stopped darting about in mania. Finally, when Afroze settled her gaze on Halaima, it was a steady gaze. The exhaustion of holding anger and hatred inside for so many years broke her glare into a soft regard. Now, the right time had come to tell.

"Why did she hide it from me, Halaima? Why did they all hide this from me?" Afroze murmured, gripping a mug of steaming tea that was set before her.

"Rosie, your mother was very ashamed. She looked at you, and all she could see was guilt."

"But it was not her fault."

"To her, everything was her fault, Rosie. She could never be a mother to you, although she told me how she would stand and stare at you as you slept. She was in too deep. She had pledged her life to fighting for a better country, yet she tortured herself that she could never be a better mother."

"She rejected me. She never wanted me near her. Now. Back then. She could never bear me."

"Rosie, she could never bear herself. Whenever your mother looked at you, she saw only the pain and suffering that her choices had brought you. Even now, you are not a child any longer. You are a woman, older than the doctor was when she had to send you away for your safety. Even now, she hides her guilt by hiding her heart. She loved you deeply. I know that to be true."

"How? How do you know that, yet I don't know it?"

"Ah, Rosie. I have a child, a daughter. I know that to my daughter, I am almost larger than I can ever be. To my daughter, I am a star in the sky. She looks at me like I can change the entire world, like I am this heroine who can fight her battles, cast away all the monsters and all the pains in this horrible world. But, Rosie … I know the truth. I am just a frightened woman, not a goddess. I am as scared of the darkness as she is. I sometimes push her away, so that she can see that I am just a fragile woman, afraid and ignorant about how to be a mother. I am afraid that if she saw me for what I really am, she would stop feeling anything at all for me. I can bear my daughter's anger, and I can bear my daughter's hatred. But, Rosie, I cannot bear my daughter's nothingness."

"She preferred my hatred? She preferred me to be angry and rile against her? All so that I would not forget her?" Afroze said, and Halaima placed her warm hand on top of the tremoring one of Afroze, nodding her head.

Afroze took Halaima's hand and squeezed it tightly. "I have been so horrible to her, Halaima."

"And she has been so horrible to you, Rosie."

"I wanted to hurt her. I … Sathie … I wanted to take away what was dearest to her."

"Sathie was never dear to the doctor. You are what is dearest to her. Both of you made many mistakes."

Afroze pulled her hands away from the warmth of Halaima's grasp and pressed the palms to her face. Her eyes burned from tears that she just could not shed. Even with all this new knowledge, she could not cry. She doubted that she ever would find tears again, because she knew that tears finally shed might heal her. "Yes, we made many mistakes. Is it too late?"

"No, Rosie. Your mother is still here. She is still living and breathing, and for that, it is never too late."

"I must go to her." Afroze stood up abruptly, the stool she had been perched on fell in a clatter to the floor.

"No. Not now, Rosie. The doctor is very tired. She is sleeping. There is time enough for it. Now you know her truth, and that is all that matters."

"But, she doesn't know that I know now, Halaima."

"Rosie. The doctor knows. She knows."

CHAPTER EIGHT

IT WAS NOT too late. Nor was it the right time. But it was the only time that they had. The awkwardness caused by decades of estrangement between the mother and her daughter was not easily dissolved away. Too much had happened, and too many things had to be said. And when there is a formidable ocean that needs to be crossed, it is never the ones who dive in and flail madly who make it to the other side. The ones who glide with an insufferable tide, the ones who stop fighting the deep, are the ones that cross safely over.

Some things are said in subtlety. Some things are best left unsaid. Explanations and apologies can come in the elusive form of glances, light touches of two hands, and in the restraint of not saying anything at all. It is sometimes best to sit quietly next to each other, asking no questions and troubling no scars.

Sylvie and Rosie.

Sylverani and Afroze.

Mother and daughter began a slow dance of reconciliation that silenced the massive roar of every single thing that could have been said and said and said.

Afroze noticed that in the morning, her mother arrived to the breakfast table unmade up with garish pastes. She was proud in her baldness and finally allowed the beautiful morning sun to fall on her scalp, dappling it and playing with skin that had been tormented by acrylic wigs. Over the next couple of days, she stopped wearing her red satin gowns with their uncomfortable ruffled collars, and just sat there in the lightest and most pleasant white kaftans. She still wore lipstick, the redder the better. She still demanded her breakfasts, those greasy plates of eggs and sausages, even though she could barely eat them.

"Why do you insist on having Halaima give you those breakfast plates, Mother?" Afroze asked her one day. She playfully pulled the plate away.

Not good for you. This food will kill you, you know.

Sylvie made a mock-angry face and lightly pulled the plate back toward her. She picked up a fork and played with the food, arranging it in a pattern. Criss-cross crisps of bacon, and a round yellow egg. Noughts and crosses.

There was an ease about Sylvie now, once the burden had been released, once the secrecy and guilt were quelled. She spoke openly now, her tone lighter, almost humorous, as she slowly cast off the darkness that being in prison had cloaked her in. Little anecdotes now slipped into conversations, and as she told snippets of her story, everyone grew braver and asked her more questions. All her years of silence fell away. Her stories healed her as she told them, and healed Afroze as she listened in rapt attention.

"When I was in prison," Sylvie began, "the prison matron was a cruel woman we called Beetle. Everyone called her that, even our warders, because when she breathed, she sounded like a 1972 Beetle starting up on a cold winter's day." The memory of Beetle and her hawking morning breaths made Sylvie giggle and turn bright red with the effort.

Bibi, seated nearby, also began to laugh. "And then? And then what, Madam Sylvie?" Bibi asked, unaware of the gravity of the story's context.

"Oh, this Beetle. She would come to our cells. We had been starving for days, given nothing. Not even water. And she would walk through the passage outside our cells, carrying a plate of her hot breakfast in her hand.

Ey, ladies, you can smell it, I know you want to have it. Crispy crispy bacon, two fried eggs with runny yolk, sausages, hot toast, and butter … Hmmmm, ladies. Anybody want some?

Aaah, we were starving. The hunger made us mad, angry, sad. Our stomachs were like huge stones inside our bodies. Bibi, you know how hungry you get if your mama doesn't make your food on time and you start to cry. Oh, we used to cry when Beetle walked around with her breakfast. And I remember I told myself that if I ever got out of this hole alive, I would eat that breakfast every day of my life. And I have, haven't I, my little Bibi girl?"

"Yes you have, Madam Sylvie. But you mustn't eat that pork thing, you know. God doesn't like that."

Sylvie laughed loudly, throwing her head back and grabbing Bibi into a cuddle. "Yes, my child. Maybe you're right. God doesn't like many things. But that fat Beetle … she certainly loved it."

"Fat Beetle, bacon eater. Married Peter Pumpkin eater …" Bibi started singing in her childlike nursery rhyme voice and stood up, walking around puffing her stomach out and parodying the image of Fat Beetle she had conjured up in her vivid imagination. And this innocent child in her most uncomplicated trusting happiness allowed the adults to veer away from their pain and suffering.

Sylvie fell into a fit of happy mirth, and soon, despite herself, Afroze joined in the laughter. As she held her belly and almost teared with silly laughter, she felt a funny ripple spread like bubbles through her stomach, which now was beginning to swell despite her trying to hide it.

She stopped laughing abruptly, her eyes widened in shock. Again, the flutter pushed against her hand.

"So, Rosie. When were you planning on telling us?" Sylvie asked, regarding her daughter with more delight than criticism.

Afroze looked at her mother from underneath thick lashes, she bit her bottom lip, looking so much like a naughty little child who was caught stealing sugar from the pantry.

"Oh, come on, Rosie. I knew from the day you almost fainted here at this table when you smelled the sausages. So, when is it …?"

Sylvie trailed off. Both Halaima and Afroze knew that she had been reminded of the incessant race against time, the race where every day was a win.

"Oh, Mother," Afroze said, and grabbed Sylvie's hand. "Here, feel this. I think she is kicking me."

Sylvie placed her hand on her daughter's belly, rounder now than when she had arrived, and although the shy little thing hiding inside refused to move at all, it was enough for Sylvie that her hand was there.

"Well, you need a darn kick," Sylvie joked, but refused to remove her hand.

"Four months, Mother. I'm four months along."

Secretly, both women counted the months to go. And both women prayed for time to be forgiving.

That night, Sylvie insisted on sitting on the back veranda, even though she was exhausted and clearly needed to lie down. Afroze sat next to her, every now and then lightly touching her belly, willing the baby to do something, anything, so that she could place her mother's hand there again.

"Rosie. I don't need a medal or a plaque with my name on it," Sylvie began.

Afroze burned with guilt for the time when she had argued with her mother for wanting such things. It was a different time then. Now she understood why her mother desired her name to be remembered.

"But Mother. I didn't mean what I said that day. I was so angry ..." Afroze trailed off, feeling horrible.

"No no, Rosie. I'm not saying this because of what you said that day. I mean it. I had this idea that I had sacrificed so much for the anti-apartheid fight, the most of all being you. I had given away years and years of my life, my sanity, my career, and my child. I looked at all the people who were given street names, buildings, and halls, even schools and parks with their names emblazoned all over them. And I thought then that one day when I am gone, you would never know all that I had done. You would never know why I had sent you away. And more than anything, Rosie, I wanted you to be able to look at a piece of metal or concrete and remember me."

"Mother, I have always preferred to look at things. Metal, concrete, brick, plaster. Those things made more sense to me than people ever did. I became an architect so that I could sanctify things that had no life, because those things could never hurt me. They were there. They would always be there. And if I created them, then they would always be with me. But, now … things are different."

Sylvie looked at Afroze, and her eyes were soft and sleepy. She understood exactly what her child was saying.

"Oh, that Sathie. He did a good thing after all, didn't he? Asking you to remain here to help build something that I could put my name on." Sylvie laughed.

With the mention of Sathie's name, Afroze blushed red, and a hot wave rose from her chest into her face. Sylvie missed nothing, and seeing this, she began to laugh softly. "You silly girl. No point in blushing now, I know all about the allure of that smooth operator."

"I … I don't know what to say to you … I *was* silly …"

"Oh, nonsense, Rosie. You are a woman, and you are beautiful. Sathie couldn't help himself. You little flirt, you had the poor man in rapture from the second he set eyes on you. Don't worry, had I been in your place, I would have done the same myself."

Afroze looked with twinkling eyes at her mother, and both stifled a little merry laugh.

The night was a warm one. The buzz of insects seemed amplified in the swollen heat, and in the distance bullfrogs sang an orchestra. In unsion, both women looked toward the dark shape of the khaya. An unsaid thread between them buzzed in amplified significance as well.

"So, no school, no crèche, no clinic with a plaque … What do we do with the khaya? Any ideas?" Afroze mused out loud, casting a side glance at Sylvie.

"Hmmm … Well, I have the best idea of all." Sylvie said.

The same night, Halaima walked out of the garden shed carrying a large can of petrol, pumped from one of the two service stations in town, which was to be used to power the generator during the incessant power outages that plagued Brighton. She walked around the perimeter of the khaya, sloshing the sweet-smelling liquid here and there, ensuring that it coated the crumbling walls. She muttered aloud about safety and craziness, but she did it anyway. There was something about it that made her feel good.

She bravely went inside the awful little building with no assistance of light, and poured what remained of the petrol over the piles and piles of papers. They were the doctor's personal journals and medical records of all the people that had come to this place, struggle heroes, many now long dead. But many still lived, and they were the ones who remembered nothing. They forgot so quickly, and there was nothing noble in that.

There in that room, Sylvie had stitched up bullet holes, shrapnel and stab wounds, signs of terrible torture. She had nursed them and fed them and then bundled them off into the night to fight for yet another day. A better day. Now the room was filled with their ghosts. No one remembered who they were, and even if they were the most lauded men and women in the new rainbow land, no one cared much for the nights of their suffering because they stopped caring a long time ago. Now, in the new free land of South Africa, only a sparse selection of fighters were given the gift of feeding on the gravy that the painful struggle had finally acquired. Many old stalwarts, who had lost limbs and love to emancipate the country from the fetters of white domination received nothing in return for their losses. The coffers of the country were raided by men and women of lesser stature and activist history. They grew corrupt, fattened on the meat of the true heroes. Suddenly, the deep words of social unity and equality became whispers inside the halls of capitalism.

Halaima emerged from within the dark place and walked swiftly into the house. She returned, carrying in her hands a small pack which she pushed into the doctor's waiting hand. Afroze helped her frail mother down the veranda steps, and slowly they made their way over clods and clumps of Brighton earth; and when they came to stand near the ugly building, Afroze held out her hand. Onto her flat palm her mother placed a box of matches.

The blaze was enormous. All three women, standing in the safety of the house, were shocked that they had not burned themselves up in their craziness. The fire crackled and whooshed, it wheezed and threatened to spread. But the night was still. Windless. And the flames confined themselves to devouring the horrid little building. Everything burned. Nothing remained. When the people from the town looked up to the little hill on which the doctor's house stood, they saw the glow lighting up the night sky.

The men from the town rushed to the blaze, muttering to each other about what the crazy doctor had done now. They arrived too late. The khaya was razed to the ground. The fire had been fueled and fed by the papers containing those stories that would never go down in history books.

The men shook their heads when they saw the three women standing in the doorway of the house, standing unafraid and proud. They knew that the fire would not touch them.

In the days and months that followed, Afroze grew larger as Sylvie grew smaller. Sylvie smiled often; she spoke little. She enjoyed little silly games with Bibi, and spent long afternoons sitting quietly next to Afroze. Mother and daughter spoke sometimes, exchanging brief words and phrases that meant more to them than the longest of conversations. Sylvie had her chance to feel the strong kicks that protruded from Afroze's stretched belly. She giggled like a child when she felt them, her eyes full of wonder at the life that would soon come into the world.

Sylvie left the world quietly on a peaceful Sunday afternoon, bathed in sunlight. Afroze was sitting next to her, reading to her from a book of poetry. The gravel in Afroze's voice, brought on by a swollen belly that pushed her diaphragm upward, was hypnotic, and from a soft sleeping place, Sylvie slipped away.

Halaima and Afroze clung to each other, sisters in grief as they said goodbye to the woman that had conjoined them. They dressed her in a chiffon sari, the color of butter, one she had been saving. Maybe Sylvie had been saving that sari for her daughter. But it suited her so beautifully, in her final eternal sleep. Afroze applied bright red lipstick to a mouth that was surely smiling.

There was nothing large and official about the final salute to Doctor Sylverani Pillay, activist and comrade. No one came to make speeches. No flags were flown at half-mast. No one wrote of it in books and articles. She had come, she had served, and she had quietly left.

And when Sylvia Moomina entered the world two months later, it was a bright and beautiful day.

"Here, hold her, Halaima," Afroze said to her tearful sister, handing over her treasure to willing arms.

Halaima looked in rapture. She saw the doctor's strong chin, she saw the doctor's cheekbones.

"Rosie, she is beautiful. I am going to miss you."

Afroze could see, in Halaima's moist eyes, fear lurking. It was the fear of one who knew she had lost her place. There was no need for her now.

"Oh, Halaima, don't be silly. Where are you going? This house belongs to you now." Afroze said lightly, and Halaima stifled a loud sob that escaped her trembling lips. Her eyes, screwed up with tears that she had been quelling for so long, asked questions.

"This cottage was never home to me. You've loved it more than I ever could, Halaima. Where I saw walls and bricks, you saw beauty. I could never love this place like you do. It is yours. Live here, and be a family."

EPILOGUE

AFROZE BHANA DROVE her car through the streets of Cape Town. She pushed the gear into a roaring second, and the car flew up a steep hill. The loud revving of the engine woke the sleeping baby in the seat next to her. Afroze made soothing sounds as the infant began to fuss.

She stopped before the facade of a familiar home. Outside, on the small lawn, sat Ismail and Moomi. They sat close together, almost in a cuddle. Ismail was reading the newspaper to Moomi, who nodded earnestly at all he was saying. They looked up at the woman approaching them, carrying a baby wrapped in a soft, white shawl.

The Cape southeaster began to awaken. It was going to be yet another windy Cape Town day. Afroze stopped and looked at her parents, marveling at the myriad colors of the house fronts, jewels in her necklace of heritage. In the light of a morning sun, the houses blazed. She cooed to the child, admiring the plain, unadorned architecture of simple homes.

AUTHOR'S NOTE

IN EARLY 2014, long before my debut novel was even considered for publication, I was charged with transgressing the laws of my profession as a therapist. My charge, brought upon me by a professional medical body, was one of unprofessional conduct, of acting outside of my scope of practice by practicing my profession without a supervisor present during my session with a patient. Charges were brought against me because of one patient who I had seen, the one time I had contravened the laws of my regulatory body, and I was guilty on all counts. I fully admit my guilt, and always did during the hearings and trials I faced over a two-year period, and still face currently.

The patient's name was Jane, but of course this is not her real name.

I was called to see Jane by a concerned relative, who had exhausted all other avenues and had heard of me through a grapevine that I did not even know my name had been bandied about in. It seemed I had earned a reputation as a last resort, the one to go to when all else failed.

In a tremulous voice that spoke almost apologetically, hushed, and secretive, Jane's relative begged me to go to see her cousin, telling me that Jane was in a nursing home, had been diagnosed with schizophrenia, was violent, had stopped eating and moving and lay in her bed for weeks, deeply silent and deeply depressed. Every therapist who had been called in to see Jane had been either chased away by her in a violent rage or had simply not turned back after one initial visit. At that point, I was given no further information on the history of Jane. The relative remained tight lipped, telling me to read the file. I sensed that she thought I would refuse immediately if she disclosed any further information; she had been down that road before. She hedged her bets on telling me nothing much, hoping I would go, meet Jane, and then read that dreaded file. And that was it.

I was fully aware that I was only allowed to see patients in a specific setting with my supervisor present. These were the laws. But I willingly and of my own volition ignored those laws and went to the nursing home without informing my supervisor, my practice manager, or my colleagues. There is something of the maverick in this act, but also something in the never-been-told quality in Jane's story. It unfolded in my mind over the very faint, simple telephone conversation and it resonated with me. Maybe I am, like most writers, a sucker for a secret. And I realize that may make me a selfish healer, a collector of peoples' pain, but I had never seen myself that way. I only believed strongly that there was something to be learned and shared with the world with every story.

I did go to Jane. I did read her file, after a tussle with the management at the nursing home for access to it. Producing my certificate to prove I was a qualified therapist wielded a tiny window of opportunity, and I began to discover Jane in the words written by others about her.

The story of this old woman then made me decide to chance it, to break the law, transgress the rules of my council, and eventually place my entire professional reputation in jeopardy. I risked losing my license. But I was not even able to stop myself. There was no medical reason why I should not see Jane. I was fully qualified to do so. But being immersed in writing my debut novel I had forgotten to renew my practicing license by a simple act of nonpayment of an annual fee. It was nothing but a signature and a payment that separated me from being a practicing therapist with over fifteen years of experience and one who had to see patients only under the supervision of someone, anyone who could have easily qualified a year ago. I did not possess the one three-line piece of official lettering. Far after the payment was due I found a crumpled-up reminder notice to pay my fees or risk losing my license—that page that I had let lie at the bottom of my overflowing desk. It was completely my fault. In the eyes of the law, I was guilty of all charges, and it changed my life forever.

I arrived at the nursing home, a dark, brown house hidden behind high walls, set on a suburban street full of homes that boasted beautiful trellises of climbing orange and yellow Cape Honeysuckle, swing sets in front yards and busy buses that drove with a whining whirr of wheels that only poor people's buses can make. Loud rap music droned in the air. Teenagers stood on the street corner, smoking and whistling at schoolgirls. And right in the middle of all this life sat this home, filled with cast-away mothers, waiting for a visit, or to die. Whichever came first.

I was regarded with suspicious eyes, as I entered this home, the caregivers and matron wondering what secrets I had come to expose. And they behaved with the demeanor of women who had many secrets to keep in that place, behind those high, brown walls.

They took me to Jane. In a dormitory-style bedroom lined wall to wall with metal cots, the stench of stale urine hung in the air. On the furthermost cot, underneath a massive pile of ragged, old quilts, a tiny head poked out. In the dim light I could almost think there was a baby lying there, curled into a fetal position. The windows were set high on the walls, the dark, brown metal frames creating a dramatic break between ceiling and wall, and even in the heat of that January summer day, the dark, plain drapes were drawn erratically, letting slivers of sunlight in but blocking most out.

Slowly as my eyes adjusted to the gloom, I realized that most of the other cots were filled with sleeping women too, some snoring loudly, some just moaning in their sleep. It was ten o' clock in the morning. They should have been awake, outside in the sunshine, gardening or chatting. But they all lay in the darkened room, sleeping.

I will not engage in the details of my treatment of Jane. Needless to say, she met me with great force and resistance to any attempts to pull her out of her sickbed and into some semblance of movement. There were no "aha" moments, no large breakthroughs, no sudden shifts that changed anything about the landscape of this old woman. Throughout the time that I was allowed to see her—and this time was short lived, as someone reported me to my professional body and I was stopped from all practice—the extent of my therapy only saw some slight changes in her behavior.

I suppose I could console myself that in my last few sessions with Jane, before I was pulled off her case and hauled off into trial, she managed to sit out of bed and stare forward, able now to take a spoon of soup to her own mouth occasionally. The last day I saw her, she told me she wanted to read a book. But before I could get her one, I was barred from any further visits. Her desire for a book inside the musty world into which she had been thrown was a breakthrough in my eyes. The breakthrough was not dramatic, and sometimes I find myself explaining to my family, who I placed under extreme strain due to the many trials and hearings I had to endure, that what I did was somehow worth it.

Jane had been an anti-apartheid activist. She had been in the military wing of the African National Congress (ANC), the Umkhonto we Sizwe, or the Spear of Africa, and had been one of the many women who had learned hard combat skills in Lesotho and Angola. The ANC was a banned organization in apartheid-era South Africa. And yet many activists, like Jane, had answered the call of the great comrades Nelson Mandela, Walter Sisulu, and Ahmed Kathrada, who were sentenced to life imprisonment on Robben Island, and who had begun a precisely designed call to action. Many people the world over know about the ANC—and they obviously know the name of its most famous father, the late Dr. Mandela—but not many people, even in South Africa, know of the depth and supremely planned logistical threads of the Congress. I suppose now that the country has been freed from the shackles of apartheid, most people care not for the details of how it was done. Yet in the country's current state of disarray, the people who fought for the freedom of the nation and equality for all South African citizens of every color are now the politicians in power. The African National Congress remains the ruling party, but the dissent and anger toward the ruling party and more especially the elected head of the country is rampant throughout the country. Corruption, misappropriation of government funds meant for the poor, lies and silencing of journalists and writers who try to expose this, is the order of the day. Rhetoric between political parties amount to empty words. It is the poor people, mainly black South Africans, who still suffer the lack. They suffered it at the hands of a racist law called apartheid, and they suffer it now with growing capitalism and exploitation of resources. Many politicians of the ruling party, the ANC, feed the people fustian speeches and flowery promises of grandeur, expecting the most vulnerable (like women and children) to satisfy their hungry bellies on these words. The leader of the country is an unapologetic businessman. The age when politics spoke for democracy is declining, bringing in a new order of faux-democracy. The new order is money, and this money never trickles down to the people who need it.

Although no legal convictions have resulted from this dishonesty, the people of the country are slowly engaging in a new struggle. This new struggle is a fight against the venality of power and money.

It is a slow fight. The poor and disenfranchised have remained as poor and as neglected as they were under the apartheid regime. The ideals of Dr. Mandela, and the words of the Freedom Charter and New Constitution, are ignored in favor of unethical business dealings and unlawful conduct. The wealth of the country is not spread equally, and the poor grow poorer as government funds are stolen.

After her time in Lesotho and Angola, Jane had tried to return to South Africa when the struggle was at its height in the mid-seventies, but had been detained several times without trial. After being released from prison, she then had spent many days in exile in Angola and Swaziland, running from safe house to safe house. She had been shot several times. She had been tortured. She had been fed mind-altering psychiatric drugs and then been withheld them when she fell into their dependency. She had learned the atrocious skill of bush surgery, and had often had to collect the shattered bones and limbs of her cadres.

Jane lost many things. She lost her marriage to the struggle, she lost her ability to have children, she lost her potential to live and work due to her injuries, most of them unseen and without visible evidence. Mainly, she lost her sanity, and after all had been said and done, her mind fractured completely into a schizophrenic mess. This mess, described in her ugly folder in only clinical detail, looked away from how she had got there; it focused only on medical descriptions of her current behavior. There was no doubt that Jane was schizophrenic, but after such a life, a mind is a fragile thing. And yes, it broke and failed her when the time finally came for her to return to a life of normality.

When the country had finally become a free and fair democracy and Mandela had been released and then elected our first democratic president, Jane's was one of the many names that were never remembered. Like many freedom fighters before her, she had given her life to a struggle and had ended up with nothing. Her activism meant nothing; she was pushed into a nursing home by young people who barely knew what she had endured.

Had I not gone to see Jane, alone, without a supervisor who did not want to take on a "headache case," then no one in this world would know this woman called Jane had fought hard, lost much, and walked this Earth as a warrior.

Activists like Jane are still alive, littered all over this land. In depressing, cheap nursing homes and low-income apartments that they do not deserve to die in. Poverty stricken, forced to go to humiliatingly incompetent government hospitals for treatment for injuries they sustained when they battled for our freedom, and forced to survive on barely nothing to fill their bellies. One avid stalwart of the struggle told me, as I delved deeper and deeper into the hovels that housed our heroes after my meeting with Jane, that a packet of cheap watered-down soup was his only meal every day.

South Africa is a dichotomous land, a land of two faces. There is a fast-growing upper class of the nouveau riche activists-turned-politicians, and then there are those such as Jane who don't wear their activism like gold crowns. They eat watery soup and guard the secrets of our way forward behind their rheumy eyes. Lest we ask … Lest we forget …

ACKNOWLEDGMENTS

Thank you:
My family

Thank you
Maria Cardona
Maia Larson
Ujala Sewpersad
Thohida Mohamed Kader
Junaid Ahmed (R.I.P—November 2016)

Thank you

ray, e.d., i.b.